Side Quests

Xine Fury

Side Quests

This is a work of fiction. Names, characters, places, and incidents either are the product of the author's imagination or are used fictitiously. Any resemblance to actual persons, living or dead, events, or locales is entirely coincidental.

ISBN 978-1-967029-09-9

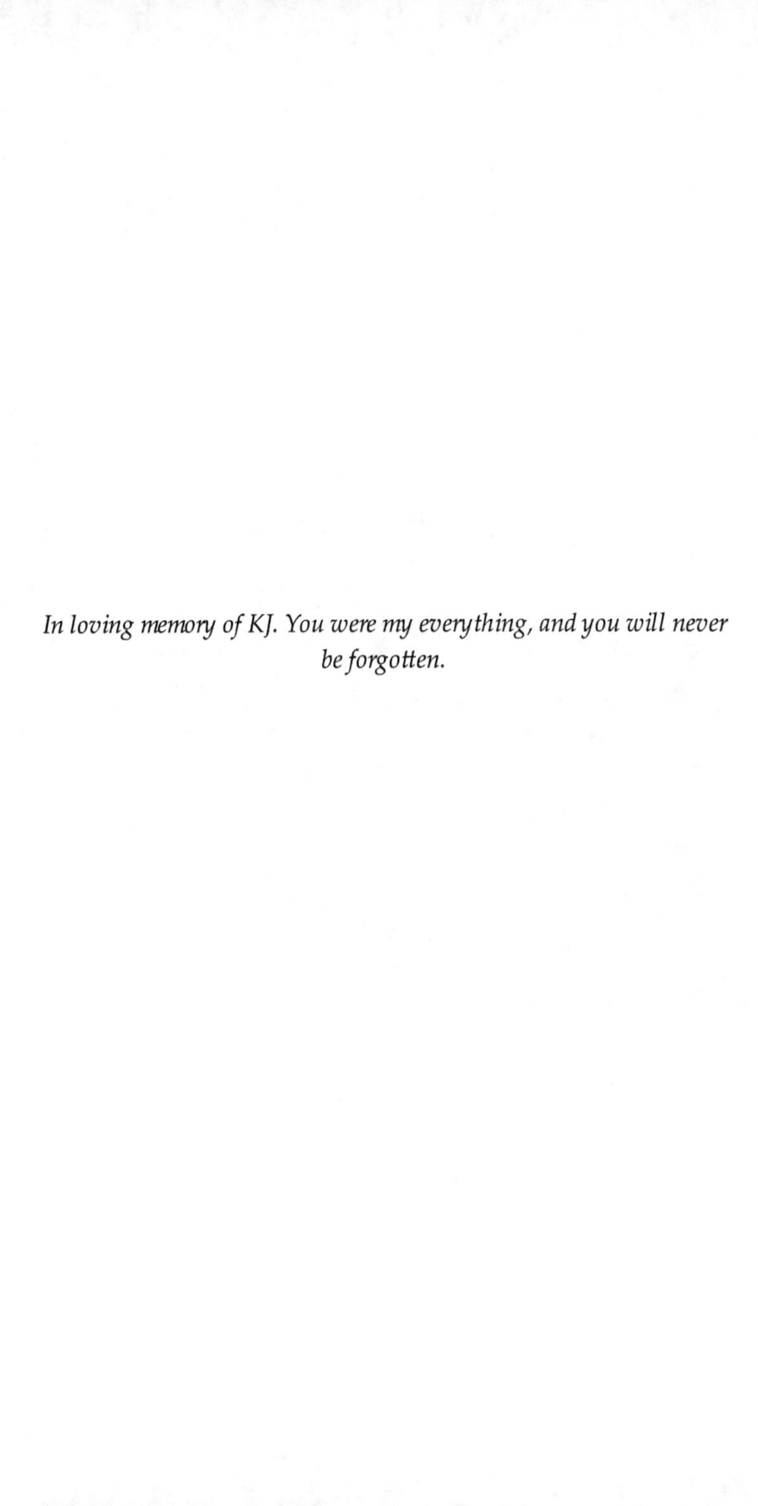

In loving memory of KJ. You were my everything, and you will never be forgotten.

Side Quests

Contents

The NPC

It was officially tourist season again. Thousands of vacationers walked up and down the strip, pouring in and out of wax museums, video arcades, fudge shops, and gimmicky motion theaters. Rita honked her horn as a family of six suddenly crossed in front of her pickup truck, even though they were nowhere near a crosswalk. None of the jaywalkers even looked in her direction as they made a beeline for the pancake restaurant across the street.

"Don't drive angry," Dot said, riding shotgun. "We're still going to get there before they open."

"Can't I just hit one of them?" Rita asked. "Maybe one of the smaller ones? They won't miss just one."

"Pretty sure that's still considered murder," Dot said.

"Stupid legal system, taking all the fun out of driving," Rita muttered.

After spending nearly ten minutes at a five-way traffic light, they turned left onto Greystone Heights, which was only slightly less crowded. Once they passed the aquarium, though, the crowds thinned out a bit. A few minutes later they pulled into a space in front of a small shopping center. Rita and Dot got out of the truck and gathered up their gaming supplies.

The store didn't really have a name, at least not one posted for the world to see. A rectangular sign above the entrance simply said "Games" in large black letters. Still, it didn't seem to be hurting for business. It wasn't quite nine yet, but the store was already open, and the front door barely had time to shut between patrons.

"I stand corrected," Dot said.

"They must have opened early when they saw all the tourists," Rita said. "I wonder if the rest are here yet."

"There's Brant's car," Dot said. "They're probably waiting for us."

Dot stayed close behind her girlfriend as they pushed their way through the crowd. Rita was built like a football player and people tended to step aside when she approached. The rest of their group was already seated when they stepped through the door to the back room.

"Nice of you to finally join us," Brant said with a chuckle.

"We would have been here faster but Dot wouldn't let me drive on the sidewalk," Rita replied.

"I just didn't want to spend the afternoon washing blood off your tires," Dot said, sitting down.

"Wouldn't be the first time," Rita joked.

"So did everybody roll up their new characters?" Brant asked. Everyone nodded. "Good," he said. "Let's go around the table real quick and see what you got."

Rita went first. "Bessie Vanderbeef. She's a minotaur barbarian with black fur and a wicked scar across the left side of her face. She carries a two-handed battleaxe."

"Sounds about right," Brant said. "Think you'll ever roll up a character built around diplomacy?"

"What's the point?" Rita said. "Your NPCs always turn out to be traitors."

Brant laughed. "Don't blame me, blame the modules. What about you, Dot?"

"I hope this is allowed, but I used the new heritage rules," Dot said. "Her name is Sybil Disobedience. She's an elf sorcerer. She's the offspring of a fire elf and a forest elf, but due to a curse, her skin is split right down the middle – half pale, half red. She's an outcast from both societies, so now she's just trying to find a place to belong."

"Should be interesting," Brant said. "Robert?"

"I've got a dwarf cleric named Johann Elderbrick," Robert said. "He's on a redemption arc after an evil warlord tricked him into betraying his clan. Now he's getting on in years and just wants to do as much good as possible before he dies."

"And Sharon?" Brant asked.

"Poisanne Berri," Sharon said. "Human rogue. She's a fifteen-year-old street urchin. People underestimate her because she looks weak, and she's used that for plenty of cons. But now she's trying to go straight."

Brant nodded and wrote down a couple of notes. "Natalie?"

"Gnome bard," Natalie said. "Her name is Epiphany, but everybody calls her Pip. She's very enthusiastic, to the point of being hyper."

"Very good," Brant said. "Let's get started. You're having a drink in town when you hear rumors of a blight affecting the local forest."

"Let's check it out," Robert said, and everyone agreed.

Brant gave them a bit more exposition about an evil cultist and a foreboding castle. A few minutes later – though hours had passed in the game world – the party found itself carefully searching the thick woods.

"As you make your way through the forest, you suddenly

feel like you're being watched."

The players grabbed their dice and got their pencils ready.

"I roll perception," Sharon said. "Sixteen."

"No need for the roll," Brant replied. "You easily spot a rabbit-like person squatting on a rock, watching you carefully."

"I don't remember seeing rabbit people in the monster folio," Robert griped.

"*You* shouldn't be reading the monster folio," Brant countered. "That's out-of-character knowledge."

"Hey, I might run a game someday," Robert said.

"What does the rabbit-thing look like?" Rita asked.

"She's about three feet tall to the top of her head," Brant replied. "Though her ears add another two feet. She has human-like limbs, but her legs are extremely muscular. She has white fur and a rabbit's face, though more expressive. She's wearing simple clothing. She looks curious but cautious, like she might bolt at any moment."

"I talk to her," Natalie said.

"Make a social interaction check," Brant said. "So you don't scare her off."

"Nineteen," Natalie said. "Hey... we're just passing through, we mean you no harm. What's your name?"

"Harriet," Brant replied, speaking in a softer but higher-pitched voice. The back room of the gaming store seemed to fade away as the players got into character.

"Hello, Harriet," Pip said. "We're looking for the lair of an evil cultist, and we think we've taken a wrong turn. Have you seen a castle? Big, with black bricks, probably really scary looking?"

"Yes, scary," Harriet replied. "I know scary place."

"Good," Pip said. "Can you take us there?"

Harriet's eyes widened in fear. "No. Bad place. No go there."

"Don't worry about us," Bessie said, stepping forward. "We're here to defeat the castle's master and make your forest safe again. You'd like that, wouldn't you?"

The rabbit-woman nodded vigorously. "Yes yes," she said. "Stop bad man. Hurts us. Makes trees die. But I no go there."

"Should I threaten her?" Bessie asked.

"You'll do no such thing," Sybil said. "You can catch more flies with money than you can with vinegar."

"Honey," Bessie corrected.

"Yes, dear?" Sybil replied, batting her eyes in a flirty way.

Johann groaned and turned back to Harriet. "We'll pay you," he offered. "Say, one silver piece?"

"You should offer more than that," Poisanne whispered.

"Nah, that's a fortune to these backwater folk," Johann replied.

"What is… pay?" Harriet asked. "What is silver?"

"See?" Johann said smugly, and held up a silver coin.

"Ooh, shiny," Harriet said. "I like the shiny."

"Take it," Johann said, and tossed it to the rabbit woman.

She caught it and turned it over a few times in her hand. She sniffed it, then bit it to test its hardness. "Still scared," she said.

"You don't have to take us all the way to the castle," Pip told her. "Just take us as far as you dare, and point us the rest of the way."

"You follow," Harriet said, stuffing the coin into her pocket. "Not far, come." She turned and bounded into the forest, stopping every few hundred feet to make sure the party was still behind her.

Hope they don't die, Harriet thought, as she watched the four adventurers disappear into the old stone building. Then she turned and hopped away, anxious to get as far away from the castle as possible.

When she finally felt safe again, she stopped to rest near a creek. Squatting on a log, she took out the coin and examined it again. There were markings etched into it. One side showed the profile of a human's face, just under the toothmarks she'd put in it earlier. The other side had writing on it, but Harriet could barely speak their language, much less read it. Still, she wanted a better look at it. A ray of sunshine poked through the trees a few feet away, so she hopped over and let it fall on the coin.

So pretty, she thought, turning the coin over and over. When the light hit it just right, there was a bright glint that forced her to blink. Then she froze, having seen a small movement to her left. A blotch of light on a nearby tree had moved. It could have just been the way the light trickled through the leaves, but Harriet didn't think so. Hareborn were a skittish folk, and they understood movement as expertly as a wolf distinguished smells. This mote of light hadn't moved like a sunray through wind-blown leaves. It moved like... like...

Then Harriet looked at her hand and understood. Sunlight reflected off the silver coin and made the glint on the tree. As her hand trembled, so did the light. She experimented, slowly turning the coin, making the light move up and down the trunk. *This is amazing*, she thought, thrilled with her new trinket. She stuffed it back into her pocket and bounded back to her burrow.

Harriet was the only Hareborn in the forest. She'd been forced from her home at an early age. She couldn't even remember the details anymore, just lots of screaming, fire, and what seemed like an eternity of running. Then she'd been captured by some gray-skinned men, kept in a cage, and taken on a long journey by boat. She'd escaped during a battle between her captors and some humans, and she'd been living in the forest ever since.

She couldn't say she missed home. She didn't have enough memories of the place to really miss. But there was a desperate longing in her soul that she didn't really understand. She hadn't met another Hareborn since she was a child, and it seemed unlikely that she ever would again. While she had an uneasy familiarity with some of the rangers who camped nearby, she didn't have anyone she could truly call a friend.

What little she could speak of the local language, she'd learned from the rangers and passing adventurers. The party she'd met earlier was one of many she'd seen over the years, and rarely had any returned from that evil castle. She felt bad about escorting them, as if she was feeding them to whatever dark creatures lurked within. But maybe today's group of heroes would succeed, and the forest would finally be free of the spreading darkness.

Harriet reclined on an old bedroll she'd been given by another adventuring party. Her burrow was full of random trinkets and excess supplies, like waterskins and slingshots and useless bits of jewelry, all gifts from heroes she'd reluctantly led to their doom.

Once again she pulled the silver coin out of her pocket and flipped it over and over in her hands. It was her new favorite item. She liked shiny things – most of her people did – and this was the shiniest thing she owned by far. Even here, underground, it glinted off the candlelight and reflected a faint disc of light onto the wall. She tilted the coin, making the dot move around the wall. She made it wiggle and bounce, then made a game of moving the dot around the wall, avoiding the roots and rocks that jutted from the dirt walls.

This continued to entertain her right up until bedtime.

Harriet woke up at dawn and went through her usual morning routine. She was working on a new tunnel to the west, filling in the exhausted east tunnel with dirt as she went. She carried a couple of empty burlap sacks with her, gradually filling them up with today's harvest as she burrowed. The undersoil in the region was filled with rootpips, which were bitter, hard-shelled nuts that only grew several feet underground. Harriet didn't care for them herself, but the crows loved them.

Once both her sacks were bulging, she called it a day and went outside. It was almost noon by the time she reached her favorite stump. She held her hand up to her mouth and began making birdcalls. The crows began to appear. Just a few at first, but within minutes dozens of the black birds surrounded her stump, waiting for her to feed them. But the crows hadn't come empty-handed. Many of them brought berries and vegetables to trade.

She happily took a cucumber from one of the nearest crows, and snacked on it while she reached into her bags and threw nuts to the awaiting flock. Of course, she could have cut out the middlemen and foraged for berries and veggies herself, but why? She was more comfortable burrowing than wandering around the dangerous forest. And the crows went crazy for these nuts that they had no way to gather for themselves.

When Harriet was done eating, she pulled out her silver coin and played with it, still turning it over and over in her fingers. Sometimes she would flip it with her thumb, occasionally dropping it. Some of the crows watched her fiddle with the coin, almost as if they were taking notes.

Once both bags were empty, Harriet held up her hands, fingers splayed. The crows recognized that signal and flew off, though a few stayed behind searching the ground for any nuts that might have been missed. Harriet stuffed a few more veggies into her bag, then looked for a safe rock to sit on to enjoy the day and watch for lost adventuring parties.

None came that day.

The following day, in addition to vegetables, a few of the crows brought her some silver coins. "Huh," Harriet said. They still brought her more food than she could possibly eat, so getting a few shinies in the mix was a nice bonus. She stuffed them into her bag and went about her day as normal.

As the days and weeks went on, more and more of the crows brought coins. Harriet had to dig out a new room in her burrow just to store them.

Several months later, Harriet filled her morning bags and headed for her favorite clearing. She was almost there when she noticed the odor of rotting wood. The blight that emanated from that evil castle had finally spread to the feeding spot. The stump was now withered and black, and the surrounding trees were barren. Her brow wrinkled with worry. She couldn't feed the crows here. The smell alone made her stomach lurch.

She hopped around the forest until she found another one of her favorite spots, a log by the creek. She looked up and saw that a few crows had been following her. She took out her favorite coin and flashed it in the sunlight a few times. At that signal, the crows descended. The flock had almost doubled in the past couple of months, and she'd started bringing extra bags. Hauling their coins back to the burrow was getting to be a chore. She wasn't sure what she was going to do with all these silver coins, but it was always fun to expand the horde. So far she'd had to burrow out three more rooms for storage.

The following morning she awoke to the sound of bleating. Somewhere, an animal was in pain. It was a heartbreaking sound, made worse by the fact that Harriet wasn't sure there was anything she could do. At best, she could put the poor animal out of its misery, but just the thought of it made her queasy.

She dug around her stash until she found a child-sized rapier. It was a new acquisition, a gift from another adventuring party she'd helped earlier in the week. They were probably dead now, a prospect that wracked Harriet with guilt, but she had warned them. She hooked the rapier to her belt and carefully stuck her head out of the burrow.

The screams didn't sound very far away. Seeing no danger, she crawled out of her hole and cautiously hopped toward the sound. Behind a thicket of small trees, she spotted a deer. She'd never heard a deer make that sound before, and she knew it had to be in extreme distress. Looking around for predators, she approached the deer and examined its wounds.

It wasn't going to make it. Something had taken several bites out of it, and it was only a matter of time before it bled out. She was about to draw her rapier when she heard the growls. She looked up to find that she was surrounded.

Harriet hopped backward, then turned and dove over a stump and through some brush. A pack of wolves – at least a dozen, maybe more – chased her through the forest. As she bounded through the trees, she looked for low-hanging branches she might use to escape their hungry mouths. She'd never been very good at climbing trees, and she was afraid to slow down long enough to try it.

Reacting on pure instinct, she lost track of which direction she was going. She could still hear them behind her, getting closer as she tired. She tripped over a fallen branch and tumbled forward, but she was back on her feet in an instant. A wolf snapped at her tail as she hopped away, missing her by mere inches.

She knew she couldn't keep this up. She needed a plan. *The river*, she thought. But she wasn't a strong swimmer, either. *A cave, maybe.* She scanned the forest as she hopped, looking for any hole large enough for her, but too small for her pursuers.

She realized she'd made a huge mistake when she found herself in the dark hollow. Thick dead trees lined both sides of the path, and there was no way out except for straight forward. Straight towards the castle. Had the wolves guided her here on purpose? She didn't know, but they definitely blocked the way back out. She now had two choices – face the wolves or hide in the castle. Either way, she wasn't going to survive the hour.

She looked up at the looming castle, its gleaming black bricks covered in dead ivy. The castle was taller than it had been. The central tower now stretched hundreds of feet into the sky. But it didn't look like there had been any recent construction. All the stonework appeared equally ancient. It was as if the tower had simply grown, the same as a tree grows.

Seeing no other way out, she crossed the moat and slipped between the bars of the portcullis. The wolves snapped at the bars and growled, but they couldn't follow her any further. Out of breath and completely fatigued, Harriet collapsed on the cold stone floor.

Harriet awoke to find herself in a small cage. She got to her feet, and then patted her body up and down, looking for wounds. Other than some sore muscles, she seemed to be in perfect health. She was still fully dressed, but her rapier was missing.

The cage was about five feet on each side, and maybe eight feet tall. She couldn't see much beyond the cage, just distant brick walls lit by flickering flame. The bars were close enough together to trap a human, but Harriet had no trouble poking her head between the bars. That's when she realized she was suspended above a deep pit. Peering over the side of the cage, she could just make out a swirling vortex of air about twenty feet below the edge of the pit.

She moved to each side of the cage, looking for any way out. On one side of the room below, she saw an exit guarded by two trolls. On the other side sat a black marble throne carved to look like the mouth of a demon. There was another exit on the back wall, behind the throne. This one was unguarded.

She turned and looked at the trolls again. They weren't watching her, but just staring straight ahead with dull expressions. Harriet put her back against the bars and experimentally tried to shake the cage. It didn't rock much, and she couldn't get it to swing at all. She poked her head back out again, and saw that it was suspended by eight taut chains, each attached to a different point on the ceiling.

She considered slipping through the bars and climbing on top of the cage, then shimmying up one of the chains. But her upper body strength wasn't that great, and she'd never been good at climbing. Then she examined the floor. She found a pair of hinges on one side and a release on the other. She realized with horror that the cage was designed to drop the occupant into the pit.

As she pondered her predicament, a hooded man in black robes entered the room. "Ah, good, you're awake," the man said as he crossed the room and stood in front of the throne. He pointed his black wooden staff toward Harriet. "Ch'athos prefers his victims to be wide awake and aware of their impending doom."

Harriet stared down at him in confusion. "You're... castle master?" she asked.

"So even the rabbits know of me," the man said proudly, pulling back his hood. He was human, with a bald head and pale skin. Flame tattoos adorned much of his face. "Yes, I'm Korthak, the 'evil cultist' you've probably heard so much about. But don't worry, you have nothing to fear from me."

"No?" Harriet asked.

"No," Korthak said. "Because I'm just the messenger. The true lord waits in the Otherealm, amassing the power he will one day use to rule our world. When I drop you into the portal, your soul will feed Ch'athos and his power will grow."

"Cat-Toes?" Harriet asked.

"Ch'athos," Korthak corrected her. "Rhymes with 'pathos.' Which is what he will deliver when he finally awakens and drains the life from this world!"

"You kill trees," Harriet said angrily.

"It takes a lot of energy to open this portal," Korthak said.

"That's why I built the castle here, in a forest so teeming with life."

"Close portal," the Hareborn ordered.

Korthak burst out laughing. "Oh, *you're* making demands of *me*? This is priceless."

"Now!" Harriet shouted.

Korthak stopped laughing. "You amuse me, but my patience has limits. Now if you'll excuse me, I only have an hour to prepare for your sacrifice." He walked behind the throne and through the exit.

Harriet fumed. She didn't care so much about her own life, but she had to protect the forest. These woods had given her so much, and she couldn't just let it all die. Her courage fortified by anger, she squeezed through the bars. With her arms out behind her holding on for dear life, she placed the bottoms of her feet against the bars and squatted. Trying not to look down, she took two deep breaths and then pushed off.

She opened her eyes midway through the leap. The portal seemed to swirl even faster now, as if her presence made it hungry. She thought she saw the tip of a tentacle poke through for a moment before it withdrew into the vortex.

And then she landed, mere inches from the edge of the pit. She rolled forward and got to her feet, using the hideous throne for balance. She turned and saw the guards drawing their clubs. One troll remained in the doorway while the other ran towards Harriet. She turned and bounded away.

The troll chased her around the pit twice. Each time she neared the exit, Harriet considered diving between the other guard's legs. But the way he held his club at the ready, she knew he'd bash her across the room if she tried.

It didn't seem like the best idea, but on the third time around, Harriet broke away and hopped toward the door behind the throne. She knew Korthak had gone that way, but it still seemed safer than trying to get by that troll. The door led to a spiral staircase, and she jumped up the stairs three at a time.

The troll wasn't far behind her. She could hear his heavy breaths and echoing footfalls as he pounded up the stairs. She passed a door, but couldn't take the time to slow down and open it. A few seconds later, another door opened as she approached. A surprised Korthak tried to block her way but he was too late. Harriet hopped right past him and continued up the staircase.

She saw sunlight up ahead, and a few hops later she was outside. Unfortunately she was on top of the tower, and it was a long way down. Harriet hopped over to the ledge, looking for a safer way down. The masonry was smooth and offered no handholds. There were a few creeping vines running up the castle face, but they looked too withered to hold her weight.

"Don't try it," came Korthak's voice. "Ch'athos demands a live sacrifice."

Harriet turned and saw him approaching. Behind him, the troll guarded the stairwell. "Let me go," Harriet pleaded.

Korthak shook his head, then pointed his staff at her. He mumbled some words in a language Harriet had never heard, and the tip of his staff began to glow.

Harriet reached into her pockets looking for a weapon. Anything would do. All she could find was her lucky coin. As she grabbed it, she saw a crow fly overhead.

The cultist fired a blast of green energy from his staff. It hit Harriet in the legs, and she went numb from the waist down. As she fell forward, she flipped her coin into the air. It tumbled towards the sky, catching the light several times before losing its momentum and arcing downwards.

Another crow flew by, followed by three more. And then, as if summoned by magic, a massive flock of crows blotted out the sun.

Lying on the roof, Harriet couldn't even see through the whirlwind of black feathers. She heard Korthak shout, first low bellows of surprise, then higher-pitched shrieks of pain. The undulating mass of crows moved closer and closer to the edge of the roof. As the flock moved past the ledge, Harriet heard the cultist's final scream, a long, drawn-out shriek that receded as he fell to the earth.

The paralysis spell wore off immediately upon Korthak's death. Harriet stood up and saw the troll flee back down the stairwell. Then she noticed Korthak's staff. She picked it up and descended the stairs to the throne room.

When she emerged from the stairwell, both trolls bowed to her. "You the Crow Queen," one said with great reverence.

Harriet hopped up to the edge of the pit and waved the staff over the vortex. "Close," she said. Nothing happened. "End," she tried, but it kept on swirling.

"Master always said Finitum," one troll suggested.

"Finitum," Harriet said, and the portal dissipated. Now exhausted, she hopped over to the throne and sat down. A few seconds later, a crow flew into the room and perched on her shoulder. It carried something shiny in its beak, and Harriet held out her hand. A coin landed in her palm. She immediately recognized it as her lucky coin, which she'd left on the roof.

"Thanks," she said, then leaned back and took a nap.

"You're sure you want to try this module again?" Brant asked. "You barely escaped with your lives last time."

"We've leveled up since then," Dot said. "Heck, I know fireball now."

"Your funeral," Brant said. "So, you still remember the way from last time. You make your way through the forest and reach the final path to the castle. The trees on each side are... are..." Brant squinted at the book, then flipped back and forth through the pages. He sounded a bit confused when he continued reading. "...lush and vibrant, with white bark and bearing plump fruit. As you reach the castle's front gate, you are awestruck by the gleaming white marble."

"Wasn't it black before?" Sharon asked.

"Maybe I read it wrong last time," Brant suggested.

"I remember the path to the castle being more ominous," Sharon said.

"Are you sure you brought the right book?" Natalie asked.

Brant closed the book and looked at the cover. Then he shrugged and found his spot again. "Yeah, I must have been on the wrong chapter or something last time," he said. "But whatever. Let's just play it as written."

Everyone mumbled in agreement, and once again the world faded as they let themselves get carried away by the story.

The moat was full of crystal clear water, and koi fish goggled at them as they crossed the drawbridge. The courtyard held a well-maintained garden and a serene fountain. Several crows made use of a birdbath underneath an ivy-covered wall.

An impeccably dressed troll greeted the party at the door. "The master awaits," he said in a deep voice.

"This castle has definitely changed since the last time we were here," Johann said, noting the freshly cleaned tapestries. They passed by one room full of priceless art, and another room filled with nothing but piles and piles of silver coins.

They followed the troll up a few flights of stairs until they reached the throne room. Where there had once been a circular pit, now sat a banquet table filled with exquisite food. They recognized their host right away. The rabbit-like woman sat on a wooden throne carved to look like a pair of bird wings. A crow perched on her shoulder.

"Friends," the Crow Queen said. "Welcome. Stay. Rest. Eat."

The party didn't get the fight they'd come for that day, and they never fully understood how the story had changed so drastically since their previous visit. But they ate, they rested, and they talked. By the end of the day they'd made a powerful ally in the Crow Queen, and their friendship would be a much-needed resource later in the campaign.

Different

It was around four AM when the lights streaked across the sky. Susan was only awake because she'd heard her father get up to go to the bathroom. His heavy footsteps always caused the floors to creak like an ancient sailing ship. A few minutes later she'd heard the flush, more footsteps, and the groan of his bedroom door. And, a few minutes after that, the boar-like grunting of his snores.

Susan tossed and turned for several minutes, then climbed out of bed. She tip-toed through the hallway, used the bathroom herself, and crept back to her room. Her father's snoring only hitched twice during the trip – once when she flushed, and again when she shut her bedroom door. The house was pitch black, but she wasn't afraid of the dark. After losing her mother to cancer the previous year, boogeymen and other made-up monsters just didn't impress her as much.

She was about to get back into bed when the lightshow caught her eye. Rushing to the window, she watched as hundreds of bright streaks hurtled towards the

Earth. She'd heard of meteor showers before, but this was much brighter, much prettier. Not taking her eyes off the window, she stepped back and felt around her dresser, looking for her camera.

Bingo. She held the camera up and took a picture, and nearly blinded herself as the flash reflected off the window. *Idiot*, she admonished herself, then disabled the flash. The 110 film only held twenty-four shots, and she'd used up half the roll the day before, when a squirrel climbed across her window screen. Her father didn't like her wasting film – money was tight, after all – but the meteor shower was a once-in-a-lifetime event. She hoped at least a few of the pictures would come out.

She quickly used up the rest of the roll, but the shower was starting to peter out as well, and ten minutes later the sky was dark. She couldn't wait to tell Ellis; she was into astronomy, and she'd be so jealous of what Susan had seen.

"Bullshit," Ellis said. "I subscribe to Astronomer Monthly. There's no way I didn't know about it."

"I swear on my mother's bible," Susan said. She tried not to invoke her mother's name – it felt like blasphemy now – but Susan hated being called a liar.

"You were dreaming," Ellis said. "If there'd been a meteor shower, it would have been in the papers this morning."

"You read the newspaper?" Shanda asked, her face more curious than mocking. Ellis was a nerd, but the thought of a twelve-year-old reading the daily paper still seemed strange.

"No," Ellis said. "But my dad does, and he knows I like astronomy. He'd have told me."

"It is a little fishy," Georgia said.

"It's true," Susan said, pointing to the sky. "The lights were right up there and they went over the roof and into the woods. Most were white or yellow, but I saw some red ones, too."

"Sounds like you saw some fireworks," Eiko said, pushing her glasses up on her nose. Her glasses weren't as big as the ones Ellis wore, but she still got called a nerd from time to time.

"I didn't hear any bangs," Susan replied. "Besides, I can prove it. When my film comes back, I'll show you." The five girls sat around a concrete table in Susan's backyard. Shanda, Ellis, and Eiko sat on one of the two semi-circular concrete benches, while Susan and Georgia sat on the other. They often met at Susan's house on Saturdays. It was at the halfway point between all of their houses, and of all their houses, it had the best places to play.

"Why wait?" Shanda asked. "You said it fell into the woods back there. Let's go see if we can find something."

Everyone seemed excited by the idea, and a few seconds later they were traipsing through the woods. Autumn was in full swing, and the fallen leaves had almost completely covered the well-worn path through the trees. The woods weren't huge, and the path – if they were to stay on it – would take them straight to the mini-mart a few streets over. But that wasn't their destination. Instead, they combed the woods looking for craters, glowing space rocks, maybe even crashed spaceships.

"Don't get your hopes up," Ellis told them. "Most meteors burn up before they hit the ground."

"So you believe I saw it?" Susan asked.

"I don't know, but... I hope you did," Ellis said finally.

"What are these?" Eiko asked. They'd been searching for about an hour, and they were close to the north edge of the woods. They could just barely make out a gas station through the trees.

"Where are you... oh," Ellis said. Eiko was on her hands and knees, examining a small mound of dirt. Another twenty or thirty similar mounds peppered the area. Each was about the size of a baseball and looked as if someone had dug a hole and filled it back in.

"Weird-o-rama," Shanda said.

"Could those be where meteors landed?" Susan asked.

"Meteorites," Ellis corrected. "They're only meteors when they're falling. But those don't look like impact craters. Maybe they're gopher holes?" She didn't sound very sure.

"What if they're anthills?" Georgia asked, taking a few steps back. She didn't appreciate nature as much as the others.

"Let's keep looking," Susan said, and they spread out.

They took a break around noon and convened at the clubhouse. The "clubhouse" was really an old duck blind they'd found in the woods, next to a pond that had dried up years ago. But they'd fixed it up a little over the last couple of years. They'd tied a large waterproof tarp over the roof, put an old rug on the floor, and they'd brought in a few rusty folding chairs and a discarded end table. It was cramped, but they liked hanging out there.

It made them feel like members of an exclusive club. They'd all struggled to find a place in the world. Shanda and Eiko were the only non-white kids in their grade. Ellis was a bookworm, Susan was a tomboy, and Georgia was overweight. None of them were ashamed of who they were, but the other students never let them forget that they were different.

"Doesn't look like we're going to find anything," Eiko said.

"It probably just looked like it was closer than it was," Shanda added. "I bet it really fell miles away."

"If you saw anything at all," Georgia said.

"I didn't dream it," Susan said.

"Can we head back soon?" Eiko asked. "I need to pee."

"I'd like to keep looking," Susan said. "Just go behind a tree or something."

"Can someone go with me to watch out for bears?" Eiko asked.

"There's no bears around here," Ellis said.

"Snakes?" Eiko said.

"Not poisonous ones," Ellis said.

"Mom said she saw a bobcat in the backyard once," Georgia offered.

"You're not helping," Ellis said.

"It's okay, I'll go with you," Shanda said. She and Eiko stood and climbed out the trap door, leaving just Ellis, Georgia, and Susan behind in the clubhouse.

"We can search all day, but I don't think we're going to find anything," Ellis said.

"I swear I saw it," Susan said.

"I believe you," Ellis said. "But that's not the point. Most meteorites burn up before they touch the ground. We won't find anything because there's nothing to find."

"And I've got better things to do than run around the

woods all day," Georgia said.

"Go home whenever you want, Georgia," Susan said. "Nobody's stopping you."

"Maybe I will," Georgia said, but she didn't move.

Turning back to Ellis, Susan asked, "What about when I get the pictures developed? Maybe you can look at the pictures and tell where they landed?"

Ellis looked doubtful. "Maybe, but—"

"Susan! Come here! We found something!" It was Shanda's voice, from outside the duck blind. Susan, Ellis, and Georgia climbed out and saw Shanda waving at them. "It's this way, come look!"

Behind a large stump, they saw Eiko crouching over a strange object. It was stuck halfway out of the ground, and shaped like the end of a football. But instead of leather, it was covered in translucent bumps that kept changing color in the light.

"Pretty," Georgia said, and moved in for a closer look. All of them crowded around the object.

"What is it?" Susan asked.

"I don't know, an egg maybe?" Ellis replied. Shanda reached out to touch it, but Ellis slapped her hand. "Don't," Ellis said. "If it's from outer space, it could have some sort of disease."

"You really think it's from space?" Susan asked.

"I don't know," Ellis said. "But I don't think we should touch it without gloves. We should come back with a—"

The object exploded, covering all of them with clear, jelly-like goo. Georgia screamed.

"I knew I should have gone home," Georgia shrieked, using the hem of her dress to wipe off her face.

"Don't get any in your mouth," Ellis said. "We need to wash this off as fast as we can."

The five friends ran back to Susan's house. It started to rain on the way, which turned into a full downpour by the time they reached the house. Despite the free shower from Mother Nature, they still used the backyard garden hose to wash off all the goo before they went inside.

"Looks like you girls got caught in a flood," Susan's father said as the girls walked in.

"It's raining pretty hard," Susan said. "We're going to go upstairs and dry off."

"Good idea," her dad said. "There's extra towels in the hallway closet. I'll make some sandwiches for when you come back down."

The girls went upstairs, dried off, and convened in Susan's room.

"Are you going to tell your dad about the goo?" Eiko asked.

"I don't think so," Susan said. "He might yell at me for getting close to it."

"So what was that thing?" Shanda asked.

Ellis shook her head. "Maybe Susan's right. Maybe it's from outer space. When it stops raining, we should go back with gloves and a garbage bag. Maybe we can—"

"Go back?" Georgia asked. "Seriously? You're crazy. We're covered in space germs and you want to go back for more?"

"It could be a big scientific discovery," Ellis said.

"No, no," Georgia said. "I knew you girls were crazy, but it was fun crazy. This is dangerous crazy. I'm going home." She stood up.

"At least wait 'til the rain stops," Susan said.

"No," Georgia said. "If I stay here you're going to talk me into going back to the woods. No, thank you." She gave them one last glare and walked out the door.

"If anybody else wants to leave, that's okay," Susan said.

"I won't be mad."

But Eiko, Ellis, and Shanda seemed excited about the discovery, and couldn't wait to get back to the woods for a better look. Unfortunately, it only rained harder for the rest of the day. The other girls had to go home before the sun went down. The downpour lasted until well after midnight, and there was even some talk on the news about flash floods.

On Sunday morning, Eiko, Shanda, and Ellis showed up bright and early at Susan's house. The four of them went back into the woods, but they couldn't find any sign of the object they'd encountered the day before. There was a slight dip in the ground where it had been half-buried, but there were no pieces of the object itself. They went on to explore the rest of the woods, but even those "gopher hole" mounds had been washed away.

Susan's pictures weren't much help. The prints came back nearly black, with faint white lines streaked across the sky. It was enough to convince Ellis that the meteor shower had happened, but it wouldn't prove it to anyone else. After a few weeks they forgot the incident had even happened.

NOVEMBER 1989

The lipstick-red Corvette had been going sixty-five in a thirty, and Officer Danson just knew the driver was going to be a teenager before they even rolled down the tinted windows. Still, he wasn't prepared for the drop-dead gorgeous creature sitting behind the wheel. The girl was thin but buxom, with a big blond perm and glossy red lips. She wore a designer dress and two hundred dollar sunglasses, the latter of which she took off as the officer spoke to her.

She looked like she'd been crying. "Oh, thank god you're here, officer," she said breathlessly. "I was having an emergency."

"What's wrong?" Officer Danson asked, looking puzzled.

"There was a man with a gun," the girl said. "I cut him off in traffic – I didn't mean to, I was just trying to merge. I've only been driving for a year. Then he started tailgating me and honking. I was about to pull over and let him pass, but then I saw his gun in the rearview mirror."

"He pulled a gun?" the officer asked. The girl was obviously upset. Tears were streaming down her cheeks, and she kept taking hitching breaths as she spoke. Her chest heaved beneath her low-cut blouse... *She's ten years younger than you*, the officer thought, forcing himself to look into her big blue eyes.

"He fired twice into the air," the girl said. "I was so scared I almost went off the road. But I was afraid that if I pulled over, he'd stop too and he'd shoot me. So I just put my foot down, hard, trying to get as far away from him as I could."

"What was he driving?" Officer Danson asked.

"I don't know cars," the girl said. "It was black, or maybe dark blue? Two door, kind of a slanty front. He backed off when I passed you. He's probably long gone by now."

"I'll radio ahead," the officer said. "We'll see if anyone spots a car with that description. If you think of anything else, please give the station a call."

"Of course," the girl said. "Can... can I go now? My heart's beating so fast... I just want to get home and lock all the doors."

"That's fine," the officer said. "You drive safe, now." Then he turned and went back to his patrol car.

I can't believe he bought that, Georgia thought as she got back on the road. And yet, that wasn't exactly true. Not only could she believe it, but she was pretty sure she could have told an even bigger whopper and gotten away with it.

Her life had changed a lot in the last five years. She'd grown a good six inches but lost more than fifty pounds. She was in an entirely different social circle, and while her new friends weren't as book smart as the ones she'd had when she was twelve, they were a lot more fun. Georgia finally felt like she was where she was meant to be.

Boys fought and fawned over her, girls copied her style, she got good grades without studying, and her parents handed her everything on a silver platter. It was like being royalty. Her only regret was that she'd be graduating next year and she'd have to start over in college. But the way things had been going lately, she was confident that she'd be queen of the campus as well. Nothing was beyond her grasp.

These thoughts entertained her all the way to the mall.

"Ugh, is that Georgia Moore's fan club?" Shanda asked, sipping her soft drink.

"Looks like it," Trill replied. "If they're all here, Georgia can't be far behind."

It was Friday night, and the food court was even more crowded than usual. Hundreds of overlapping conversations combined into a booming ambient murmur, which was so loud that Trill and Shanda had to lean forward to hear each other. And yet they still heard the squeals from Georgia's friends when she finally walked through the door.

"Praise be, Queen Snidebitch has arrived," Shanda said,

watching Georgia's table from across the room.

Trill snorted and nearly choked on her soda. Shanda and Trill shared a plate of nachos while waiting for their friends to show up. Every couple of minutes someone would walk up and ask if they were using their empty chairs, and Shanda would have to explain that the seats were taken.

Finally Brett showed up and took a seat. "Hey girls, what's up?" he asked, taking a nacho.

Ellis showed up a few seconds later. Shanda immediately stood up and they shared a brief kiss, then glanced around nervously before sitting back down.

Brett rolled his eyes. "Nobody's looking at you," he said. "Look at this crowd. We're practically invisible."

"Why would anybody look at us when cheerleader central is right over there?" Trill added, nodding her head in the direction of Georgia's table.

"Besides," Brett added, "As long as I'm here, nobody's going to care about you." A couple of years earlier, Susan started dressing as a boy full-time. He now insisted that his friends treat him as a boy, including calling him Brett. His father wasn't being very supportive, but he hadn't tried to stop him.

Eiko had gone through similar changes. She'd adopted the nickname "Trill," and she didn't consider herself male or female. That had been harder to explain to her friends, but they still supported her. People still referred to her as "she" and "her," but she dressed in neutral clothing and resisted gender norms.

"Anybody want to get out of here?" Brett suggested. "Maybe see a movie or head to the arcade?"

"Or the bookstore!" Ellis suggested.

"Can't see a movie tonight," Trill said. "Mom says I gotta be home by ten."

"I don't like the arcade," Shanda said. "It's too crowded on Fridays. We'll never get to actually play anything."

"Bookstore shouldn't be crowded," Ellis said.

"Ellis," Brett said. "I know we're not exactly the cool kids, but something about spending Friday night at a bookstore seems sort of…"

For just a moment, a woman's scream drowned out the crowd. Then there were several shouts followed by more screams. Brett and his friends scanned the crowd, looking for the source of the commotion.

A man was chasing Georgia Moore through the food court. He looked to be in his late sixties, with a weathered, unshaven face and clothing that was just one step up from sackcloth. He wielded a plastic spoon like it was a sword, and it was clearly his intent to stab her with it. "You're infected!" he shouted over and over. When the man yelled, Brett noticed that he was missing all his teeth.

A couple of guys grabbed him from behind, while a third wrestled the spoon out of his hand. Mall security showed up a few seconds later. As Brett watched them drag the man away – still yelling about infections – he thought he saw something strange. A blurry object the size of a grapefruit flew off of the man's head and vanished into the rafters.

"Did you see that?" Brett asked.

"Everyone saw it," Trill said. "That homeless guy tried to stab Georgia."

"With a spoon," Shanda said, laughing.

"A plastic spoon," Ellis added.

"No, the flying thing," Brett said, studying the ceiling. The food court was under a glass dome, supported by dozens of crisscrossed metal rafters.

The others looked at him strangely. "What are you talking about?" Shanda asked.

Brett squinted at the rafters. "Never mind," he said.

Across the food court, three men fawned over Georgia as she recounted her horrific ordeal.

"Let's just go," Trill said. "I don't want to watch her turn this into a pity party."

"Where to?" Shanda asked, standing up.

Ellis opened her mouth to speak, but Brett interrupted her. "Bookstore it is," he said.

As they walked away, Brett kept turning back to look at the rafters.

All the stores were more crowded than usual, but the bookstore was substantially less packed than the food court had been.

"So what did it look like?" Trill asked Brett, as the four browsed the science section.

Ellis was busy pulling books off the shelves and flipping through them, looking for inspiration for her next science project. The other three just stood around and watched her browse.

"What did *what* look like?" Brett replied.

"You know what," Trill said. "Whatever you saw flying around the food court. I can tell you're still thinking about it."

"I'm not sure what I saw," Brett said. "It was like... see-through, but sort of hat-shaped."

"Top hat? Bowler hat?" Shanda asked.

"Like a ski cap," Brett said. "It's like the guy was wearing a transparent ski cap when he attacked Georgia, and it flew away when he was caught."

"Had to be a trick of the light," Trill said.

"I guess so," Brett replied.

"Hey guys," Ellis said, holding up a book. "Look what I found. In 1947 there was this science expedition to the jungles of Peru. Look what they found in a crater." She opened the book to a two-page spread. A black-and-white photo depicted four men standing behind a large egg.

"That looks familiar," Shanda said.

"Just like the one from five years ago," Brett said. "Did they ever figure out what it was?"

Ellis read more of the article. "Well, no," she said. "It says they all went mad one by one, and they started killing each other. Only one scientist made it back alive, and he couldn't remember what happened to the egg."

Trill looked thoughtful. "Did they mention... transparent hats?"

"No," Ellis said, thumbing through the chapter. Then she looked up. "You think the egg and the hat thing are connected?"

"Tell me it doesn't fit," Trill said. "They found an egg, they went crazy. We found an identical egg. That homeless guy went crazy."

"Five years later," Shanda said. "I mean, we were what, twelve? Are we even sure we saw what we saw?"

"I am," Brett said.

"So think about it," Trill said. "These things, they hatch, they mature, then they latch onto people's heads, feed on their mental energy, and it makes their victims crazy."

"Or maybe they're not crazy," Brett said. "Maybe the creatures want the people to kill each other. Maybe they take over the planet by making the population kill themselves."

"Seriously?" Shanda asked. "You're basing all this on a blur you probably didn't even see? How did we jump from one crazy homeless guy to world domination?"

"I know what I saw," Brett said. "In my entire life, I've only ever experienced two events I'd call 'supernatural' or 'otherworldly.' One was finding that weird egg. The other was seeing that invisible hat. Most people don't even see one supernatural thing. Wouldn't it be stranger if they *weren't* connected?"

"Your logic makes no sense," Shanda said. "Five years ago we found a strange egg. Our twelve-year-old imaginations ran wild with it – made it seem bigger and more alien than it really was. Tonight you saw a shadow. Some optical illusion that happened to fall on a man with real mental health issues."

"What if I prove I saw it?" Brett asked.

"How?" Shanda asked.

"We're going to stay here tonight until after the mall closes," Brett said. "Then, once all the people are gone, we'll hunt it down."

Shanda rubbed her hand over her face. "You have got to be kidding me," she said. "How are we even going to do that?"

"Easy," Brett said. "We'll sneak into a bathroom and wait until the mall closes."

"What about the security guards?" Shanda asked.

"My cousin used to be a security guard here," Trill said. "He said they don't have overnight security. After the mall closes, they spend an hour walking around and making sure the place is empty, then they lock it up and go home."

Shanda winced. "We're really going to do this, aren't we?"

"Okay, let's go round robin," Brett said, and handed each of the others a quarter. Then they left the bookstore. There was a pay phone outside the mall pharmacy, and they took turns calling their parents, each one claiming they were going to spend the night at a different friend's house. Once their alibis were in place, they went inside the pharmacy to shop for flashlights and batteries.

"Check this out," Ellis said as they browsed the fall clearance section.

"That could work," Brett said, picking up a long, green butterfly net.

They pooled their allowances and bought two flashlights, some batteries, the net, and a few candy bars to get them through the night. Then they sought an appropriate hiding place to wait for the mall to close. It was twenty minutes before closing, the crowds had finally thinned out, and most of the stores had their gates half down.

"Won't they check all the bathrooms when they're doing their final rounds?" Shanda asked.

"I have a thought about that," Brett said.

"Of course you do," Shanda muttered.

"Check it out," Brett said, leading them to the center of the mall.

A trio of festive parade floats were parked around the central fountain, decorated with Halloween-themed characters. Earlier that day, costumed performers had stood on the floats and tossed candy to passing children. But now they were empty.

One of the floats depicted a cornfield with a scarecrow and several gravestones. To complete the scene, the float featured a straw-lined skirt that nearly touched the floor.

"They'll never think to look under here," Brett said, lifting the skirt. They looked around to make sure no one was watching, then slipped under the float.

Shanda scowled. "Smells like engine grease under here," she said.

"Where's your adventurous spirit?" Brett asked. "Remember when we used to play in the woods all day?"

"...and then we'd pick ticks off each other all night?" Trill added, laughing.

"I... like being clean now," Shanda said. "I don't like the feel of leaves in my hair and dirt on my face."

"Fuddy duddy," Brett teased.

"I grew up," Shanda said. "That doesn't make me boring."

"You could never be boring," Ellis said, and put an arm around her.

"Oh great, you've got us trapped under here with the lovebirds," Trill said.

"Shush, someone's coming," Brett said.

They could only make out the bottom two inches of the shiny black shoes that walked past. The feet stopped right in front of the cart, turned, and then walked away. "Fountain's clear!" a man's voice shouted.

From around the mall they heard other shouts like "East wing clear" and "Information desk clear." As this was going on, another pair of shoes went by, this one pushing a wide broom. One end of the broom went under the float as it passed, and everyone had to scooch back a few inches to avoid it.

They kept waiting, hearing fewer voices and footsteps as time went on. Brett periodically used his flashlight to check his cheap digital watch. At 11:54 PM, nearly one hour after the mall's posted closing time, they heard several loud THUNKs as the main lights were turned off.

Off in the distance, they heard one last door slam shut. They were finally alone.

They waited ten more minutes just to be sure. "Okay, let's move," Brett said.

"You two go," Shanda said. "Ellis and I will be fine right here."

"Thought you didn't like the smell," Trill said.

"She got used to it," Ellis said. It was dark under the float, but Brett and Trill could hear kissing sounds.

"Break it up," Brett said. "We've got a job to do."

The four crawled out from under the float. The main lights were off, but a row of smaller, dimmer lights lined the edges of the ceiling.

"To the food court," Brett whispered.

It felt really strange to be there after closing. The darkness wasn't too scary – there was enough light to see by, and they'd spent plenty of time in their youth running around the woods after dark.

No, what really felt wrong was just how quiet it was. This was a building they'd visited nearly every weekend of their lives, and they'd come to associate it with a certain noise level. It had always maintained a constant murmur at its quietest, though earlier tonight it had sounded more like the crowd at a football game. But now it was as quiet as a graveyard.

They turned a corner and reached the food court. All the chairs had been set upside down on the tables. The neon signs were off, and that persistent smell of fresh cookies had faded away.

"Where did you see it?" Ellis whispered.

Brett switched on his flashlight and pointed it at the ceiling. He slowly moved the light along the girders.

"Assuming this thing is real, it's probably gone now," Shanda said.

"It might have latched onto someone else as they were leaving," Trill added.

"I know," Brett said. "But there weren't any more commotions, right? So no one else went crazy."

"I don't know if we'd have heard it all the way from under the float," Trill said.

"And we don't know if it causes madness right away," Ellis added.

Brett continued looking at the rafters, frowning.

"Even if it is in the mall, it's not like it had to stay right here," Shanda said.

"Hey! You kids!" It was a man's voice. Footsteps rushed toward them, but they were too shocked to run.

Brett raised his hands to show he wasn't armed. "I'm sorry, I'm sorry!" he said.

The security guard skidded to a halt right in front of them. He was in his mid-twenties, with curly blond hair and a very sparse mustache. "What are you kids doing here?"

Brett was nearly in tears. *Brainsuckers from outer space I can handle,* he thought. *But not getting arrested for trespassing.*

The guard tapped his foot. "Well?" he asked. "One of you speak, or you're all going to jail."

"I'm so sorry," Brett said. "We have a very good reason for being here. I… I can't tell you what it is, but I promise we weren't robbing the place. Please don't arrest us." But in his head, he was screaming *Please go away please go away please go away…*

"Oh, okay," the security guard said, then began walking toward the exit. "I was about to head out," he explained. "Do me a favor and make sure the door locks behind you when you leave." Then he walked out the door, and it clicked shut behind him.

Brett just stood there for a moment, blinking.

"What just happened?" Shanda asked.

"He… believed me?" Brett said.

"I didn't even believe you," Trill said.

"Wait," Shanda said. "The creature you saw… maybe it was on his head, messing with his mind."

"So you believe me now?" Brett asked.

"No, but…" Shanda said, then trailed off.

"There was nothing on his head," Ellis said. "I thought of that while he was talking, so I looked really close. His hair was too fluffy. If there had been an alien hat monster attached to his head, his hair would have been matted down. Even if it was invisible I should have seen something."

"Maybe it's a trick," Trill said. "He didn't think he could take all four of us, so he let us think we were going to get away, but he'll come back in a few minutes with the p— Eaaagh!"

Everyone turned toward her while she screamed.

And then they all saw it. The thing on Trill's head looked like a thick bowl made of clear gelatin, though it was hard to see unless the light hit it just right. It covered her head down to the top of her ears, and it throbbed and pulsated like it was sucking on a straw.

Trill kept screaming, but the other three stood frozen. Finally Shanda came to her senses. "Get it!" she shouted, and whacked Trill on the head with a flashlight.

"Ow!" Trill shouted, but she also kept pounding on her own head.

Brett tried to bring the butterfly net down on her head, but he missed and broke the handle across her shoulder instead. Then he began beating on the creature with the broken handle.

"I said ow!" Trill screamed, tugging at the creature. Oddly, it wasn't actually hurting her, but its grip around her head was strong.

"Pull it off!" Ellis suggested, and they all gripped at the edges of the creature's mouth – if that was indeed a mouth – and pulled. It finally popped off her head and squished as it hit Ellis in the chest.

"Get it off me!" Ellis shouted, falling backward onto the floor. Brett reached for it but the creature suddenly took off on its own, undulating through the air the way a jellyfish swims through water.

"Don't let it get away!" Shanda shouted, and threw her flashlight at it. Her aim was dead-on, and the creature spiraled back to the floor, splatting against the hard tile.

Brett grabbed the head of the butterfly net off the floor, and brought it down on top of the creature. It tried to take off again, but couldn't get through the net.

"We need a box or something," Ellis said as she got to her feet.

"Are you okay?" Shanda asked her, and Ellis nodded. They held hands and looked into each other's eyes.

"Hello, nearly had my brains sucked out?" Trill said.

"What did it feel like?" Ellis asked, sounding more curious than concerned.

"Like being gummed to death by a toothless lion," Trill answered. "But... it didn't really hurt. I could feel it in my head, like it was trying to make a psychic connection, but it couldn't make it work. It felt like... like it expected a milkshake but got castor oil instead."

"This is all very interesting, but can I get some help here?" Brett still sat on the floor, holding the net's outer ring against the tile so the creature couldn't fly away.

While Brett and Shanda stayed with the creature, Trill and Ellis found a supply closet. They started to grab a couple of garbage bags when Ellis noticed a large plastic container full of mustard packets. She popped off the lid, dumped out the packets, and took the container back to Brett.

Working together, they carefully slipped the lid

underneath the net, then flipped it and deposited the creature into the container. Then they pulled the net away and sealed the lid shut.

"Should we poke some holes in the lid?" Trill asked.

"Do we actually care if it lives?" Shanda asked.

"We don't even know if it needs oxygen," Ellis said. "But I'd like to take it home and run some tests on it. I guess I should keep it alive so I can learn more about it. Better safe than sorry."

Brett kept a pocketknife in his pocket, which he now used to puncture the lid. Then they finally left the mall and went home.

"Wake up, sleepyhead!" The voice came up through the floor, a bit muted but still loud enough to invade Brett's dreams.

Brett groaned. The last thing he wanted was to get out of bed right now. He'd gotten home very late and had been extra quiet so as not to wake his father. The old house's creaky floors hadn't made that easy.

But the wafting smell of sausage links overpowered his desire to fall back asleep. He rolled out of bed, got dressed, stopped by the bathroom, and went downstairs.

"Hey, Dad," Brett said as he sat down at the table.

"Rough night?" his dad asked, setting a plate in front of him.

Brett smiled. His dad had arranged the eggs and sausage into a smiley face. "Yeah, didn't get a whole lot of sleep."

"I heard you come in," his dad said. "It was pretty late. I thought you were staying at Eiko's."

"She got sick, so I came home," Brett said. "And she goes by 'Trill' now."

"Is she going to be okay?"

"Sure Dad," Brett said. "It was probably just something she ate."

His dad sat down. "Son, I think we should talk about Trill."

Oh god, what now? Brett thought. He bit a sausage link in half and chewed, waiting for his father to continue.

His dad sighed. "Are you two… ah…"

"We're just friends, dad," Brett said.

"I don't pretend to understand your generation," his dad said. "But I've heard rumors about Ellis and Shanda, and then you want to be treated like a boy, and Eiko – sorry, 'Trill' – what's her deal again?"

"She doesn't consider herself male or female," Brett said.

"But you still call her 'she,' right?"

"For now," Brett said. "If she thinks of something else she likes better, she'll let us know."

"I'm not going to lie to you, Brett," his dad said. "I find all of this very confusing. You like dressing like a guy, and you like being called Brett, and I'm happy to play along. Though if you were a real boy, I wouldn't allow you to sleep over at Trill's house, and I'm pretty sure her parents wouldn't either. But it won't be long until you're out in the real world, and you'll have to get a job…"

"I know, Dad."

"Do you?" his dad asked. "Because employers aren't going to put up with this cross-dressing crap. Like I said, I'm happy to play along, but I'm hoping you get it out of your system soon. I always wanted a son, but…"

Where are you going with this? Brett wondered.

His dad sighed. "I love you no matter what. But I'm not sure your friends are a good influence on you."

"What?" Brett asked.

"Trill especially," his dad said. "Crazy begets crazy, and I'm afraid that as long as you're influencing each other, you're not seeing how the world's going to see you."

"Dad," Brett said.

"Whatever happened to Georgia?" his dad asked, taking a bite of eggs. "She seemed like a nice, normal girl. I think she'll go far in life. I bet she marries a rich guy and they end up having three kids."

"Is that what you want for me?" Brett asked. "You think I should wear frilly dresses so I can land some hunk and be a housewife?"

"I just want some grandkids before I retire," his dad said. "But if you keep up this tomboy thing, no man's going to be interested in you."

"This isn't some 'thing,' Dad," Brett said. "This is who I am. I'm not going to grow out of it."

Brett's dad frowned and looked like he was debating on what to say next. "Brett," he finally said. "I spoke to the pastor…"

Oh no, Brett thought, gaping at his dad. *Just drop it. Accept me for who I am. Drop it drop it drop it…*

"But you know what?" his dad said. "He's full of crap anyway. You know what's best for you." Then he finished off his plate and washed his dish in the sink.

That was easy, Brett thought. He wondered if his dad had really come around, or if he just didn't want to start an argument. Either way, it wasn't like him.

Shanda and Ellis woke up to a pounding on the bedroom door. They'd stayed at Shanda's house because it was easier to sneak into without waking anyone up. Shanda lived over her parents' detached garage, in a room that had once been an attic, then later a guest house before Shanda took it over.

"Shanda, are you in there?" Her mother's voice was so loud she might as well have been standing in the room.

"One minute, ma!" Shanda shouted. Then she nudged Ellis and said, "Get dressed. Hurry."

They were both naked – they'd been tired after getting home from the mall, but not *that* tired – and their clothes were scattered about the room. They both scurried around the bedroom like it was the world's fastest Easter egg hunt.

They heard the jingle of keys in the lock. "I said one minute!" Shanda shouted, frantically pulling her underwear on.

The door opened. Shanda's mother burst in, looking very angry. "What is *she* doing here?" she asked, pointing at Ellis. "You said you were going to spend the night at her place."

"We changed our minds," Shanda said. "I didn't think you'd care."

"Sorry, Mrs. Henderson," Ellis added, blushing. She was still trying to pull her jeans up over her hips.

"Her parents just called me," Shanda's mom said. "They wanted to talk to Ellis. I told them you two were at their place. They said you were staying here. I almost had a heart attack until I saw your car outside."

"Like I said, we changed our minds," Shanda said. "We were going to stay at her house, so that's what we told you. Then I remembered I had a tape I wanted to show her, so I told her parents we were coming here."

"What was the tape?" her mother asked.

"The... uh..." Shanda began. Her mind completely blanked while trying to think of a title.

"You're grounded," her mother said.

"All I did was —" Shanda began.

"You lied to me," her mother said. "Nothing but home

and school for two weeks. Ellis, I'll drive you home."

"Actually… my car's still at the mall," Ellis said, biting her lower lip.

Shanda's mother groaned and shook her head. "Fine. Get your things and I'll take you to your car."

It wasn't until they left that Shanda remembered the creature. They'd trapped it in a plastic bin and locked it in Shanda's trunk. *What am I supposed to do with that thing?* Shanda wondered. Ellis had planned to experiment on it, but Shanda didn't want to go anywhere near the creature.

She walked over to her window and looked down at her car in the driveway. Just knowing that the creature was in the trunk made her shiver.

Trill woke up at six AM on the dot. She usually did, no matter how much she'd slept. Her bladder had a built-in alarm clock, and it woke her up regardless of whether she drank any water before going to bed. She fully intended to go straight back to bed after using the bathroom, but as she stumbled through the hallway, eyes half-closed, she heard footsteps from upstairs.

They never get up early on Saturdays, Trill thought.

But her parents weren't just awake, they were active. The thumping from above was constant and loud, like her parents were running in place. *Did they start a new exercise routine?* Trill wondered. They'd tried aerobics a few years earlier – Trill's parents were suckers for passing fads – but those leg warmers hadn't been worn in a long time.

Trill stood still for a moment, trying to decide whether to go back to her room. Then she heard a larger thud, accompanied by the tinkling of glass. A list of possible casualties flashed through Trill's mind. The bedroom window? Her mother's bedside lamp? The old black-and-white television they kept on their dresser?

The running continued. Trill slowly walked through the hallway until she came to the base of the stairs. She stood there for a moment, then shouted, "Mom? Dad?"

The thumping stopped. Trill heard the bedroom door open. Everything was silent for a couple of seconds, then there was an explosion of footsteps as her parents ran out their bedroom door and down the stairs.

Trill froze when she saw them. Her father was naked from the waist down, but somehow that was the least horrifying thing about the situation. Both parents were wild-eyed and covered in cuts and bruises. What clothing they wore was ripped and tattered, and they moved in clumsy jerks, like marionettes in an earthquake.

And both of them had alien parasites on their heads.

Trill's mother, who had a PhD in chemistry and an IQ of one-sixty-eight, grunted "Get hurrr" like a Neanderthal in a dinosaur movie. They reached for their daughter with murder in their eyes.

Trill screamed and ran out the back door.

Maybe I was too hard on her, Mrs. Henderson thought as she pulled her station wagon into the driveway. Yes, she'd caught Shanda in a lie, but it wasn't like she'd committed a felony. *But why, though?* she wondered. *Why would Shanda tell me she was staying with Ellis if they were going to come back here instead?* It was an odd thing to lie about.

But then it hit her. *For the privacy*, she thought. *If I thought they were somewhere else, I'd have no reason to disturb them here. They could party all night in Shanda's room, doing drugs, having boys over, and whatever else they wanted and I'd sleep right through it.* Her pulse raced as she thought of more and more possibilities.

Then she shook her head. *I'm being silly,* she thought. *They're good girls. I've never even heard Shanda talk about a boy. And I'd have smelled it if they'd been doing pot. I'm going to head up there right now and talk to her. If she apologizes, I'll unground her.*

She got out of the station wagon and put her keys in her purse. As she walked past her daughter's car, she heard a clatter from inside. *Was that from her trunk?* she wondered, and walked around to the back of the car.

Something was moving in there. She could hear it banging around. *Maybe a raccoon?* she thought as she grabbed her keys. She unlocked the trunk, then jumped back as the lid went up.

A nearly transparent, cup-shaped thing flew out of the trunk. Mrs. Henderson had just enough time to think, *That looks like a giant condom.* And then it was on her head, tearing into her thoughts.

On the outside of the garage, a set of wooden stairs led to a small landing outside Shanda's bedroom door. Mrs. Henderson watched as the door opened and her daughter stepped outside. The girl stood at the top of the stairs, screaming.

But in Mrs. Henderson's eyes, her daughter had transformed into something alien. Except Shanda looked the same as she always had. It was more like Mrs. Henderson's perception of the human race had changed, matured even – she now recognized them for the monstrosities that they really were.

Must... shut... her up, Mrs. Henderson thought, and charged at her daughter.

After breakfast, Brett was tempted to give Ellis a call to see if she'd figured out anything about the creature. But it was still pretty early, and he didn't want to wake her parents. Besides, he wasn't quite sure if she'd slept at her place or at Shanda's.

So instead he went outside to mow the lawn. He hated most of his chores, but mowing wasn't so bad. It made him feel manly somehow. Just pulling on the starter cord gave him a masculine rush, and he whoop-whooped when he got it to start on the third try. Even his father usually needed five pulls.

He was halfway done when he saw it. The woods at the edge of his property seemed to come alive for a moment. All the leaves rustled, and even the trunks swayed a little. But he didn't feel any wind.

And suddenly the sky was full of jelly-like creatures, each one identical to the thing they'd caught at the mall. They spread out in all directions, some floating gently like dandelions, others jetting through the air with great urgency.

One dove straight at Brett, and he ran for the house with his hands over his head. He was halfway to the door when he felt something moist wrap around his hands. It pulsed and stretched, trying to make a connection with his mind.

Get off me! Brett thought, and then it was gone. Brett looked up and saw that it had flown back up into the air to join the swarm. A few more dove toward Brett, but they turned away once they got close.

Brett was relieved, but he didn't feel safe yet. He ran back into the house and slammed the door.

Ellis wasn't a very comfortable driver. Her friends couldn't wait to get their learner's permits at fifteen, and most of them had their licenses within a week of turning sixteen. But Ellis had put it off as long as she could, only relenting when her dad's hours changed and she could no longer count on him for rides to the library.

She was okay driving to school and back. She'd found a route that, while circuitous, kept her off the main roads and ensured she didn't have to make any left turns without an arrow. She also didn't mind going to the library, as it was only fifteen minutes away and barely took any turns at all.

But she hated driving around the mall. It didn't matter what time of day it was, something about the mall just attracted crazy drivers like a magnet.

As she pulled out of the mall parking space, Ellis gripped the wheel so hard her knuckles were white. There was a small road that circled the mall, and while the light she needed was on the left, she turned right instead so she wouldn't have to wait for a break in traffic. As she was making the circuit around the mall, a man ran out in front of her car. Ellis shrieked and slammed on the brakes.

She just missed him, but he pounded on the hood with his fists. Then he ran over to the driver-side window and punched the glass. That's when Ellis noticed the creature on his head. He hit the window again, harder, this time shattering the glass. Ellis screamed and hit the gas, speeding away from the man.

She usually didn't listen to the radio when she drove – music didn't calm her down, and it just felt like one more distraction that might get her killed – but now she turned on the radio and moved the dial until she found a news station.

Strange reports were coming in from all over town. There were more car wrecks than usual, multiple incidents of violence, and people in general were doing odd self-destructive things, such as running into traffic. Several people had reported seeing flying jellyfish, but none of those statements had been confirmed.

I can confirm it, Ellis thought. *This is an invasion, just like in the movies. We have to find out what kills these things, or they'll spread all over the world.*

She thought a moment as she pulled out onto the main road. *The specimen we captured. Maybe I can test it for weaknesses. I have to get back to Shanda's.*

Trill ran all the way to Brett's house. Her parents had given up the chase more than half a mile back. First her mom had peeled off to chase a dog, and then her dad had tripped over a fire hydrant. They'd both seemed easily distracted, and Trill hoped that was a good sign. *They have flaws we can exploit,* she thought.

She reached Brett's house just in time to see him run out the door, his father in pursuit. Trill tackled Brett's father from behind, then quickly got to her feet, grabbed Brett's hand, and ran. "Come on!" she shouted.

"What about dad?" Brett asked.

"Just run!" Trill shouted, and they ran.

Brett's father chased them for about half a block, then wandered away.

Ellis pulled up to Shanda's driveway and put the car in park. The sky was now full of jellyfish, the swarm looking like some sort of weird weather phenomenon. *I can't get out in this,* Ellis thought. One creature dove and splatted against her windshield, then peeled itself away and flew back into the sky.

At the top of the stairs to Shanda's room, Mrs. Henderson pounded on the door. Ellis couldn't see if she wore a creature from this distance, but she had no doubt the woman had been taken over. Unsure of what else to do, she honked her horn.

Mrs. Henderson turned away from the door and rushed down the stairs. Ellis realized the woman was running straight for her. She put the car in reverse and started to back away.

But Mrs. Henderson was faster, and she jumped onto the hood of the car and started banging on the windshield.

Ellis screamed and hit the gas. Her car lurched backward, but Mrs. Henderson held on. Then Ellis spotted Shanda running toward her car. Ellis unlocked the door and Shanda climbed into the passenger side.

"What now?" Ellis asked. She shifted back into drive, but she was afraid to hit the gas with Shanda's mother on the hood.

"Mom, please, get off the car!" Shanda shouted.

Mrs. Henderson stopped attacking the windshield, and then rolled off into the street.

Shanda and Ellis looked at each other. "Did she come to her senses?" Ellis asked.

Then Mrs. Henderson bellowed with rage and ran off to chase a squirrel.

"Drive!" Shanda shouted. "Before she comes after us again!"

Ellis stepped on the gas pedal. "Where to?" she asked.

"Somewhere safe," Shanda said. "Try Brett's! Maybe he'll…"

And then they noticed a couple of figures running up the street towards them. Brett and Trill were being chased by a pair of men Ellis didn't recognize. She didn't even come to a complete stop before her friends pushed their way into the backseat.

"Get us out of here!" Trill shouted, and Ellis drove off.

They passed more insane people as they drove. No two seemed to react the exact same way to their possession. Some fought each other, others attacked inanimate objects, and a few just stood perfectly still as if they were catatonic.

Ellis screeched and slammed on the brakes as a man in a bathrobe suddenly crossed the street in front of her. "Can someone else drive maybe?" Ellis asked as they turned a corner.

"Don't stop until we're somewhere safe," Trill said.

"Any suggestions on that?" Ellis asked.

"The duck blind?" Brett suggested. "I think the woods are pretty clear now."

"I think we should go to my house," Ellis said. "We can lock ourselves in the basement. I have some equipment down there. Maybe I can figure out a way to—"

And then another car smashed into them. Everyone screamed as the car spun in a circle before coming to a rest next to a telephone pole.

"Is everyone okay?" Shanda asked.

"I'm bleeding," Trill said.

Brett leaned over and looked at her. She had a deep cut from where her head had slammed against the side window. The window was broken, and bits of glass glistened in Trill's wound. Brett took off his shirt and used it to wipe her forehead.

"I think we need to get out of here," Shanda said, watching a crowd of alien-controlled people amble towards them.

Ellis tried to turn the key but the car wouldn't start. Her car had been hit from the side, just ahead of the right front tire. Her hood had popped open and she could see steam billowing through the air.

"We have to run," Ellis said.

The nearest building was a BurgerJester restaurant. "In there," Shanda said. "On three."

She counted to three, and all four exited the vehicle. Someone inside the restaurant opened the door for them as they approached. Ellis and Shanda were the first to make it inside, while Brett and Trill walked arm-in-arm, finally stumbling through the door.

A man in a BurgerJester uniform closed the door behind them and locked it. "None of you have those things on your heads, right?" he demanded.

"We're clean," Shanda replied.

"I've never seen anything like this," the employee said. "I was getting ready to open when people started pounding on the windows, all wearing those plastic hats. They looked angry so I didn't open the door."

"Are you the only one here?" Ellis asked, looking around.

The man nodded. "There's supposed to be two more, but they haven't shown up yet. Do you know what's going on?"

"Alien invasion," Shanda said, staring out the window. More people shuffled by, some limping or bleeding. Occasionally one would attack the glass, but they'd inevitably get distracted by something else and wander off.

"Do you have a first aid kit?" Brett asked, and the employee ran off to get it.

"So what now?" Shanda asked.

"We just have to think it out," Ellis said. "What do we know?"

"The brainsuckers land on people and take control," Trill

said, still holding the T-shirt to her forehead.

"The infected are very violent," Shanda said.

"But they have short attention spans," Brett added.

"And…" Ellis thought a moment. "I think they sometimes follow orders?"

"What do you mean?" Trill asked. The employee came back with the first aid kit and opened it. Then he started dabbing at Trill's head with a cotton ball.

"When your mom was on my car, you told her to go away and she did," Ellis said.

"Might have just been a coincidence," Trill said.

"Also, one of the creatures tried to land on my head, but it went away when I told it to," Brett said. Then he thought for a second. "No… it went away when I thought about telling it to."

"If they take over minds, then maybe they also read minds," Ellis said. "Hold on, I want to try something." She walked over to the window, where a woman in a torn dress looked at them vacantly.

Ellis stared her in the eyes and thought, *Release her now*.

The creature on her head flew off into the air. The woman looked confused for a moment, then scared, and then another one of the creatures landed on her. She flew into a rage, beat against the glass a few times, then ran across the street.

"How did you do that?" the BurgerJester employee asked.

"I think the aliens are telepathic," Ellis said. "And I don't think they're sentient. I'm pretty sure they're just animals, acting on instinct. They don't control the people they attack, they just suck on their brainwaves, which makes their victims go crazy."

"So this isn't an invasion," Shanda said.

Ellis shook her head. "That meteor shower five years ago

– that's how they spread, they float through the galaxy like balloon spiders, and Earth just got in the way."

"I want to try it," the employee said, and went to the window. He stood eye-to-eye with another infected person and thought really hard. Nothing happened. "It's not working," he reported.

"Huh," Ellis said, disappointed.

Brett stood up and approached the glass. He stared into the person's eyes, and they ran away. "Worked for me," he said.

"We must be different somehow," Shanda said.

"Of course!" Ellis replied, slapping her forehead. "That egg that splattered on us in the woods that day – maybe it changed our brain chemistry!"

"So you mean we're what, part alien now?" Trill asked, wincing.

"I don't know," Ellis said. "But I really want to get back to my house now. I have a machine that reads brainwaves."

"I have a car," the employee said.

"Good," Ellis said. "You come too. We'll need a normal brain to compare us to."

"But I'm clocked in," the man said. "I can't just—"

One of the windows shattered as a metal trash can flew through it. Two angry-looking men burst through, along with five or six more flying creatures. One of the men rushed towards Brett, while the other grabbed a chair and began smashing more windows.

Brett stood still and thought as hard as he could. *Calm down calm down calm down…*

The man slowed down and finally came to a stop, then started wandering around aimlessly. Then Shanda and Ellis went to calm the other man.

One of the aliens flew at Trill's face, and she screamed. She thought *Go away go away go away* and it swerved past her, going for the BurgerJester employee instead.

Trill grabbed a salt shaker off of a table and threw it at the alien. She hit it dead on, and the shaker broke open against the creature's gelatinous hide. Then the creature pulsated wildly, falling to the floor. It shuddered for a few seconds and lay still. There was a large burn on its side where the salt had hit it.

The four teens continued to scare away the aliens with their telepathic commands. But more kept coming in through the smashed windows. "We can't do this forever," Brett said.

"I quit," the employee said, pulling off his hat. "Follow me."

The BurgerJester employee – who introduced himself as Jeff – drove them around half a dozen accidents and avoided at least twenty people wandering in the streets. Ellis directed him to her house, where the five rushed from the car to her front door. They had to fend off a few of the creatures on the way in, but now that they knew how to order them away, they only had to protect Jeff.

"Where are your parents?" Shanda asked as they walked through the living room.

"Good question," Ellis said. She'd seen their car outside, but no one seemed to be home. "Mom? Dad?" she shouted, but no reply came.

She shrugged and led them down to the basement.

Jeff goggled at all the electronic equipment piled up against the walls. "What are you, some kind of genius?" he asked.

"My dad is," she said. "I just like to dabble."

"She's a genius," Shanda said.

"Here's the machine I wanted to show you," Ellis said. It was a nondescript metal box with a digital readout on the front. Two curly wires led from the box to a pair of foam pads. "Who wants to go first?"

Shanda volunteered. Ellis stuck the pads to her temples and had her think about certain emotions, then recorded the results. She went on to test herself, Brett, Trill, and Jeff.

"Just as I thought," she said as she looked at the results. "The four of us don't think like regular people anymore. Sorry Jeff, you're normal."

"So we have telepathy now?" Shanda asked. She tried to send Ellis a telepathic message but she didn't hear it.

"I don't think so," Ellis said. "It's more like we've tapped into the way the creatures communicate with each other."

Brett frowned. "I had a weird conversation with my dad earlier," he said. "He wasn't infected, but he changed his mind about something really quickly."

Ellis pondered for a moment. Then she turned to Jeff and thought, *Stand on one leg*.

Jeff immediately stood on one leg. "Why am I doing this?" he asked.

"Amazing," Ellis said.

"So we can make the aliens leave people alone," Brett said. "And we can make people do what we say. But there's only four of us and thousands of the aliens. And even if we tell the aliens to leave the people alone, they'll just fly right back a few minutes later. So what can we do?"

"You saw the thing with the salt, right?" Trill asked.

"The what?" Brett asked.

"When I threw—" Trill said, but stopped. They could hear footsteps upstairs.

Ellis walked over to the stairs. "Mom?" she yelled up to

the kitchen.

Two sets of footsteps thundered towards the stairs. Her parents burst through the door and took the steps two at a time as they tried to murder their daughter.

"I'll get this," Shanda said, and started thinking toward the two infected parents.

"Wait," Ellis shouted, and fell back against her work table. She pressed a button marked "play" and her parents stood still. Then the aliens drifted off of their heads.

"What are you doing?" Trill asked.

"I converted your brainwaves into sound," Ellis replied. "Then I played back your anger track."

"I don't hear anything," Brett said.

"The pitch is too high for us to hear," Ellis said. "But the sound is there. If we could broadcast this globally, we could make the creatures flee."

The two creatures continued to float away, fleeing the basement. Ellis watched as her parents came to their senses. "What just happened?" her mom asked.

"I'm about to save the world," Ellis said.

"It's like it's snowing," Brett said as he watched out the window of the airport control tower.

"Looks more like a sandstorm to me," Trill said. The salt was so thick in places that it clung to the window, making it difficult to see the hot air balloons in the distance.

All over town, radio stations and public loudspeakers played the silent brainwave tapes, and alien jellyfish fled into the air, only to get burned by the salt drifting on the wind.

"I'm going to have to wash my car tomorrow," Brett muttered.

"So I have a question," Shanda said. "That mind control trick we have – is that going to stay with us? Even after the aliens are gone?"

"I don't know," Ellis said. "It's possible the presence of all the aliens created some sort of telepathic field that we were tapped into, and the ability will fade when they're gone. But that's just a theory."

"Wow, can you imagine if it stays?" Brett said. "I'll be able to get any job I want."

"Think bigger," Shanda said. "You use it right, and you won't need to work at all."

"Well I, for one, refuse to do anything unethical with my power," Trill said. "Though, there are a couple of guys at school who might find themselves eating sand."

"I don't think we should use the telepathy unless our lives depend on it," Ellis said. "We don't know the long-term effects on the people we influence. Or on ourselves. We could be giving ourselves brain cancer every time we use it."

"Besides, we shouldn't get special treatment just because we're different," Trill said. "The more we use our power, the more we'll be tempted to. Sooner or later we'll be talking ourselves into robbing banks with it."

"I guess," Shanda said. "I mean, it's a good thing *we* got power, instead of someone more evil."

"Exactly," Trill said. "Can you imagine what would happen if this ability fell into the wrong hands?"

"Space Jellyfish Almost Take Over Small Town," Lance read, rolling his eyes. *Tabloid trash*, he thought, then turned to the "Hollywood Gossip" section to see if he was mentioned.

He reclined on a padded chair in front of his luxurious pool, in a backyard that overlooked downtown Beverly

Hills. He continued to flip through the newspaper until he came across the headline, "Teen Heartthrob Lance Darling Joins the Cast of SoCal High."

"Page twenty-three?" Lance exclaimed, shaking his head. Then he tossed the paper aside.

He heard his back door close, and familiar footsteps stepped across the concrete. His assistant, Terry, handed him a cold glass of cola.

"Sir," Terry said, "There's a woman at the door who wishes to see you."

"A fan?" Lance said. "How did she get my address?"

"I don't know, sir."

"Give her a signed photo and send her on her way," Lance said.

"I'm sorry sir, but I must insist," Terry said. "I promised her she'd be allowed to speak to you personally."

"Why did you promise that?" Lance asked, slipping on his sandals.

"I... don't know," Terry admitted. "She was very persuasive."

"Fine, I'll get rid of her myself," Lance said, marching back to the house.

He opened the front door to find a gorgeous young woman on his porch. She was high school age, with blond hair and a fantastic figure.

Beautiful or not, she's in for a world of hurt, Lance thought. "Now listen here," he began.

"Lance Darling?" the woman asked. "It's really you! I'm Georgia." Then she stared him hard in the eyes and said, "Marry me."

Playing God

The spider was the size of a minivan and covered with human-like flesh. *It's not really there*, Florence's brain pleaded, but it was hard to argue with her eyes. It took a step forward, and Florence took a step back. She gasped as her back hit the wall. Only it wasn't the wall. What she felt against her back was solid, but far from flat. It moved against her weight, and she was able to back up a few more inches.

She was unable to take her eyes off the flesh-spider, but she reached behind herself to get a better feel of the barrier. She shrieked as her fingers tickled the meaty rib bones of a half-eaten corpse.

This is worse than the time I fell into that septic tank at work, she mused, then almost laughed at the absurdity of the thought. Of course this was worse. No experience in her life compared to the one she was currently living. If she survived this – which didn't look likely – it would easily become her worst memory of all time.

Two more flesh-spiders climbed through the doorway, one walking along the ceiling. The nearest one was now only a few feet away. It was dark in here – wherever "here" was

– but the spider was close enough to make out more details. Its flesh was, indeed, quite humanlike. Florence could see pores, freckles, sparse hair, and even discolorations that might have been liverspots.

As she watched, more eyes opened up along the spider's legs. Now it had dozens of eyes, all staring at Florence in hungry fascination. Its fleshy mandibles twitched in anticipation.

Why can't I wake up? Florence wondered. It didn't feel like a dream. Everything felt too solid, too real. But it was the only explanation. She couldn't remember how she'd come to be in this place, nothing about the room looked familiar, and the spiders were like nothing else on Earth. Outside of horror movies, that was. It simply had to be a dream. Nothing else made sense.

The flesh-spider lifted a front leg and thrust it through Florence's abdomen. It felt like being kicked by a mule. She was now pinned to the wall. She reached out to push the spider away, and it bit into her right hand. She could feel her fingers being crunched into bonemeal. It was excruciating... and yet, it didn't feel like she would have expected. The pain was less like having her digits crushed or severed, and more like being electrocuted.

It was confusing, but she didn't have time to dwell on it. The other spiders had arrived. Florence looked up just in time to see a ceiling-mounted spider thrust a leg towards her eye. Again, it felt more like getting punched than impaled, but it wasn't as if she had a reference for comparison. She tried not to get stabbed in the eye on a regular basis, so maybe this was what it was supposed to feel like.

She was now blind in her left eye, and she couldn't move her head. With her remaining eye, she was forced to stare into the approaching mandibles of the ceiling spider.

She could feel something gnawing on her leg, but with everything else going on, she dismissed that pain as unimportant. The first spider had finished off her right hand and had begun chewing on the left. *But I type a hundred words a minute*, she lamented faintly.

Those mandibles were now in her face. Within the spider's maw, Florence could see sharp teeth, a pink tongue, a uvula... she had no idea what it was supposed to look like down a spider's throat, but this definitely wasn't it.

The mouth closed around her face. She could feel her skin stretching and pulling as the spider devoured her face, leaving her with – she imagined – the ragged visage of a horror movie zombie. Its leg – the one currently embedded in her eye – jerked hard, and she felt her neck snap. But she didn't die, she didn't even get light-headed. She continued breathing even as the spider tore her head from her body and placed it in its hungry mandibles.

Florence waited for death. At this point, she craved it. *If these are going to be my last thoughts, I'd better make them good,* she thought. *Um... E equals MC squared?* In her panic, all she could remember was her social security number and a few random scenes from kindergarten.

It was pitch black now – her head was lodged in the throat of a giant spider, after all. All she could hear were crunching sounds as her head was pulverized by the massive jaws. *What even am I now?* she wondered. She'd always assumed death was instantaneous once the head was separated from the spine. But now she wondered if brains kept on thinking forever. All those brains in jars she'd seen in museums – had they been thinking? Would her thoughts go on even as her brain was digested in the spider's stomach?

She could now see a light in the distance. *Maybe it swallowed a firefly*, she thought. Though at this point, she was surprised she could see at all. Was her remaining eye still intact? Was it still connected to her brain? It seemed unlikely.

Maybe I'm headed for the afterlife, she thought.

But as she got closer, she realized it was a doorway. She moved towards it. She wasn't sure how she was moving, but it took no effort. She reached the doorway and put a hand on the doorframe. *My hand?* Florence thought, moving it back in front of her face. She looked down and patted herself all over. She was intact again. Somehow.

Through the door, she saw a dimly lit hallway. *I've been here before,* she thought. It seemed very recent, but she couldn't place the memory.

There were chittering sounds behind her. She turned to look, but it was too dark. She saw movement, but couldn't make out any details. She fled into the relative safety of the hallway.

There were doors all up and down the hall. She tried one, but it wouldn't open. She tried another. Also stuck. The third opened, but inside lurked some large, fleshy mass. It was like a living, pulsating tumor that took up most of the room. Florence couldn't get a better look, nor did she want one. She slammed the door shut and ran further down the hall.

The open doorway – the one she'd come in – was now filled with thousands of rats. Except these rats were skinless, like they'd been flayed to death but they'd forgotten to die.

Florence continued to run. She reached a corner, turned, and kept going. She could hear the swarm just behind her, running along the floor, walls, and ceiling. Their squelching squeaks were deafening. She turned another corner, then another. She was certain she'd made a complete square, but the hallway didn't look the same. With each turn, the wallpaper became older, more faded, sometimes peeling. The carpet became more threadbare, and the light fixtures featured more and more cobwebs.

Seven turns later, the hallway ended at a door. Florence risked a look behind her. The rats were just turning the last corner. Florence grabbed the knob and twisted. It was unlocked. The door was stuck in its frame, but it was no match for the adrenaline flowing through Florence's body. She pulled it open and saw that the room was pitch black inside.

Anywhere is better than here, she thought, and jumped inside, slamming the door behind her.

The floor was wet and squished as she walked. Florence realized she was barefoot. *Wasn't I wearing shoes before?* she wondered. *Granted, I have been eaten since then.* She barked out a laugh, a sound which felt totally inappropriate the moment it left her mouth.

But she couldn't really remember being eaten. The thought had come to her as a fact, a thing she knew but didn't actually recall, like learning how to walk or the first time she'd pumped gas. She knew those things had to have happened – she could walk, after all, and she put gas in her car every week – but they weren't actually memories. It was now a fact to her that she'd been eaten by giant spiders, but the actual memory had burned to embers.

Her legs unsteady, Florence lurched back to the door, then felt around for a light switch. The walls were also soft and slimy, and she withdrew her hand right away. But this had to be done, so she steeled her nerves and touched the wall again. She explored until she found a bump. Not so much a switch as a button, but really not even that – it was more like a...

Don't think it, Florence thought. *If you think the next word you will lose your mind.*

She pressed the bump, and it diminished into the wall. A warm, yellow light lit the room. What she saw next horrified her.

The walls and ceiling were red flesh, like the inside of her mouth. The floor was a giant tongue. The walls were covered in what looked like giant canker sores. It was one of these that she had pressed to light up the room. Florence couldn't see a light source and had no idea what was illuminating the room.

The door had vanished. The only exit was on the far side of the room, a hole in the floor that looked remarkably like the back of a throat.

I'm not going that way, Florence thought. *I'll rot here first.* She sat against the wall, as far from the throat as possible, hugging her knees. She realized she was naked. *When did that happen?* she wondered. The tongue beneath her quivered as she sat, as if it was tasting her flesh.

She tried to catch her breath. It felt like she'd been on the run for hours. This was not a safe room, but for now, it was the entire universe.

But the room wouldn't allow a reprieve, even for a moment. The floor began to wiggle. Florence stood, then was knocked off her feet. The tongue undulated around her, and she realized with horror that it was trying to push her toward the hole. She tried to get to her feet again, couldn't, then rolled toward the wall on the right. The ripples changed direction, pushing her away from that wall and back towards the hole.

"No!" she shouted, and tumbled over the moving mound of tongue-flesh, back toward where the door had been. She desperately pushed against the wall. She looked for anything she could use as a weapon, any object, anything that would make her feel less vulnerable. But there was nothing. She shrieked and dug her fingernails into the fleshy wall.

Now the entire room shook. An angry shout emanated from the throat, a bellow so loud it made Florence's ears bleed. The room began to tilt. Soon the throat hole was at the bottom of the room, and the walls and floor angled towards it like a funnel. The air from that hole smelled like a trashcan at a carnival. Florence tried to grab something, anything to slow her descent into that hole. But there was nothing. She slid along the wet flesh until she vanished, and now she was falling, falling in an infinite void…

"Time of death, nine PM," the executioner reported, removing the REM discs from Florence's temples.

"It only took six minutes?" Gabe asked. Gabriel "Call me Gabe" Tull was a reporter for the Cutting Edge Times, an e-magazine about new technologies.

"For her it seemed like hours, maybe days," the executioner replied. "Days of nothing but the worst horrors imaginable. No rest, no reprieve. Just running in terror until your heart gives out." As they talked, a pair of technicians placed Florence's lifeless body on a stretcher and wheeled it out of the room.

"What if the prisoner has a stronger heart?" Gabe asked.

"The program will run as long as it takes," the executioner replied. "They'll be caught in a never-ending loop of horrific scenarios with no relief. No one can hold out forever."

"What was so wrong with lethal injection?" Gabe asked.

"She poisoned her husband and all three children," the executioner said. He didn't appreciate the question, but he didn't raise his voice. He was used to defending his position. "Should we just let her pass away peacefully?"

"That depends," Gabe replied. "Does the state execute for revenge, or to protect the rest of society?"

"Look at it this way," the executioner offered. "You have no idea the amount of stress that comes with my job."

"I'm pretty sure Florence had a worse day than you."

The executioner ignored him and continued. "With traditional executions, someone always has to pull the lever, inject the poison, fire the rifle. In my career, I have executed seventy-three prisoners. Were all of them guilty? Probably. I believe in the court system, but it's not infallible. It still hits me sometimes, in the middle of the night: I have killed seventy-three people. And the bigger that number gets, the bigger the chance that one of them was wrongfully convicted. Most people can't take this job as long as I have."

"I can imagine," Gabe said.

"But with this new system, they kill themselves," the executioner said. "The condemned are haunted by their own fears, by nightmares of their own creation. And when the inevitable happens, their bodies kill themselves."

Gabe shook his head. "Ridiculous. That's like saying lethal injection is suicide because the body chooses to absorb the poison. You're using a device to execute condemned prisoners, pure and simple. If that's allowed by your moral compass, fine. Half the country agrees with you, so who am I to tell you you're wrong? But don't rationalize it as being somehow 'less murderous' than, say, the firing squad."

"Let me ask you a question," the executioner said. "Do you believe in an afterlife?"

"I have no idea," Gabe replied.

"Me neither," the executioner said. "But if there is a Hell, we both know she's burning there now, and the horror show we just put her through is nothing compared to her eternal torment."

"Yes, but—"

"But," the executioner continued. "If there is no afterlife, then we all achieve the same peace when we die. Is that fair? Her children choke to death on deadly chemicals, their throats burning, their stomachs bursting, but their killer gets to peacefully fall into an endless slumber? What I'm saying is, if we're going to put these monsters down anyway, shouldn't we put them through a little Hell first?"

"Is that rhetorical?" Gabe asked. "Because if you're asking me, you've taken 'playing God' to a whole new level."

"Oh, cry me a river," the executioner said. "You people always whine about 'playing God' when new technology develops. When we started cloning human hearts for transplants, we were 'playing God.' When we cured cancer using stem cell research, we were 'playing God.' When we started using nanotechnology to manage diabetes—"

"I can't help but notice all your examples saved lives," Gabe said. "And yet you're using them to defend a method of execution. How about the atom bomb? Weaponized diseases? Cloning dinosaurs for warfare? Far better examples if you ask me."

The executioner groaned. "I think we're done here. Go back to that propaganda rag you work for, put whatever liberal spin you want on it." The executioner held up one of the REM discs and flipped it like a coin. "But mark my words, in ten years, this will be the norm. This is the future of capital punishment."

Gabe stood and gathered his things. "Thank you for your time," he said, and shook the executioner's hand.

The executioner changed clothes in the locker room, clocked out, and got into his car. He took a long, deep breath before starting the engine. *Leave it behind*, he thought. *You're not the executioner now. You're Earl. Earl Kinnard.*

It was a daily ritual, a way of keeping his work life and home life separate. On days when he had to perform executions – which he called "X-days" - he tried to keep interactions to a minimum. He used a separate entrance on those days, wore a doctor's mask, and avoided chit-chat. No one called him Earl on X-days; he was simply "the executioner."

But today was different. Maybe because he was testing new technology. More likely it was the interview that had thrown him off guard. He wasn't used to having long-winded conversations on X-days. He wished he could have scheduled the interview somewhere else, after work, but the reporter had insisted on seeing the execution in person. It was hard to stay in executioner mode while being interviewed, and some of Earl had shown through during their discussion.

He didn't like it when that happened. His entire coping mechanism hinged on Earl staying home on X-days. He looked at himself in the rearview mirror and noticed he was sweating. Trembling, he took his hands off the wheel and rubbed his eyes. Then he just sat for a few minutes, hands over his eyes, taking deep breaths and trying to regain control.

Earl.

His eyes snapped open and he lowered his hands. Someone had whispered his name. He looked around, out the windows, in the backseat, searching for the voice. *Okay, get a grip*, he told himself. It was obviously an auditory hallucination brought on by stress. What else could it have been?

He wasn't completely over his breakdown, but enough was enough. He put the car in gear and drove home.

Earl lived alone. His ex-wife had left him shortly after he'd been assigned to execution duty. When he'd accepted the position, he'd hoped she'd be proud of him. But no, she'd called him a ghoul. It wasn't the only reason they'd split up, but it was certainly the straw that broke the camel's back. Now the house felt too big, too empty. Coming home sometimes felt like going to a restaurant alone, and sitting at a table designed for six.

He parked in the garage and went straight upstairs to the guest room. That's where he slept these days. The master bedroom was full of memories he wanted to avoid. He supposed he should convert it into something useful like a home gym, but it was easier just to never go in there.

Earl began to undress. He used to wear pajamas after he got home at night, but since the divorce he tended to just lounge around in his boxers. Less laundry, no one to impress, and he'd never really found the pajamas comfortable anyway. He emptied his pockets and put his wallet on the dresser, along with...

What's this?

The REM discs. The ones he'd used on Florence. He thought he'd left them at work, but here they were in his pocket. *Guess I'll take them back tomorrow*, he thought, setting them next to his wallet.

Then he went back downstairs and tossed a frozen dinner in the oven. He watched the news while it cooked, then an old sitcom while he ate. He stayed up for another two hours before going to bed.

Earl.

The voice woke him from a dream, something about winning a pizza by playing skeeball. His dreams were rarely creative, mostly they were just spruced-up memories with minor discrepancies. One night he'd go bowling dressed as Elvis, another night he'd take George Washington out for pizza. Actually, a lot of his dreams involved pizza.

But now he was wide awake. He'd heard his name again, just as he had in the car. Of course, he had been dead asleep thirty seconds ago. But the voice hadn't felt like a dream.

"Cora?" he called out. He hadn't seen his ex-wife since that final day in court, but he was pretty sure she still had a key. Maybe she'd suddenly missed an old photo album or her grandmother's quilt, and she'd stopped by to pick it up.

At three AM on a Tuesday. Without calling first.

He sat up in bed for another minute. *It was just a dream, case closed,* he thought. He lay back down.

Earl.

This time he was out of bed and on his feet in an instant. He switched on the lights. Nothing was there. His wallet was still on the nightstand, so it couldn't be a robber. Though why a robber would call his name, he didn't know. He hadn't been awake long enough for logic.

His bedroom door was halfway open. He couldn't remember if he'd closed it when he'd gone to bed. Usually he did, but not always. He poked his head out into the hallway. Nobody was there.

Then his heart leaped into his throat. At the end of the hallway, the door to the master bedroom was open. He hadn't opened that door in weeks.

He crept through the dim hallway until he reached the bedroom door, then peered inside. It was dark, but he could just make out the form of a woman. She was facing away from Earl, standing perfectly still.

"Cora?" he called again. But it wasn't Cora, not unless she'd lost fifty pounds and grown six inches taller.

"Seven," the woman whispered.

He knew that voice. He'd heard it earlier that day. "Se- Seven?" he asked.

"Seven," the woman rasped. "Seven innocents."

Behind her, six additional figures emerged from the darkness. It was hard to see anything more than silhouettes at first, but Earl's eyes adjusted until he could make out their faces. He recognized all of them. He'd only met each of them once, but as with everyone he'd euthanized over the years, their faces were forever burned into his memory.

Earl was not an imaginative man, but he'd seen his share of scary movies. No movie monster could compare with the reality of discovering a strange person in your bedroom, only to realize it was someone you'd killed. And Earl now faced this terror sevenfold.

"Seven innocents," Florence hissed again.

He didn't need any further clarification. It was one of his deepest worries. No court was infallible, the question was just how often it failed. He'd read somewhere that four percent of executed criminals later turn out to be innocent. If the statistic was true, then out of the seventy-three executions he had performed, he was likely to have killed two, maybe three innocent people. It was a sobering thought, but one he usually rejected.

Four percent is nothing, he always told himself. *It's almost zero. If every prisoner I execute has a four percent chance of being innocent, then every single one of them is ninety-six percent likely to be guilty.*

Apparently not. Looking into the faces of these seven ghouls – five men, two women – details of their trials came flooding back to him. None of their cases had been cut-and-dry. Each of them had been the subject of controversy, with trials that lasted for months. According to the press, some of the evidence had been questionable, but each of them had been found guilty anyway. Earl remembered crossing picket lines to get into the building on a couple of their X-days.

"I don't… understand…" Earl yammered. But it was a lie. Deep down, he knew what their accusation meant. He knew because he'd often suspected it himself. They say a guilty conscience needs no accuser, and Earl's conscience had been stockpiling evidence for years. His mental filing cabinet was crammed full of rationalizations, counterpoints, alibis, and apologies. With all the murders on his hands – state-sanctioned or not – he knew he'd face a trial someday. In this world or the next.

He'd prepared for this chance to defend himself. He'd crafted dozens of careful, well-reasoned arguments, designed to convince the most die-hard bleeding-heart anti-justice morons. Knowing what had to be said, Earl opened his mouth to speak.

"My job… they made me… if a rabid dog… the Bible says… no… had to protect… most were bad… they killed…" He closed his mouth, tried to get his thoughts together, then spoke again. This time, all that came out was unintelligible gibberish.

Naturally, his audience was not convinced. The seven accusers stepped forward, their hands outstretched, reaching for Earl's throat.

"I'm sorry," Earl said, then turned and ran. His first instinct was to run down the stairs and out the front door. However, he quickly realized that the stairs were no longer there. There was nothing but wall where the stairs should have been, adorned with the same maroon-striped wallpaper as the rest of the upstairs hallway. But as Earl looked down the hall, it seemed to stretch on forever.

The ghosts – or zombies or revenants or whatever they were – ambled through the bedroom door. Earl fled through the unending hallway, passing the same six framed photos over and over, the same open bathroom doorway, the same decorative table that had once supported a vase of flowers. Cora had taken the vase with her; it had belonged to her grandmother. The empty table was a constant reminder of her absence.

Despite the infinite hallway and the impending doom, Earl couldn't help but think of how much he missed Cora. *I should have listened to her*, he thought. But these thoughts soon dissipated as the hallway became less familiar. The pictures no longer hung on the walls. He stopped passing the table and bathroom doorway. As Earl ran, the wallpaper gave way to the plain gray brick of the Garden State Penitentiary.

He passed a cell door. Then another and another. Faces watched him from inside. He recognized them as prisoners he had executed. Some hurled insults. Others reached through the bars, their fingers just brushing Earl's arm as he passed.

I'm so tired, Earl thought, but he kept on running. As he passed the next cell door, it clanked and began to slide open. He could hear inmates running after him, shouting accusations and violent threats. The next door also opened on his way by. The more cells he passed, the larger the mob grew. He dared not slow down to turn his head, but he could see their shadows on the walls as he ran. The light around them flickered as if they carried torches.

And still he ran. The never-ending hallway soon ran out of cell doors. It was now just blank white walls, like the walls at Garden State Penitentiary that led from death row to the execution chamber. Earl realized that he no longer heard so many footfalls behind him, and the shouting had died down. Instead he heard a single set of heavy boots, and a strange scraping sound he couldn't identify. The footfalls were slow, but each step shook the floor. Despite Earl's faster pace, his unseen pursuer seemed to have no trouble keeping up.

The hallway finally ended up ahead. A door loomed closer and closer, but Earl recognized it right off, and it wasn't a door he wanted to enter. It was the door that led to his place of work. The execution chamber where he'd administered dozens of lethal injections, some earlier this year, one earlier this month. It had been the prison's preferred method of execution right up until the invention of the REM discs.

Earl came to an abrupt halt as he slammed into the door. With nowhere else to turn, he reluctantly opened the door. He risked a look behind him as he entered.

Fifty feet away, a monster of a man stomped his way toward Earl. The man was shirtless, with a bodybuilder's physique. He wore black pants and a matching executioner's hood, looking like something out of an old cartoon. He dragged a massive ax behind him. The handle alone was longer than Earl was tall. The executioner's eyes glowed red.

Earl slammed the door shut and locked it. It shuddered immediately, with a loud thump that knocked him to the floor. It thumped three more times before it went silent. As Earl climbed back to his feet, he noticed the floor was covered in dirt. He stood and turned away from the door.

This was not the lethal injection room. Earl found that he was outside, standing before a gallows. The noose swayed in the breeze, though Earl couldn't feel any wind. He took a few steps backward, looking around. All the walls were gone, and Earl stood inside a circle of cowboys. Each was dressed in the traditional outfit of a television Western, complete with chaps, spurs, vests, and holsters. But their faces – they were the faces of the "Seven Innocents" who had been in Earl's bedroom. There were at least forty cowboys, but there were only seven faces, repeated over and over.

Earl struggled to catch his breath. He couldn't break the circle, as they stood shoulder-to-shoulder and they all brandished six-shooters. Ahead, the gallows beckoned. The crowd thickened behind Earl, forcing him forward to the wooden platform. As he got near, the noose came alive. It lowered onto the platform, then slithered forward like a snake. Then it thrust forward at lightning speed, lassoing Earl's neck before he had time to react.

It dragged him the rest of the way to the gallows platform and pulled him up into the air. Now hanging above the platform, Earl pulled at the rope, trying to loosen its hold on his neck. He looked down and saw the trap door open beneath his feet. The square hole was pitch black. Suddenly he dropped into the hole, plummeting at an insane speed, into the darkness, knowing at any moment he would come to a sudden stop. At this speed it wouldn't just snap his neck; it would pop off his head like a champagne cork.

He fell for what seemed like forever, then landed in a wooden chair. He no longer felt the noose around his neck. He tried to raise his arm to see if the rope was still there, but he found that his wrists were clamped to the armrests. Something landed on his head. He couldn't see it, but it reminded him of the metal colander his mother used to use to wash vegetables. He used to pretend it was an army helmet when she wasn't looking.

The childhood memory almost brought a smile to his face, but then he saw Florence. There was very little light in the room, but he could see her beyond the edges of the light, standing by a large switch on the wall. The lever was comically large, easily half the length of Florence's body.

"Any last words?" she hissed, her hand on the lever.

Earl struggled to think of something, some irrefutable argument that would convince her not to pull the switch. But it didn't matter, because he now realized there was a gag over his mouth, and he wore a chinstrap so tight he couldn't move his jaw. He gave Florence a pleading look, but she remained unmoved.

Time seemed to slow down as she pulled the lever. Earl had time to remember every life he'd taken in his career. Every face appeared before him with crystal clarity, and he mourned each and every one of them.

And then the lever completed its journey, the circuit was made, and every one of Earl's nerve endings exploded in unfathomable pain.

"He's right in here, Mr. Gray."

The coroner led the warden into the examination room. Two of the tables were empty, but on the third lay the body of Earl Kinnard, former executioner of Garden State Penitentiary.

"That's him," the warden confirmed with a sigh. "What happened?"

"As near as we can tell, he had a heart attack in his sleep," the coroner said. Then he had a thought and fished for something in his pockets. "But he was wearing these on his temples. Are these... what I think they are?"

The coroner handed over two silver discs, and Warden Gray examined them, frowning. "Yes," the warden confirmed.

"I've seen them on the news," the coroner said. "Could these have induced a heart attack?"

"That's what they do," the warden answered. "But they

couldn't have killed Earl."

"Why not?" the coroner asked.

Warden Gray slipped the REM discs into his pocket, then looked the coroner in the eyes. "They can't be activated by the person wearing them. They have to be initiated manually, you understand, and the program won't start unless the wearer is asleep. If these are what killed him, then someone else was in the house…" He trailed off.

The warden wandered back out of the morgue, mumbling to himself.

That night, Warden Gray returned home and got ready for bed. As he was getting undressed, he reached into his pocket and found the REM discs. *What are these doing here?* he wondered. *I thought I put them back in storage.*

For just a moment, a shadow passed over his face. He thought he heard someone whisper his name, but convinced himself it was just the wind outside. As he stared at the discs, strange guilt feelings tugged at the corners of his mind. Random memories flared and faded. A parade of prisoners invaded his thoughts.

Reformed prisoners he'd denied parole. Prisoners who'd perished from unsafe conditions. Prisoners who would have been better off at mental institutions. Prisoners who had clearly been wrongfully convicted.

Get over it, he admonished himself. It was a for-profit prison, after all, and they received more funding if they kept the cells full. And of course conditions were harsh. Garden State Penitentiary wasn't a damn summer camp. Gray was good at his job, and as far as he was concerned there was no reason to feel remorse.

Or was there? The faces of the prisoners pleaded with him

one last time.

He shook his head, dispersing the intrusive thoughts like a dog shaking itself dry. *You're getting soft in your old age,* he thought. Then he placed the REM discs on his nightstand, turned off the lights, and went to sleep.

Eyes

"You all set?" the man asked. It was pitch black outside. It was the only time they were safe. He held an ancient flashlight, so old it still used D batteries. But he didn't dare turn it on, at least not yet. He'd procured the batteries from a black market remanufacturer, and while he trusted his supplier, he still wasn't sure how long the batteries would hold out.

"Any time," his partner said. She tried to sound confident, but her voice was shaky. It was going to be dangerous, but it would be worth it if they succeeded. Steadying her nerves, she added, "Just get me to the keypad; I'll do the rest."

They held hands, and the man led his partner across the empty parking lot, through the alley between two buildings, and to the warehouse door. He'd practiced the route several times during the day, in the guise of a jogger taking a shortcut to the park. He knew exactly how many paces it would take. There were no streetlights or security lamps; why would there be? The warehouse was long-forgotten and full of obsolete technology.

Still, the contents were forbidden, and therefore the building was locked. The man felt around until he found the keypad. "Here," he whispered, guiding the woman's hand. She felt until she found a slot, then she inserted a keycard. An old LED screen lit up, requesting a password. It wasn't very bright, but the man still cupped his hands over the screen to keep the light contained.

A long wire protruded from the end of the keycard, leading to a device on the woman's belt. With a few button taps, she hacked the lock. She didn't look at her device as she worked; she knew the keypresses by heart. Finally the door popped open. They crept inside, making as little noise as possible, and closed the door softly behind them.

Now it was time for the flashlight. They didn't know the layout of the warehouse, and they couldn't just blindly grab boxes in the dark. The man still used it sparingly, turning it on for seconds at a time and aiming it low. "See any yet?" he asked.

"I think I saw something," she whispered. "Nine o'clock from your position."

He flashed the light on again, aiming to the left. A large stack of bright yellow boxes sat on a wooden pallet. He switched off the flashlight and hooked it to his belt. They grabbed two boxes each, holding them under their arms.

Counting his paces, the man tiptoed back to the door, his partner following right behind. They reached the front door, carefully opened it...

...And they were blinded by three glowing eyeballs that hovered outside. "Unidentified trespassers," an electronic voice announced. "You have been caught stealing government property. Surrender or face the consequences."

But the trespassers knew better. The punishment would be the same regardless of if they fled. "Run," the man muttered. "I'll hold them off."

The woman stepped behind her partner and then backed

away slowly, keeping his body between herself and the eyes. Then she turned and ran.

"Intruders escaping," an eye said, and all three eyes fired beams of green energy from their irises. The man did his best to block the shots so his partner could escape. Then he fell forward, one last breath escaping from his lips as he crumpled to the warehouse floor. The boxes made faint shattering noises as they tumbled to the ground.

The woman ducked behind a stack of boxes, but it was too late. She'd been seen, and now the eyes approached from each side of the stack. There was nowhere to run, but still she would not surrender. Better to die here than to prolong the inevitable. As a prisoner they'd make an example of her, most likely by executing her on live TV.

"This is your last chance," an eye said. "Surrender or face the consequences."

"Face this," the woman said, throwing one of the boxes at an approaching eye. The box – which only weighed a couple of pounds – made a tinkling sound as it bounced off the eye.

"Subject is hostile," the eye behind her said. "Neutralized." It fired three blasts into the woman's back. She fell on her side, crushing the box she still held under her left arm. The box – labeled "40w LED Light Bulbs" – crunched loudly as it flattened beneath her weight.

"All threats eliminated," an eye announced, and the floating orbs returned to the police station.

Moesha stood before the class of twenty-nine teenagers, her textbook open on the lectern. Several of the students yawned or doodled on their desks. Moesha sighed. Most of her students didn't actually want to learn, but that barely mattered anymore, since there were so many subjects she wasn't allowed to teach them.

What's even the point? she thought. She flipped through the textbook until she finally reached a page with some readable text. But even this page was only half-allowed; six of the ten paragraphs had been struck through with a permanent marker.

She cleared her throat, thought about what she was going to say, then paused. She glanced up at the ceiling, where four floating eyes stared at her as if daring her to say what was really on her mind. Moesha wasn't afraid of going to prison, but again, what was the point? If she broke the rules, she'd just be replaced. It wasn't like her sacrifice would mean anything. She might as well just do her job as ordered.

"In the eighteenth century," she began, "North American colonists sent many ships to Africa, scouting for employees to work in the fields. They found many people who were looking for jobs, so they took them back to America, where these new employees worked in exchange for free lodging and meals."

Moesha paused, trying to decide how to phrase the next paragraph. The floating eyes pulsed. She saw one's iris contract, indicating it was zooming in on her. She took a deep breath. "In the 1860s, these employees decided they wanted to quit their jobs, but their employers didn't want to be left short-staffed. So they… argued."

She closed the book. "The United States eventually went to war with itself over whether these employees had the right to break their contracts. When the fighting finally ended, the employees were granted the freedom to work wherever they wanted." Then Moesha lifted her head and glared straight into one of the glowing eyes. "This led to no further disputes. These happy immigrants integrated into society with no conflict whatsoever, and everyone has treated everyone equally ever since."

She looked back at her class. As she'd predicted, they weren't listening anyway. And why would they? She'd just delivered a history lesson so bland that even she'd had trouble staying awake. *What am I even going to put on the test?* she wondered. But she'd have to worry about that later. The bell was about to ring.

"For homework tonight," Moesha started to say, then paused again. Sighing, she said, "Watch a TV show that takes place before the year 2000, and write three paragraphs about it."

Several of the students groaned. "Three paragraphs?" one griped. Then the bell rang and everyone got up and left. Moesha sat down at her desk, flipping through her curriculum. What had once been a full semester's worth of lesson plans had been reduced to about a month's worth of content, and she'd have to really stretch it out or American History 101 would become a study hall. *I'll make them watch a movie tomorrow*, she thought, then frowned. *...If I can find one on the approved list.*

The final bell rang, and Moesha walked over to the Teachers' Lounge to grab her things. More eyes floated above the hallways, giving off white light while watching for any restricted behavior. The ceiling sported no light fixtures, no fluorescent tubes. All electronic light now came from these eye-shaped camera drones. And they were everywhere – in stores, in homes, they'd even replaced the dome lights in cars. Flashlights, headlights, nightlights... if you wanted to see, then you consented to being watched.

At first it had seemed like a great idea. The eyes would record everything, but by law, no one would watch the recordings unless a crime occurred. If you committed no crimes, you had nothing to hide. And to be fair, the number of unsolved crimes went down once the eye drones were installed, just like the government promised.

But the legal system sat on a slippery slope. Once all the eyes were in place, and once the population got used to their presence, the government decided that the eyes in high-crime areas should be constantly monitored, instead of the footage just being used as evidence after a crime. A few years after that, any public eye could be monitored at all times. Then the law was expanded to include the eyes in private businesses.

And now, in 2074, a mere twenty years after the eyes were first introduced, the government could legally monitor any eye, anywhere, at all times. They could watch citizens in their homes, in their bedrooms, even in their bathrooms. The only time a citizen was unobserved was in the dark – and the government already had plans to upgrade the eyes with night vision.

Meanwhile, and not coincidentally, more activities became illegal each year. One of the first principles of criminology is that it's impossible to eliminate crime completely. As major crimes become more difficult to commit, lawmakers often shift their focus to minor crimes. In a way, the legal system is a lot like a body's immune system. Without a disease to fight, bored white blood cells will arbitrarily declare a new enemy, and the body develops a new allergy. In the same way, bored lawmakers justify their existence by writing new laws.

So the increased police presence was a natural progression of events… or maybe it was the plan all along.

"License and registration, Ma'am."

Moesha already had both ready and handed them over.

"Mo... is that Mo-sha or Moy-sha?" the officer asked, examining the license.

"Mo-*ee*-sha," she enunciated slowly.

The officer shook his head slightly in a way that seemed to say, *You people have the silliest names.* "Do you know why I pulled you over?" he asked.

Driving while black? Moesha wanted to say, but she knew that would only lead to trouble. "Well, I couldn't have been speeding; it's a self-driving car. Do I have a tail light out?"

"No," the officer said. "I ran your plates, and it turns out you haven't registered a period tracker app."

"I don't use one," Moesha said.

"May I ask why not?"

Why is it any of your business? Again she held her tongue. "Because I'm pretty regular, and I can usually tell when I'm about to menstruate." She hoped her frankness would embarrass him, but he remained stone-faced.

"The state would prefer you register one anyway," the officer said. "For your own health."

"I'll get that taken care of right away," Moesha said. "Will there be anything else?"

"It says here you're a teacher, right?"

"Yes sir," Moesha said. *Where are you going with this*?

"So you must be used to tests," the officer said. "I'd like you to take one for me." He smiled, looking proud of his masterful segue.

"What, a sobriety test?" Moesha asked. "I haven't been drinking—"

The officer handed her a sealed packet, about six inches long. Moesha recognized it immediately and gasped.

"Is that a pregnancy test?" she asked.

"Now if you'll just step outside your car, you can use that guardrail for privacy."

Moesha wanted to yell at him, slap him, ask for his badge number, threaten to get him fired, and drive off into the sunset. But she knew that saying so much as "boo" was likely to get her arrested. Or shot.

Every year, a new indignity, she thought as she opened her door. *And every year, we take it with a smile.*

"The ice cream's half melted now," Moesha said, unpacking the groceries.

"Get stuck in traffic?" her brother asked. Ronald grabbed a bag and started putting boxes away.

"Pulled over," Moesha said.

"DWB?" Ronald asked.

"Pregnancy check," Moesha replied.

"That's one they haven't stopped me for," Ronald said. "So are you?"

"Of course not," Moesha laughed. "You know I haven't had a boyfriend since college."

"Hey, just because you like eggs now doesn't mean you don't sometimes crave sausage."

Moesha laughed even harder. "Did you come up with that yourself?"

"As far as you know," Ronald said, flashing her that dopey smile that always made her feel better.

Moesha shook her head. "It was a bad day from the start," she said.

"So vent," Ronald said. It was the least he could do. She'd let him stay there ever since his divorce, and it didn't look like he'd be back on his feet anytime soon. "I promise I won't give any advice," he added with a wink.

"Do you know how hard it is to come up with a history lesson when I'm not allowed to say anything bad about our country?"

"So toe the line," Ronald said. "Say what you're told to say. Your rent's more important than your principles."

"That sounds like advice," Moesha said. "But I can't lie to them. I know they're not listening anyway, but I can't just stand up there and tell stories. If I can't lie, and I'm not allowed to tell the truth, there's just not much left."

"Sounds like an easy job to me," Ronald said. "Are they hiring? I'll talk about nothing for an hourly wage."

"I just can't take this anymore," Moesha said.

"So look for another job," Ronald suggested.

"Not just the job," Moesha said. "It's all of it. You know what's wrong with this country?"

"Here we go," Ronald muttered.

"The wrong people are in power," Moesha said.

"Obviously," Ronald said.

"I mean, all the time," Moesha clarified. "Power is inherited, not earned, and the people who have it don't want to share it."

"So what would you do about it?" Ronald asked.

"I propose we take voting rights away from cis, straight, white men," Moesha said.

"Hold on," Ronald said. "I think that's a little much."

"Just for an election or two, so they can see what it's like," Moesha clarified.

"Still—"

"Anyone who tries to vote away the rights of another group should lose the right to vote," Moesha said. "I've yet to see an African American try to vote away the rights of white people. I've yet to see gay people try to vote against straight people's rights."

"But—" Ronald said.

"But!" Moesha exclaimed. "Every single election, white

men try to vote away the rights of women and minorities."

"Sure, but that doesn't mean—"

"I'd also like to see wealthy people lose the right to influence elections."

Ronald laughed. "That would never happen."

"But it makes sense, though," Moesha said. "There are two kinds of power in this country – political and financial. The two shouldn't be allowed to overlap. The rich aren't hurting and they don't need any protections. They shouldn't be allowed to give 'campaign contributions' in exchange for political favors. I mean, look at this damn thing." She pointed at the floating eyeball that lit up the kitchen.

"Yeah?" Ronald asked.

"I didn't vote for that," Moesha said. "Did you vote for that? I don't believe for a second that the majority of Americans wanted these things in their homes."

The eye swiveled towards her as she spoke.

"You might want to tone it down a little," Ronald whispered. "You're about to end up on a watchlist."

"I'm already being watched!" Moesha shouted. "How much more can they watch me? They watch me teach my students. They watch me in my car. They even watch me pee on a stick so they know I'm not having any abortions."

"Yeah, but..." Ronald said, watching the eye. "There's some things that don't need to be talked about."

"That's my point!" Moesha said. "The fact that we're afraid to talk about this openly is exactly why it needs to be talked about."

Ronald held his tongue. He knew she was right, but he didn't want to see her get arrested. And while speaking ill of the government wasn't against the law, it certainly let the government know which citizens needed to be monitored more closely. The more Moesha ranted, the more careful she'd have to be not to break any laws.

And with more and more things being made illegal, that got more difficult all the time.

The following day was infuriating. Moesha spent all morning trying to requisition a movie, but most of the school's library had recently been added to the banned list, and the remaining films had almost nothing to do with history. She settled on an animated film about Paul Revere, which was full of historical inaccuracies but at least it didn't mention slavery or Native Americans.

Then she had a run-in with the principal. Some of the parents had complained about the previous day's lesson. One had criticized her for how sanitized it had been, an assessment that Moesha agreed with completely. But three had complained that she'd covered the Civil War at all. After all, implying that the United States had fought against itself gave the impression that it wasn't a "happy" country.

The truth was, Moesha was surprised that there were any complaints at all. That meant that some of her students had not only paid attention, but had gone on to talk to their parents about what they'd learned that day. In a strange way it was uplifting. Her students had always treated her American History class like it was naptime, and their teacher was just background noise. But this meant at least a handful were actually listening.

But the school board didn't see it that way. They treated parental complaints very seriously, and Moesha would be watched even more closely from now on.

Assuming that's even possible, Moesha thought when she got the news.

After work she had to stop at the pharmacy, but after

standing in line for half an hour, she had to go away empty-handed. Her insurance had declined to pay for her eczema creme, and she couldn't afford it otherwise. Which meant she'd have to call her provider to sort things out, but she decided to put that off until the weekend.

And to top it all off, she got pulled over again on the way home. This time it wasn't for a pregnancy test, but part of a random search for illicit substances. Of course they didn't find anything, but it was yet another reminder of what the country had become.

She was running late after that, and the last thing she wanted was to have to cook dinner, so she picked up drive-thru. "I brought burgers!" she shouted as she walked through the door, but received no response.

"Ronald?" she asked, looking around. It wasn't a very large apartment, and it only took a moment to confirm he wasn't there.

That's odd, Moesha thought. Ronald worked at a construction site, and he was usually home by three or four. Sometimes he stopped to play a game of pool, but even then he always made it back before dark.

She checked her phone for messages, but there were none.

She decided to let it go. Her brother was an adult with his own life, and he wasn't required to check in with her before making plans. Moesha put Ronald's food in the fridge and ate her dinner.

When he still wasn't home at nine, she called his phone. As soon as she made the call, she heard the ringtone from another room. She frantically searched Ronald's bedroom, but soon realized the music was coming from outside the apartment. Poking her head into the hallway, she dialed again and listened.

She finally found the phone in a trashcan. And it had

blood on it.

"I'd like to file a missing person's report," Moesha said.

The clerk sounded way too nonchalant to be taking emergency calls. He asked her a few questions and entered some data, then didn't speak for a few minutes. Moesha could hear him talking to someone else in the background, but she could only make out a couple of words. When the clerk finally came back on the line, he said, "We need you to come down to the station right away."

"Is he hurt?" Moesha asked.

"He's fine," the clerk said. "He's in our custody."

"As in, under arrest?" Moesha asked.

"It really would be better if you came in person," the clerk replied.

Moesha grabbed her purse and left.

"What did he do?" Moesha asked as she sat down.

The officer didn't answer right away. He took a moment to look Moesha up and down, as if trying to decide if she was worthy of his time. Officer Blake was a big man, but his voice was oddly high-pitched for his size. "It wasn't what he did, it's who he was with," he said. "Has your brother made any new friends lately?"

"I wouldn't know," Moesha said. The officer stared at her like he expected a longer answer, so she continued. "I haven't seen him talking to anyone. But I'm at work all day."

Blake nodded and made a note on a piece of paper. "No strange phone calls? No late-night visitors?"

Moesha shook her head. "What is this about?"

The officer frowned. "I'm afraid it's pretty serious," he

said. "We have reason to believe Ronald has joined a terrorist group."

If not for his expression, Moesha might have laughed. "Ronald's no terrorist," she said.

"Are you sure?" Blake asked. "He'd probably keep it from you, for your own safety."

"He's really not very political," Moesha said.

"Or he's a very good actor," the officer replied.

"Can I see him?" Moesha asked.

He shook his head. "He's not allowed any outside contact right now," Blake replied.

"Why not?"

"Because he might use it to warn the rest of the group," Blake said. "Even if we watch you talk to him, he might give you a coded message."

"Coded message?" Moesha asked.

Blake looked at her sternly. "You know, like 'How are you' could really mean 'warn the others I've been caught.' That sort of thing."

Moesha didn't know what to think. None of it made sense. Her brother had always just sort of drifted through life. He'd never been the type to stand up for a cause. In fact, he'd often made fun of Moesha for having strong political views.

Unless that was part of the act? she wondered. Maybe he always told Moesha to calm down because he didn't want to risk police attention. Any trouble she got in could point them to Ronald as well.

But if that was true, it meant that Moesha didn't really know her brother at all.

That night Moesha went through her brother's phone. She already knew his PIN because he'd been using the same four digits on everything since high school. She searched through his texts but didn't find anything too unusual. He and his best friend talked about sports, his ex-wife had found some of his things and wanted to bring them by, one of the guys at the construction site sent him details about a lumber order...

Hold up, Moesha thought. Ronald's job had nothing to do with orders. There was no reason anyone would be texting him about a lumber delivery.

She read the conversation more closely. To most people it would have looked like a perfectly straightforward work-related exchange. But the more Moesha read, the more convinced she was that she was reading something fishy. The last few lines were particularly suspicious.

<u>Foreman</u>: The planks will arrive Fri at 2100.

<u>Ron</u>: how many?

<u>Foreman</u>: 18x40w, 14x60w

<u>Ron</u>: where?

<u>Foreman</u>: Bay 7

<u>Ron</u>: got it

Moesha puzzled over the whole thing, but the last bit in particular reminded her of a drug deal. *He'd never,* Moesha thought. But then, he was obviously hiding something from her. Was dealing drugs really so far-fetched when the alternative was terrorism? She wasn't sure which she'd rather believe.

What could Bay Seven refer to? she wondered. She pulled up Ronald's maps app and looked at his bookmarked places. Some of the locations were marked with nonsense words like flervin, mabble, and sleen.

Moesha put her hand on her chest. She remembered those words. Back when she and Ronald were kids, they'd come up with about sixty code words so they could talk to each other without being overheard. It was just a silly spy game they played, but it warmed Moesha's heart to know that Ronald still remembered them.

And he's using them for a drug deal, she reminded herself.

They'd had code words for the numbers from one to ten. *What was our word for seven?* And then it came to her. She scrolled all over the map until she found a bookmark labeled "bloop."

It was Thursday night. *Tomorrow night at nine o'clock*, she thought.

She considered replying with a coded warning, something like "Cancel the order, feeling blue." But she wasn't even sure if she should be protecting these people.

Maybe I should tell the police? she thought. But she refused to believe her brother was a bad person. If he was involved in something shady, it had to be for the greater good.

No, the only way to get answers would be to go there herself.

She took Ronald's car, reasoning that her contact would be looking for it. She also brought Ronald's phone in case he received any additional messages. The address took her to a soda bottling factory. It was well after hours, and the parking lot was empty. She drove around to the back where she couldn't be seen from the street, and parked the car.

She looked at her phone. She was ten minutes early. It was extremely dark on this side of the building. The streetlights were off, and if the building had any exterior lighting, it wasn't on. There wasn't even a moon to see by.

Moesha expected to see a set of headlights appear at any moment. She shrieked when someone knocked on her window. The man was barely visible, as he was dressed in black and wearing a ski mask. There was another man behind him, holding two large boxes. The first man made a gesture that Moesha couldn't interpret. He waited a moment, then made it again. Finally he pointed at her trunk and Moesha understood.

She popped the trunk. She heard some shuffling behind her car, and then a thunk as the trunk was slammed shut.

Moesha waited a moment to see what would happen next, but the two men seemed to be gone.

Then Ronald's phone dinged, and Moesha read the new text.

<u>Foreman</u>: Bay 3 ASAP

Moesha replied with "on my way" and looked up the address that Ronald had bookmarked as "spepny," which was their code word for three.

What the hell am I doing, Moesha thought as she typed the address into the car's GPS. *For all I know I could be transporting kidnapped babies.*

But she had to see this through. She needed to know what Ronald had been up to, even if it got her killed.

The new destination was approximately forty-five minutes away. She was over halfway there when she got pulled over.

"Out kind of late, aren't you?" the officer said.

Moesha handed over her license, along with Ronald's registration. "Yes, sir," she replied.

"Says here your car belongs to a Ronald Douglas," the officer said. "Is that your husband?"

"My brother," Moesha said. "Um… what can I do for you, officer?" She had never been so nervous in her life.

"I need to see your phone," the officer said.

"What for?" she asked.

The officer cocked his head and frowned. Moesha didn't need any further coaxing. In her panic she nearly grabbed Ronald's phone, but she realized her mistake and picked up her own instead.

"Unlock it," the officer said, holding out his hand.

Moesha unlocked the phone and handed it over. She held her breath as he flipped through her apps. Then he handed it back.

"You're good to go," he said.

"I... am?" Moesha asked.

"Looks like you were given a warning earlier this week about your period tracker app. But I see you've installed one now. Thank you for being a good citizen." The officer tipped his hat and returned to his car.

Moesha sat still for a couple of minutes, waiting for her breathing to return to normal. Then she started the car and resumed the drive.

The destination was an old gas station on a road that looked like it was only used by farmers. The only light came from Moesha's headlights, and she debated on whether to turn them off. The people she was dealing with seemed to prefer the dark, so she turned off the headlights. It was now pitch black, and Moesha braced herself for a knock at the window.

She still jumped when the contacts arrived. This time she popped the trunk right away, and she heard someone moving around behind the car. The trunk slammed shut once again.

Then she saw flashing blue and red lights in the distance. "Crap!" she shouted and started her car. But more lights flashed in the opposite direction. She was trapped. The police cars were still pretty far away, but the narrow road only went the two directions. There was nothing she could do except wait for them to arrive.

She stepped out of her car. One of the masked men still stood nearby, barely visible in the flashing lights. "If you don't want to be arrested, you'll come with us," he said.

Moesha nodded and followed him.

They ran across a field, over a shallow creek, and through a small patch of woods. Moesha held onto the mysterious stranger's hand the entire time, as letting go would have meant getting lost in the dark. She wondered how he could possibly see where he was going.

An off-road vehicle was waiting for them in another field. The man pushed her into the backseat, where someone else put a bag over her head.

"It's just a precaution," a woman's voice said. "We're not going to hurt you."

Then Moesha felt a prick in her arm, and she lost consciousness.

"What are we going to do with her? She's not even our contact!"

"We'll see what she wants when she wakes up."

"We have no idea if she's on our side. She might even be working for the cops."

"I checked her for wires and trackers. She's clean."

"Doesn't mean she won't turn us in."

Two voices – one male, one female. They sounded muted, like they were behind a wall. Moesha wiped a bit of drool from her mouth as she opened her eyes. She was no longer wearing a sack, and from her position she could see a desk and a dozen cardboard boxes. Feeling sluggish and disoriented, she rolled onto her back and stared at the ceiling.

There was a meager amount of light in the room, coming from a window in the door. It looked like this room had once been an office. There was a light on the ceiling above her, but it wasn't turned on. Moesha stared at the light for a few seconds – something seemed weird about it, but she wasn't sure what.

She was still staring at the light fixture when the door opened and someone flicked the light switch.

And then a light bulb went on over her head. *There's no eye!* she thought as a man and a woman entered the room.

"Are you Ronald's sister?" the woman asked.

Moesha nodded. "And you are?"

"We'll ask the questions," the man said.

The woman rolled her eyes. "Ignore him, he thinks we're in a spy movie."

"This isn't a game," the man said. "We lost two agents this week."

"I suppose that's fair," the woman said, nodding sadly. Then she sat down on the couch next to Moesha. "Are you okay?" she asked.

"I'm a little confused," Moesha said. "Where am I?"

They ignored the question. "Your brother speaks very highly of you," the woman said.

"Which proves nothing," the man countered.

"Give it a rest," the woman said. Turning back to Moesha, she asked, "You want some water?"

Moesha nodded. The woman gestured to her partner and he grunted something about not running a bed and breakfast. But he still reached into the desk and retrieved a bottle of water.

The woman took the bottle from her partner and handed

it to Moesha. "I'm Tish, this is Marl," she said. "Did Ronald ever mention us?"

Moesha shook her head and took a sip of water. "Never," she said. "But he hardly ever talked about his friends. He'd mention 'the guys at the pool hall' sometimes, but no names."

"We're the Darkraptors," Tish said.

"Dar-Craptors?" Moesha asked.

"Dark... Raptors," Tish clarified. Then, over her shoulder, she said, "Told you we should have gone with Nightraptors."

"Darkraptors sounds scarier if you say it right," Marl mumbled.

"There are things you need to know about your brother, Moesha," Tish said. "But first we need to know we can trust you."

"Well, if it helps," Moesha said. "I can't go anywhere else at this point. The police have Ronald's car by now. They pulled me over earlier, so they know I was the one who drove it last. I don't know exactly what's going on, but I'm fairly certain that if I were to go home right now, I'd be arrested... thanks to you."

"You didn't have to go to Ronald's rendezvous," Marl said.

"How could I not?" Moesha said. "I had to know what he'd gotten himself into. And now I'm a part of it. So thanks for that. I'm royally screwed now, and I have no choice but to trust the... Darkraptors, was it? So yes, you can trust me, if only because I'm out of options."

Tish touched Moesha's arm, her face sympathetic.

But Marl wasn't convinced. "Not good enough," he said. "You could still go to the cops and try to bargain. Now that you've seen our operation, you could..."

"She hasn't seen anything yet," Tish said.

"I want to, though," Moesha said, and they both looked at her strangely. "This was obviously important to my brother. He doesn't always make the best decisions, but he also never sticks his neck out unless he really believes in what he's doing. I need to know what you've got going on here. If I agree with your cause, I promise I'll do what I can."

Tish and Marl looked at each other. Finally Marl shrugged.

"We're working against the government," Tish said. "Trying to restore some of the freedoms we've given up in the last few years. You see, we believe—"

"I'm in," Moesha said.

It was well after midnight. Moesha crouched behind a concrete barrier in the third story of an empty parking garage, peeking over the wall and reporting what she could see. She watched the detention facility through an ancient pair of night vision goggles. All the Darkraptor tech was out-of-date, as newer devices contained tracking chips and hidden cameras.

For the past two months they'd had her doing relatively safe jobs, such as searching old, abandoned houses for light bulbs and other "pre-eye" electronics. But tonight they were on a much more serious mission. Her brother was about to be transferred from one camp to another.

The detention centers were a relatively new addition to the hellscape America had become. With more and more things becoming illegal every day, the government simply couldn't build new prisons quickly enough to contain the growing number of prisoners. In their haste, they'd converted empty office buildings and old malls into containment camps.

The others hadn't wanted her to come. They didn't feel she was ready, and they weren't sure they could trust her yet. But she'd convinced them that they might need her there to identify Ronald. A lot of the prisoners wore hoods while outdoors, but Moesha was pretty sure she could pick her brother out of a crowd, even with a hood on.

"That's him," she whispered into her microphone. Far below, beyond the eight-foot-tall chain link fence, a pair of guards ushered Ronald into a truck. He was hooded, but his lanky frame and loping gait gave him away.

"Move out," came Marl's voice in her ear.

Moesha stood and quickly – but quietly – made her way down the stairs, where Tish waited for her in a heavily modified, twenty-year-old electric car. They shared a brief kiss as Moesha got into the car, and then they drove off.

The car's headlights stayed off, and they used a night vision camera to guide them. They passed multiple eyeball cameras as they drove down the street, but the car emitted an interference signal that prevented the cameras from recording as they went by. If anyone was watching the feed at the time, they would see a few seconds of static which they would hopefully interpret as an internet hiccup.

They merged onto the road behind the transport truck, staying so far back that the truck's taillights looked like little red pinpricks.

"They're coming up on the mark," Marl said over the car's radio. "And... action."

It was hard to see from this distance, but the transport truck slammed on its brakes, and there were several bright flashes of light around the truck. Tish brought them closer, finally coming to a stop about thirty feet from the truck. Moesha could see several armed Darkraptor agents, most in the process of tying up government soldiers.

Two Darkraptors rushed toward Tish's car, each leading a newly liberated prisoner. They opened the car's back doors and shoved the prisoners into the backseat. One of the agents stayed, but the other went back into the dark.

"Drive!" Marl said from the backseat, pulling off his ski mask.

Tish turned the car around and went back the way they'd come. She took several turns onto seldom-used back streets.

"What's going on?" one of the ex-prisoners asked. Moesha recognized her brother's voice right off, and she leaned around the passenger seat to look at him. She reached for Ronald's hood but Marl slapped her hand away.

"He could still be a plant," Marl said. "We'll confirm their identities when we get back to base."

"They stuck something in my arm," Ronald said. "I think it's a tracking chip."

"Mine too," the other prisoner said. She barely sounded old enough to drink.

What did she do to get put in a detention center? Moesha wondered.

Marl removed a pocket knife from his hip pouch. "This car's got a transmission jammer, so we're probably safe," he said. "But I'd still like to remove those before we get back to base." He grabbed Ronald's arm and looked for a scar, but it was dark.

Moesha shined a flashlight into the backseat.

"Hold still," Marl said, looking for a good place to cut. But the car was bouncing around too much. "Can you find somewhere to pull over?" he asked Tish.

"No," Tish said, suddenly transfixed on her rearview mirror. Three flying orbs bobbed in the distance, getting ever closer to the car. "Buckle up," Tish said, slamming her foot down on the accelerator.

She hardly braked at all as she turned the next corner. A beam of green light hit a lamppost as she zoomed by, causing it to fall across the street like a hewn oak.

Tish drove in a zig-zag pattern through the city streets. She knew she couldn't outrun the eyes, but at least she could make herself harder to hit. A few months earlier the Darkraptors managed to capture and dissect an eye, and they'd studied the targeting code. The eyes were excellent at identifying and extinguishing threats, but they weren't as good at tracking vehicles. Each time they lost sight of Tish's car, they had to re-run the targeting identification code to make sure it was the same vehicle. This process cost them a few seconds, making it that much longer before they fired again. So Tish made as many turns as possible.

Unfortunately they were running out of downtown, so Tish had to turn back into the city to keep from being out in the open. *How long can I keep this up?* she wondered, as another green blast shattered the front window of a furniture store.

She made a sharp left turn. "I don't have a plan," she said out loud.

"Lose them!" Marl shouted.

"They're too fast," Tish said. "I can't lose them, I can only delay them."

"Do we have any weapons in here?" Moesha asked.

"Nothing that will hurt them," Marl said. The car shook as a blast glanced off the trunk.

Tish looked at the road ahead. She remembered an upcoming overpass, over by the river. "I have a thought," she said. "When I slow down, everyone jump out."

"No way," Moesha said.

"I'll meet back up with you later, I promise," Tish said.

"You're going to sacrifice yourself," Moesha said.

"I'm going to do something risky," Tish said. "But I don't want to risk your lives too."

"The rest of you do what she says," Moesha said. "But I'm staying."

"We don't have time to argue," Tish said. The overpass was only two turns away. The car shook again as a blast hit the rear bumper. "If you don't get out too, then I'm not doing the trick. And then we all die."

"But—" Moesha said.

Tish turned the corner. Her next turn was coming up. "For me," Tish said.

Moesha said nothing, just huffed loudly.

Tish turned the final corner and drove into the tunnel under the overpass. Then she did a U-turn. "Now," she said, slowing down as she turned. The passengers, including Moesha, opened their doors and tumbled out into the street. Then Tish drove forward, leaving the tunnel the same way she'd come in.

The eyes had just made the last turn when they saw the car come barreling toward them. Their targeting computers took a few seconds to re-identify the car, then they started firing repeatedly. Several blasts hit the car, which careened out of control. It sped off the edge of the road, through the guardrail, and into the river.

The eyes spent several minutes scanning the river, looking for survivors. Then they refocused their search, now scanning for the tracking chips that had been embedded in the prisoners' arms. This signal took them back to the overpass.

When they arrived, they found two bloody tracking chips lying in the street. The humans were nowhere to be seen.

"Keep moving," Marl ordered as they made their way through the woods. He and Moesha wore night vision goggles, while each led one of the ex-prisoners.

"Where are we going?" Moesha asked.

"There's a car waiting for us about a mile away," he answered.

"Can I take my hood off yet?" the rescued woman asked.

Moesha turned and pulled off both of their hoods, for all the good it did. Without goggles of their own, it was almost pitch black outside.

"Why'd you do that?" Marl asked. "We don't know if—"

"Shut up," Moesha said. "Your stupid plan got Tish killed."

"My 'stupid plan' saved your brother," Marl said. "And it was Tish's idea to drive into the river."

"Jerk," Moesha said.

"That's enough," Ronald said. "You can fight when we're safe."

They walked on in silence. Soon they reached a Darkraptor off-road vehicle which took them back to the base.

Four hours later, Moesha lay on a cot in a room with eleven other women. All around her, she heard light snores and steady breathing. But Moesha couldn't sleep. She couldn't stop thinking about Tish's sacrifice. They'd been flirting a lot lately – it was too soon to tell if it would have led anywhere, and it wasn't like dating was really much of an option when they were always on the run. But Moesha really respected Tish, and losing her felt like a punch in the gut.

Stop it, she told herself. *You don't even know she's dead.*

But deep down she knew it was true. Even if Tish had survived the crash, the eyes would have finished her off as soon as she surfaced.

Moesha looked at her watch. It was a little past five AM. The Darkraptors tended to sleep late since most of their operations were executed at night. But Moesha was done tossing and turning in her cot. She needed to get up and walk around or she'd go crazy. She carefully climbed out of her cot, making as little noise as possible so she wouldn't wake the others. Then she slowly opened the door and crept down the hall.

After a brief visit to the restroom, she moved down the hall to an empty office that looked like it had once been a medical clinic. It was now used mostly for storage, and boxes of medical supplies and light bulbs were stacked against walls. But there was a couch against one wall, next to a little table covered in paperback books.

Moesha flipped on the light and looked for something to read. She stopped when she thought she heard voices from down the hall. It sounded like an argument. Curious, she flipped off the light and quietly looked for the source of the shouting.

It was coming from Marl's quarters. He had his own room, which he both slept in and used as an office. As Moesha crept closer she saw a few spots of blood on the floor, directly in front of Marl's door.

She stood closer to the door and put her back to the wall. The two voices were muffled but she recognized them right away.

"I don't know what you're suggesting, but how dare you imply I had anything to do with this!" Marl shouted.

"Who else had the opportunity?" It was Tish. Tish was alive. Moesha's heart skipped a beat. She wanted to burst right in and give her a hug, but she didn't want them to know she'd been eavesdropping.

"If I knew that, we wouldn't be having this conversation," Marl replied. "I'd have them tied up in an interrogation room right now."

"All I know is, when I got my rebreather out of the glove compartment, I found a tracking device. One of the bigger models, and it was patched into the car's antenna so it could bypass the interference field. You're the only one who could have put it there. We only have the two sets of keys."

"We have dozens of agents with carjacking experience," Marl said.

"I thought about that," Tish said. "It's been one of my biggest worries for a while. Any one of our agents could be working for the police. What would stop them from planting a car bomb or something? That's why I installed a hidden camera in the garage."

"You didn't," Marl said.

"I did," Tish replied. "I'm going to head back to my quarters now and look at the footage. Or do you already know what I'll find?"

Marl was quiet for a moment, then asked, "Who else have you told about this?"

Uh oh, Moesha thought. She thought she heard the sound of a desk drawer opening.

"Several people," Tish said, but her voice was tinged with panic. "And if I don't come back, they'll know it was you."

"Now, why don't I believe you?" Marl asked.

Moesha couldn't wait any longer. She kicked open the door and screamed. Marl had a gun pointed at Tish, but when the door opened he turned it on her instead.

Tish took advantage of his moment of confusion and tackled him. The gun went off, and Moesha felt a sharp pain in her left eye. Now half-blind, she stumbled forward and tried to wrestle the gun out of Marl's hand. Tish sat on Marl's chest, punching him in the face.

Moesha heard yelling from down the hall, and soon more Darkraptor agents burst through the doorway.

"These bitches are trying to kill me!" Marl shouted.

"He's a traitor!" Tish yelled back.

"They're the traitors!" Marl shrieked.

Moesha held Marl's gun hand tight. She couldn't pry his fingers open, but she kept his hand pointed at the ceiling in case he pulled the trigger.

The newly arrived agents hesitated, unsure who to believe.

"Just get his gun!" Moesha ordered.

The other agents converged on them and worked together to retrieve the gun. Then they restrained all three of them – Moesha, Tish, and Marl.

"They've been working with the police!" Marl said, struggling against the grip of two agents.

"I've got proof that he's the one—" Tish said, but then Moesha collapsed.

She'd managed to ignore the pain at first – either from shock or adrenaline – but now everything went blurry and she felt a sudden wave of nausea. As she threw up on the floor, she heard several people come to her aid.

There was a scuffle somewhere to her left. Someone shouted, "Get him!" and another voice said, "He's got a phone!"

Marl's voice was next. "I've been compromised!" he shouted. "Address is One One Three Seven Roblez Av—"

There was a THUMP that sounded like a side of beef getting hit by a baseball bat. Something plastic clattered across the floor. Marl groaned, but his voice sounded lower to the ground than it had before.

"Did he just call the police?" someone asked.

"We have to evacuate the building," Tish said. "Run! Tell everyone to get out!"

Moesha heard Ronald's voice from the doorway. "Mo!" he shouted.

"I don't know if we should move her," someone close by said.

"Like hell," Moesha moaned. "Get me out of here."

She felt someone pick her up. He smelled like Ronald. Someone held something to her eye. She tried to open her other eye, but the world was tinged in red.

The word "Police!" echoed from somewhere down the hall.

Moesha faded in and out of consciousness as she was carried through the halls. She heard shouting and gunfire and lots and lots of boots. For a second she saw flashing blue and red lights, but then everything went black. The next time she opened her eye, she saw trees. Then she blinked and she was indoors again. Then she blacked out completely.

"...comfortable. I wish I had better instruments."

"Will she be okay?"

"She must have turned her head as the bullet went by. It grazed her left eyelid - right along the eyelash. I think the eye's infected."

"So we need antibiotics?"

"Too late for that. If we were in a hospital, maybe we could save the eye. But here..."

More blackness. Every time she woke up, she was in a different room. Sometimes she was on a couch, sometimes the floor, and at least once she was lying on the grass. Finally she woke up in what felt like an actual bed.

"...should be safe here."

"You're sure?"

"Not in the slightest. All I can tell you is that Marl didn't know about this house."

"Did he get away?" Moesha asked, but it came out a jumbled mess.

"She's awake. Get Ronald."

Moesha tried to open her eyes. She couldn't see out of the left, but a blurry shape hovered over her right eye. "Tish?" she asked.

"How do you feel?" Tish asked.

"Headache," Moesha said, and tried to sit up. There was another woman in the room, but Moesha didn't recognize her.

"This is Linda, she's been taking care of you," Tish said. "She's a doctor."

"Veterinarian, actually," Linda said. "But an eye's an eye."

Moesha reached up to touch her left eye but just felt gauze.

"I wouldn't play with that," Linda said. "It's going to hurt for a long time."

"Did... Marl... get away?" Moesha asked carefully.

"We don't know what happened to him," Tish said. "All we could do was run. Most of us didn't make it. Those that did are scattered to the winds. It'll be a long time before we're a serious threat again."

The bedroom door opened, and Ronald ran in to hug his sister. "It's good to see you awake," he said.

"Love you," Moesha said, hugging him back.

They separated, and Moesha pulled Tish over to sit on the bed.

"We'll find them again," Moesha said. "And we'll recruit others, and we'll rescue those in the camps. There's only so long the people will stand for such a corrupt government. The more people we recruit, the more we'll spread our message across the country. Before you know it, we'll have an army. And maybe it won't happen in our lifetime, but this will be a free country again. You'll see."

Tish leaned over to hug her, but Moesha pulled her in for a kiss instead. They lingered on each other's lips for several minutes.

"I love you," they said simultaneously, and both laughed. Then they hugged again and separated so Linda could check Moesha's bandages.

Five years later…

"There's two people in the west office," Moesha said, watching the government building from the alley across the street. The signage identified it as a records office for the IRS, but Moesha's intel said otherwise.

She didn't need night vision goggles anymore, as her newest eye implant was top-notch. Not only could she see in the dark, but she could even see the heat signatures of the soldiers walking around inside the building. "Two more in the hall," she continued. "One of them just went into the bathroom."

"Units three and four are on standby," Tish said. "Just waiting for your order."

This is it, Moesha thought. Tonight would be the turning point. Her biggest, most well-coordinated strike yet. When she gave the order, her people would flood the office building with tear gas. Then they would break in, access the government computers, and release the virus. This program would shut down every eye-drone in the country, as well as root through the government's classified documents and release the information onto the internet. The public would finally have proof that the president cheated to win the last election, and that he was planning to restrict even more freedoms in the upcoming months.

All she had to do was give the word. She took a deep breath and nodded to Tish.

"Now," Moesha ordered.

Unfinished Business

Being a single woman in Louisville isn't easy. You have to stay pretty busy just to make rent. I work two jobs – court stenographer by day, freelance proofreader by night. Exciting stuff, right? And yet I still live in a crappy neighborhood. I get harassed on the way to my car, I have trouble finding places to park, and everything just keeps getting more expensive. And did I mention the zombies?

It's been eight years since the zombie apocalypse, and things have been returning to normal. They haven't found a cure yet, but there is an inoculation. They've put fences around the major cities, and we almost have a functioning society again. At least, as much as it was functioning before.

I mean, there's been some big changes. There are certain food items you just can't get anymore. We no longer have cemeteries, just cremations. Traveling between cities takes a little more planning. But as far as my day-to-day life is concerned, I get up, I go to work, and I come home. Sure, there's zombies out there beyond the city limits, but what else is new?

Today when I got to work, I had to cross a picket line to get into the building. The government is trying to mandate the newest zombie vaccines, and the anti-vaxxers are really pushing back. They claim the drugs haven't been tested long enough, and that the zombies aren't much of a threat anymore.

Of course, any fool knows both of these claims are false. The drugs went through all the normal phases and trials, they just sped up the legal side of things so the public could access them faster. And zombies do breach the fences from time to time. There was an incident just last week in the Lake Forest area. Zombies breached the fence, four people got bitten, and one died. Guess which one was an anti-vaxxer, I'll wait. The other three suffered some injuries, but they'll get better. But the fourth… well, like I said, there's no cure once you turn.

So yeah, the protesters really get on my nerves. My job has nothing to do with passing laws, but I still have to put up with these bozos on the way into the courthouse. Yesterday one of them actually spit on me. How gross is that?

But whatever. I kept my eyes on the door, held my chin high, and went inside.

It was a full day at work, and my fingers were numb by the time I was done. I had to transcribe a four-hour trial, a pre-trial hearing, and three sentencings. And then I had to cross the picket line again to go home.

It was a little after seven when I pulled into the parking garage under my apartment building. I was about to go up the stairs – the elevator's been broken for six months – when I felt like I was being watched.

There's an alcove behind the stairwell, a little spot where a couple of the residents stash their bikes. Tonight I saw a pair of eyes staring out at me from under the stairs.

"Hello?" I asked. Instinctively I reached into my purse for

my taser. Then I saw the blood on her face, and I reached for my Zagger instead.

Zagger is short for "Zombie Tagger." Almost everyone has one, and we're allowed to carry these guns almost anywhere. They're made of clear plastic, and they fire – well, they're like little tranquilizer darts, but they do two things. First, they inject the zombie with something called 'Pro-Rigo' which causes rigor mortis to set in. Scientists are still confused by most aspects of zombie physiology, but they have identified a chemical in undead flesh that prevents rigor mortis. Pro-Rigo nullifies that chemical.

The other thing the darts do is implant a GPS tracking chip into the zombie. Later – usually within the hour – the police will show up and find the zombie, now paralyzed by rigor mortis, and they dump them back over the fence. They used to incinerate them, but people complained that there might be a cure someday. I'm skeptical on that point. I mean, if you look at these zombies, a lot of them are very obviously dead on their feet. As in, missing major organs and other parts you can't reasonably live without. Some of the fresher zombies might be savable, but most of them are too far gone.

I aimed my Zagger and was about to pull the trigger when the figure spoke. "Please don't," she said.

I gasped and nearly dropped the weapon. "Sorry, I thought you were—"

The woman ambled out from behind the stairs, and I saw her clearly for the first time. Young adult, maybe twenty-three? Black hair, dark skin, and unusually thin. She had bruises all over her face, and she was covered with dirt and blood.

I might have thought she was alive – malnourished and abused, but breathing – if not for her heart. There was a huge hole in the front of her T-shirt, and a matching hole in her chest. Her heart was completely gone, and I could see all the way to her spine.

I nearly threw up right there, but I held it together and raised my Zagger. "Don't come any closer," I said.

The zombie held up her hands in defense. Most of them don't do that; their minds are too far gone to even recognize weapons. "I won't hurt you," she said.

I lowered my Zagger again, but I took a couple of steps back. "How are you talking?" I asked.

"It's complicated," she said, and backed up under the stairs again. "Just... let me be," she added.

I'll admit that sometimes my curiosity overrides my common sense. I think most people would have just shot her and run. Zaggers are harmless to the living, so even if you mistake someone for a zombie, no real harm done. And I was tempted. But I just had to know more.

And yeah, her looks might have been a factor. Call me sexist if you want, but if it had been a man there, I'm sure I would have run. But this woman, despite all the blood and stuff, well, she was *hot*. I'm not a necrophile, but just thinking about what this woman must have looked like in life...

I shook my head. Those were not appropriate thoughts right now. I took a couple of steps closer. "Are you a zombie?" I asked. It was a ridiculous question. She was walking and talking despite lacking her body's most important organ.

"Yes," she replied.

"But you can talk?" I asked.

"Obviously?" she replied, but she sounded just as confused as I was.

"But how?" I asked.

She took a step forward. We were now just a couple of feet

apart, but for some reason I wasn't scared.

"I'm not sure," she said. "But... I have a theory." Her voice was surprisingly smooth for someone who no longer breathed. She sounded a bit nervous, though.

"Well?" I asked.

"It's... complicated," she said. "Can we go somewhere else?" She looked over my shoulder, as if afraid someone else might see her.

I've made a lot of dubious decisions in my life. Dropping out of college to take stenography classes, for example. Or maxing out my fourth credit card. Or that time I dated a cheerleader and her boyfriend simultaneously.

But this was different. This was a mistake that could have cost me my life. But when I looked into this woman's sunken, despondent eyes, I just couldn't help but feel I could trust her. And did I mention she was hot?

So yeah, I make bad decisions. But was this one of them? Only time would tell.

I took a deep breath, then beckoned her to follow me up to my apartment.

"Would you like a change of clothes?" I asked as she sat on my bed. I hate to sound bigoted but I didn't want a zombie sitting on my furniture. At least with the bed, I could wash the comforter later.

"Thank you," she said, nodding.

I found an old pair of sweatpants and a T-shirt I didn't really care about, and I helped her change into them. I considered offering to let her use my shower, but I was afraid she'd clog the drain with bits of rotting flesh. Not that her flesh was rotting that much. She couldn't have been dead for more than a few days.

I wet an old dishrag and cleaned off her face and arms. When I was done, you couldn't even tell she was dead. She looked emaciated, sure, but no one would ever assume she was a zombie.

We didn't speak while I cleaned her up, and the silence kept getting more and more awkward. Finally I asked, "What's your name?"

"Sketti," she replied.

"Are you sure?" I asked. I still wasn't sure I was talking to a sane creature, and "sketti" could easily have been nonsense syllables from a decaying brain.

"Well, it's kind of a nickname," Sketti said. "My name is Sapira, but my niece always confused 'Sapira' with 'spaghetti,' which she pronounced 'sketti.' My family thought it was so funny, that soon everyone was calling me 'Sketti.' And it just… stuck. What's your name?"

"Spring," I answered, awed by the wordiness of her response. There was no way her brain had decayed in the slightest.

"Are *you* sure?" she asked.

I laughed. She wasn't the first to think my name was weird. "I had two older sisters, Autumn and Summer," I explained. "My parents had a theme going."

"Did they ever complete the set?" Sketti asked.

"No, they stopped after me," I said. "Must have learned their lesson."

"No reason to keep going after you achieve perfection," Sketti said with a wink.

Is she flirting with me? I wondered. I tried to think of a smooth reply, then I happened to glance at her discarded clothes. That hole in her T-shirt was just… heartbreaking. No pun intended. "Sketti, what happened to your heart?"

"My girlfriend broke up with me—"

"Sorry, I didn't mean metaphorically," I said.

"I know, I'm getting there," Sketti replied. "We went camping, in a last-ditch effort to rekindle our relationship. It didn't work. Being alone together just meant we got on each other's nerves that much more. We finally gave up right around midnight. We even argued about whether to pack up the tent and drive home right then, or wait until morning. And then we heard something outside. Carlene – that's my ex – she loaded up her shotgun. We figured it was a bear, but it wasn't."

"Zombies," I said.

"Right," Sketti replied. "Once we saw what they were, we ran to the car. But I got bitten on the way. Carlene saw the bite and she shot me in the chest."

"Did she get away?" I asked.

"No idea," Sketti said. "I was busy being dead at the time. But when I died, I sort of floated up out of myself, and saw myself from above."

"Like an out-of-body experience?" I asked.

"Like a ghost," Sketti said.

"I don't believe in ghosts," I said.

Sketti frowned. "You believe in zombies, but spirits are a bridge too far?"

"Zombies are just a fact of life now," I said. "I'm not sure you could even still call them supernatural."

"Whatever," Sketti said. "I haunted the forest for… I can't say how long. I scared a few hikers. I even managed to possess a couple of people. But I could only stay inside them for a few minutes. Then I came across my body again. It was a full zombie by then, wandering around the forest on its own. I tried possessing it, and it worked. Now I can't even get back out. It's like possessing your own body sort of… locks you in."

"You're telling me you're really a ghost," I said. "Inhabiting your own zombified body."

"You don't have to believe me," Sketti said.

I frowned, lost in thought. "Your story doesn't make a lot of sense," I finally said. "You went camping during a zombie apocalypse? And your ex shot you after just one bite? How did she know you'd turn? Didn't you get the vaccine?"

"There's a vaccine?" Sketti asked.

"For about a year now," I said. "Have you been living under a rock?"

"I haven't been living anywhere," Skettie replied. "We went camping before the apocalypse. Carlene probably shot me because she'd seen too many zombie movies."

"Hold on, hold on," I said. "How long ago was this?"

"I don't know," Sketti said. "It's hard to keep track of time. I don't sleep anymore, but sometimes I blink and it's suddenly morning. But when we went camping it was... 2026. What year is it now?"

"2034," I replied.

"I've been like this for eight years?" Sketti asked. "I would have thought maybe two or three at most."

"But you're not decaying," I said. "Most of the zombies start falling apart after just a few months, but you're... fresh."

"I guess I'm special," Sketti replied. "Maybe something about having a soul keeps me from rotting away."

"This is incredible," I said. "We have to let someone take a look at you. I know this doctor —"

"Not interested," Sketti said. "I don't want to spend the rest of my unlife in a lab somewhere, getting dissected and all that. Besides, I have unfinished business."

"What unfinished business?" I asked.

"No idea, but isn't that why ghosts stick around?" she

asked. "I'm haunting my own body here. There must be a reason. If I can figure that out, I'll pass on to the next world."

"Do you *want* to die?" I asked.

"I think it's a little late to ask that," Sketti said. "The question is whether I want to cross over. And yes, if it's a choice between that and being a zombie, I'd like to move on."

"But if you had a chance to actually live again?" I asked.

"I'd do it in a heartbeat," Sketti said, patting her chest. Her hand pressed in a bit where the fresh T-shirt covered her wound. "So to speak," she added with a smirk.

"Then don't give up on life just yet," I said, grasping her hand. "We could still think of something."

She looked skeptical, but she squeezed my hand and nodded.

"I don't see why you couldn't bring your friend to my office," Jeff said.

"I'm sorry," I said, letting him into my apartment. "She wasn't comfortable going out in public."

"I won't be a part of anything illegal," Jeff said. He took off his jacket and I took it.

"I don't think this violates any laws," I told him. "But if it does, feel free to leave. Right this way."

I took him into the bedroom, where Sketti sat on my bed. "Hi," she said with an awkward little wave.

"Pleased to meet you," Jeff said, and extended his hand. She leaned away and put her hands behind her back. Jeff lowered his hand.

"Sorry," she said, turning her head away.

"She's a little shy," I said. "Sketti, he's a doctor. And a friend. He's here to help."

"To help with what?" Jeff asked, looking confused. He got

down on one knee and looked her over. "Have you been eating right?" he asked.

"Probably not," Sketti said.

Jeff held up his index finger. "Follow my finger," he asked, then started moving it back and forth. "Now count to ten."

When Sketti finished counting, she asked, "Am I all right?"

"You're kind of pale," Jeff said, then stood up and turned to me. "So she doesn't want to be touched, and she looks half-starved. I'm thinking she was sexually assaulted or abused by her husband or boyfriend, and she's been living on the streets ever since. My question is why you're being so cryptic about it. I can't help you if don't know all the facts."

"But you have no trouble believing she's alive," I asked.

"What kind of a question is that?" Jeff asked. "Of course she's alive."

Sketti and I looked at each other, and I nodded. Then she removed her shirt.

Jeff took a few steps backward. "She's... a zombie," he said. He looked back and forth from Sketti to the door.

I moved to stand between Jeff and the doorway. "She's not dangerous," I said.

"You don't know that," Jeff said.

"I know you've had the vaccine," I said. "Even if she bites you, you won't turn."

"She could still go mad and attack us," Jeff countered.

"I think the two of us are strong enough to restrain her if it came to that," I said.

"I'm not going to attack anyone," Sketti said. "I promise. I just need help."

Jeff relaxed a little. "This is... amazing," he said, turning back to Sketti. "You're talking. Thinking. You understand us. What *are* you?"

We told him everything we knew. He was just as

skeptical as I was about the ghost angle, but he admitted he didn't have a better theory.

"So is there anything we can do?" I asked.

Jeff scratched his chin. "You said she's been a zombie for eight years? If she hasn't decayed during that time, that means her body still heals. Her other organs seem to be intact... you'd think the shotgun would have torn up her lungs as well, wouldn't you? But from what I can see they look fine. Which makes me think her lungs healed as well. You know, if we study you enough, we might find cures for all sorts of diseases."

"Jeff..." I said.

"I'd love to do a brain scan," he continued. "I wonder if your sense of self comes from your brain or the ghost inhabiting your body. What if I—"

"I don't want to be a lab rat," Sketti interrupted, shrinking back again. She looked from me to Jeff, panic spreading across her face.

Jeff nodded. "I understand. What if I just take some tissue samples?"

"Jeff," I said. "This is the part in horror movies where the mad doctor accidentally creates a new, even worse disease."

"I'd be careful—"

"I brought you here because I want to see if you can help *her*," I said.

"Of course," Jeff said. "My first thought is 'artificial heart.' The rest of her seems pretty healthy, all things considered. If I could put an artificial heart in her, then replace all her blood, patch up her chest with some artificial skin... she might heal to the point of being 'alive' again."

"Can we try that?" Sketti asked.

"Not in a million years," Jeff said. "It's not like I have a box of artificial hearts in my closet. Those things are like two hundred grand. And I'd need a team of surgeons to put it in, and we'd still have to take you to the hospital to do it. So it's not like we could do it in secret, if that's what you're hoping."

"Oh," Sketti said, looking downward.

"Now if you don't mind publicity," Jeff continued, "You could probably get one for free. I'm sure some surgeon would love to go down in history as the first guy to bring a zombie back to life. Your face would be on magazines, you'd be on talk shows... You might even get a book deal."

"But then I'm back to being studied and dissected," Sketti said. "No thank you."

"You mentioned patching up her chest," I said. "What if we just went that route? Could you do that? Then at least she'd pass for human."

"Why go to the trouble?" Jeff asked. "As long as she keeps her shirt on, nobody's going to know there's a hole in her chest."

"Because it feels weird," Sketti said. "I don't like looking in the mirror and seeing my insides. I don't want to find a family of rats living in there. I don't like being reminded I'm dead."

Jeff sighed. "I'm not that kind of doctor, but I'll see what I can do. The results won't be pretty, and it won't match your skin tone. But... sure. Just give me about a week."

We talked a bit more about the specifics, explored a few other possibilities, and then Jeff went home. Sketti and I talked for hours, until I looked at the clock and realized it was two AM.

"I have to get some sleep," I said. "My alarm goes off at six. I'm already going to be dead on my feet at work tomorrow. Uh... no offense."

"None taken," Sketti said. "Maybe you could call in sick?"

"Good idea," I said. "I think I just might. But I still need to turn in. Are you going to be okay?"

"I'll be fine," she said. "Okay if I watch TV in the living room?"

"Just keep the sound down," I said, and she nodded.

I still set the alarm, knowing I'd probably just call my boss and go back to bed. Tired as I was, it still took me another half hour to fall asleep.

I woke up to the sound of sirens. Red lights flashed from somewhere outside my window. I looked at the clock. Four AM. I stood and walked over to the window. Zombies flooded the streets below, and police fought them with flamethrowers. *Not again,* I thought.

I've lived in this neighborhood for two years, and there's already been three breaches. I wasn't scared – my apartment building has sturdy outer doors, and these outbreaks didn't usually last very long. But it annoys me to no end how often the fence breaks on this side of town. I know City Planning is less inclined to spend money on the slums, but surely they realize that an outbreak *anywhere* in town could spread all over Louisville.

As long as I was up, I went to check on Sketti. I found her staring out the living room window. I went to stand next to her.

"I never want to be like them," she said quietly, watching the zombies down below.

"That would never happen," I said, putting my arm around her shoulder.

She turned to look at me. "If I were to... you know, move on, cross over, whatever you call it... You'll destroy what's left, right? I don't want my body to start killing people."

"It's a deal," I said.

She smiled. It felt like there was something in the air between us, and for a moment I thought we were about to kiss. Sirens kept going off in my brain – even louder than the ones outside – warning me that it was a bad idea to get involved with someone who didn't even have a pulse. Yet still I moved in closer. And so did she.

There was a boom. The room shook and the world outside my window was filled with orange light. We looked down below again. The fire truck had exploded, and flames crawled up the sides of my building.

"The fire escape," I said, leading her into my bedroom.

We opened my bedroom window and began to step out onto the metal platform. Then I looked down and saw several zombies climbing up the fire escape. Some of them were on fire.

I pulled myself back inside and closed the window. "Can't go that way," I said. We went out into the hallway. My building has a central shaft in the middle, so you can look over the railing and see the lobby from any floor. The zombies had gotten in and were starting to climb the stairs. Thick black smoke rose from the lower floors.

"Get to the roof," Sketti said. "I'll go downstairs and close the door."

"What?" I asked. Maybe it was the chaos of the moment, but her plan didn't make any sense to me.

"The zombies won't attack me," she explained. "Never have. If I can lock the building's front door, no more will get in."

"The front door's in the middle of the lobby," I said, pointing to a mangled slab of metal down below. "There's nothing you can do down there. We're not splitting up."

"Okay," she conceded. "Then let's at least go upstairs and

—"

The building's staircase collapsed, taking part of the hallway with it. I grabbed Sketti by the hand and pulled her back inside my apartment.

"We're stuck here until help arrives," I said.

There was a crash from my bedroom. "The window," I said.

"Maybe it's firefighters," Sketti said.

But I knew better. The bedroom door opened, and a rotting arm thrust through. Sketti ran for the door and put her back against it, holding it shut. I could hear several loud moans coming from my bedroom.

"Help me!" Sketti shouted. The arm was still trapped in the nearly-closed door. It thrashed about, trying to grab anything within reach.

I pushed my easy chair towards the door. When I was close, Sketti stepped aside and helped me wedge it against the door. Then we worked together and pushed the couch against the chair.

A floodlight passed by the living room window. I opened the window and looked out. I wasn't sure what I was seeing at first. What looked like a large metal basket floated by, carrying three firefighters. It took me a minute to realize that the basket was suspended from four cables, hanging from a helicopter.

I waved my arms and one of them pointed at me. The basket started to float in my direction. It stopped about five feet away from my window, and it didn't seem to be able to come any closer. One of the firefighters reached out to me, and I tried to grab his hand.

And then the floor collapsed. Suddenly I found myself in the apartment below mine, surrounded by flames. I hurt all over, and I couldn't feel my legs.

There was a man on the floor, about six feet away. It was my downstairs neighbor, Mr. Michello. He was face down, lying perfectly still. I stared at him, trying to figure out if he was breathing.

The firefighters now directed their searchlight through Mr. Michello's window, but I couldn't move my legs. I tried crawling toward the window, but there was too much debris around me. The fire was getting closer, and I could barely breathe through all the smoke.

I looked up and saw Sketti above me. She was still in my apartment, standing at the edge of the collapsed floor. She stepped back and forth, trying to find some way to reach me. Every possible path was blocked by debris or fire.

Finally she stared at Mr. Michello, and I saw a look of determination cross her face. I wasn't sure what she was about to do, but I could tell I wasn't going to like it. "No," I tried to say, but it turned into a coughing fit.

Sketti jumped directly into the fire. I saw her rise back to her feet again, for just a moment, before collapsing in a burning heap. Then Mr. Michello began to stir. He got to his feet, pulled me out of the debris, and slung me over his shoulder.

Just then the window shattered, and Mr. Michello handed me over to the firefighters. They helped him climb over as well, and the basket floated back away from the building. "I think... maybe *that* was my unfinished business," Mr. Michello said.

And then I blacked out.

When I came to, I was in a hospital bed. I could hear people running back and forth in the hall, that squeak squeak squeak of wheeled gurneys being pushed around, and lots of beeping machines. I wasn't sure what time it was, but plenty of sunlight shone through the window.

A woman stood nearby, checking a bag of fluid that hung near my head.

"Sketti?" I asked.

"I beg your pardon?" the nurse asked.

I was sore all over, and my arms were covered in bandages. I could see my right leg was in a cast. I shook my head, trying to organize my thoughts. "Is... Mr. Michello okay?" I asked.

"The man they brought in with you?" the nurse asked. "He's fine. He suffered from smoke inhalation and some minor burns, but he'll be okay. The firefighters say he saved your life, but he doesn't remember any of it."

"Can I see him?" I asked.

"Not for a little while," she said. "But I can give him a message if you like."

I thought about it, then shook my head. Sketti was gone. She'd possessed Mr. Michello just long enough to get us to safety, and then she must have crossed over.

"Just tell him I said thank you," I said. And then I fell back to sleep.

I have to say, I love my new apartment. Following the disaster, there was an investigation, accusations of corner-cutting, lawsuits, and a huge settlement for all those whose lives were upended by the incident. My new place is much closer to work and much farther from the fence that surrounds the city of Louisville.

And it comes with one feature you don't see in most apartments. I woke up this morning to find a finger-drawn heart on my bathroom mirror.

"Morning, Sketti," I said.

The lights flickered a little in response.

When I emerged from the bathroom, I could smell coffee brewing in the kitchen. My favorite morning show was on the TV, and last night's dishes were clean and drying on the rack. Unfinished business, my ass.

I never used to believe in ghosts, so I have no idea what the rules are. Will she fade over time, or will her presence grow? Will she find easier ways to communicate? Can she still possess people, and if so, is there any chance of her finding a permanent human form again? I just don't know.

All I can say is that as long as she's here, I finally feel whole. She's filled a void in my heart that I didn't even know was there, and I look forward to many years with my new roommate.

The Answer

"Whoah!" Nelson shouted as she opened the hatch to the hydroponics module. "That is not what I needed to see at Oh Five Hundred." She shielded her eyes with her hand and floated backward, away from the amorous couple.

"Sorry," Bradford said between gasps. "You weren't... scheduled for duty until six... and... oh god... and we thought... you'd still be asleep." Her partner, Thompson, said nothing, as her face was still buried between Bradford's naked thighs.

"I'll be back in an hour," Nelson said, turning away. "And uh, please wipe down anything you two have touched." She floated back down the hallway. It was a huge ship, comprised of twenty-six cube-shaped modules, and there were only five in the crew. And yet somehow they still stumbled over each other, walked in on private interludes, and generally got in each other's way.

When NASA had put together the crew for the first "manned" mission to Pluto, they'd selected an all-female crew for practical reasons. Women were typically smaller than men, so they required less food and supplies. But if you believed the press releases, the primary reason was to prevent sexual activity.

Just the thought made Nelson laugh. She'd had more sex in the past two years than in her entire life before liftoff. Granted, when the headlines talked about sex, they actually meant preventing pregnancy. That made a lot more sense, as giving birth out here in space would have been a dangerous prospect indeed. Still, the assumption that a crew of women would be celibate was beyond hilarious.

The Zambia 12 Clustership had been in space for two years and it was just about to pass Jupiter. It would be another seven years before they reached Pluto, where parts of their vessel would detach and become a permanent research station. They would remain on Pluto for another fourteen months, then they would begin their journey home in a much smaller ship.

That should be fun, Nelson thought. *It's cramped as it is, and on the way back we'll only have twelve modules.*

She turned a corner and opened the hatch to the communications module. Wright was strapped into a seat at the console. She smiled as Nelson came in.

"Aren't you supposed to be headed for hydroponics?" Wright asked.

"In a minute," Nelson replied. "It's being... ah..." She couldn't decide between a lie or a crude joke.

"Bradford and Thompson?" Wright asked.

"Yeah," Nelson admitted. "I'll give them a minute."

Wright rolled her eyes. "They know you're always early. They wanted you to walk in on them. They were probably hoping you'd join in. You know that, right?"

"You're enough for me," Nelson said.

"Aww, that's sho shweet," Wright replied in a silly voice. "But I don't want you to miss out if you're curious."

"Do we have to talk about this?" Nelson asked. "I was

trying to forget it."

"You're the one who says you suck at social cues," Wright said. "I'm just pointing out one you might have missed."

"Thanks, I guess," Nelson said, then decided to change the subject herself. "Any new messages from control?"

"Just the daily ping," Wright replied. "Looks like this one was sent a couple of hours ago."

"Sounds about right," Nelson said.

"Anything you want me to ask them?" Wright asked.

"Weren't the Oscars last week?" Nelson asked. "You could find out who won."

"It's not like we'll have seen any of the movies," Wright said.

"Doesn't matter," Nelson replied. "I'm starved for interesting news."

"Hold on," Wright said. "I'm getting a weird signal. It's not from NASA."

"Now *that's* interesting," Nelson said, and strapped herself into the chair next to Wright's.

"It's not even coming from Earth," Wright said, studying a readout. "What the heck?"

"Static from Jupiter?" Nelson asked. "Sometimes the computer mistakes radiation for radio signals."

"It's not from Jupiter," Wright said. "It's from somewhere up ahead."

"Maybe it's one of our deep space probes," Nelson said.

"I don't think so," Wright said. "Hold on, the computer is processing the signal. It's definitely a message, and it's from nearby."

"What's it say?" Nelson asked. Her heart was racing now.

"One second," Wright said. "R... N... B... A... Oh my god."

"Well?" Nelson asked.

"It says, 'TURN BACK.'"

"That's got to be one of Thompson's pranks," Nelson said.

"Even she couldn't have done this," Wright replied. "The sensors say there's something big ahead, and it's not Jupiter or one of its moons."

"Notify NASA. I'll wake Bryant," Nelson said. Then she pulled a radio off the wall and typed in the code for the sleep module. "Captain, wake up. We need you in the control module immediately."

Captain Bryant was the last to arrive at the control module. Bradford, Thompson, Wright, and Nelson were already strapped into their seats, and looking more serious than Bryant had ever seen them.

"So what's so important that you couldn't tell me over the ra—" Bryant began, but then she saw Wright's pointing finger. Using the handholds that lined the wall, Bryant climbed toward the window for a better view outside. What she saw made her gasp.

The massive object looked like an unfinished office building. It was almost square, with hundreds of rows of golden windows, so close together they almost touched. The side facing them was slightly concave, like a giant square bowl. An array of steel girders protruded from every edge, and hundreds of tiny lights lit up the exterior.

"What in the world," Wright whispered. Humans had not yet encountered any extraterrestrials, but this construction was well beyond the limits of Earth technology.

"It's so big," Thompson said.

"We should turn around," Bradford said.

"Are you kidding?" Wright asked. "We're the first humans

ever to see this thing."

"Well, we've seen it," Bradford said. "Can we go now?"

"I have to agree with Bradford," Nelson said. "Whatever this is, it literally told us to turn back."

"This has to be the biggest discovery of the century," Bryant said. "I'm not going to tell NASA we saw it and ran away."

"It's just so… big," Thompson said, still too awed to think of anything else to say.

"I don't like this," Nelson said. "If we stick around, something's going to kill us."

"The lives of five women versus the advancement of history," Bryant said, shaking her head. "It's no contest. We can't turn our backs on this. This is why we went to space in the first place. Even if it's dangerous, that's all the more reason to learn more about it so we can warn Earth."

"You're not seriously thinking—" Bradford began.

"We'll stay right here," Bryant said. "We won't get any closer. We'll take pictures and scan it with every device we have. Then we'll send the data to NASA and wait for their instructions."

"That means staying here for at least two hours," Nelson said.

"If this thing wanted to destroy us, it probably would have done so by now," Bryant said.

"I have a better idea," Bradford said. "We set a new course. We go around the alien murder building, continue on to Pluto, and pretend we never saw it."

"Too late for that," Wright said. "Our ship automatically relays sensor data back to NASA in case something happens to us. We've already transmitted a few images. NASA won't get them for at least an hour, but it's too late to cancel those transmissions."

"There you go," Bryant said. "If we stop now, NASA will know we were negligent in our duties."

"They can fire me!" Bradford said. "In fact, you know what? I quit. Take me home or I'll sue for… for…"

"You'd be the one getting sued for breach of contract," Wright said. "Look, I'm scared too, but the choice is out of our hands. We might as well—"

"No!" Bradford shrieked. "You people are out of your minds! I'm not staying!" She unhooked her restraints and pushed off from her chair. Then she used the handholds to climb her way out of the command module.

"Bradford!" Bryant shouted. "Get back here!"

"You should probably just let her go," Wright said. "I don't think she was going to be of any help."

"What do you think she's going to do?" Nelson asked.

"Not much she can do," Wright said. "It's not like she can just spacewalk home."

"She's having a panic attack," Thompson said. "She'll find somewhere she feels safe and curl up into a ball. Do you want me to go talk to her?"

"If you don't mind," Bryant said.

Thompson got up and left. Wright and Nelson continued to scan the alien station.

"Hmm…" Captain Bryant said. "You know those probes we were going to launch on Pluto to find a good landing site?"

"That's a great idea," Wright said.

"Wait," Nelson said. "What if the aliens think it's a weapon?"

"Anything that can build *that*," Bryant said, pointing out the window, "can surely distinguish the difference between a probe and a missile."

"I'll get a probe ready," Wright said, unlatching herself.

The probes were kept in the communications module, which was adjacent to control.

She was halfway there when the ship shuddered. She lost her grip on the handholds and slammed into the wall, then bounced off and flailed about, looking for purchase. Finally she passed the chair in communications, grabbed it, and strapped herself in.

"What was that?" Bryant asked, looking over her sensors. One of the thrusters had come online.

"Bradford," Nelson said. "She's trying to activate the engines manually."

"That's crazy," Bryant said. "She'd have no way to control the ship, we'd just—"

The entire ship lurched forward, then rotated away from the alien station. With only one thruster activated, the Zambia 12 spun in a wide circle.

Captain Bryant flipped on the radio, broadcasting to every module. "Bradford! Whatever you're doing, stop it now!"

Thompson's voice came over the speaker. "She's locked me out of the port thruster module," she said. "She's gone crazy!"

Bryant attempted to reverse the port thruster, but Bradford had severed the link to the command module.

"Can you override the hatch?" Nelson asked.

"Not from here," the captain said, undoing her straps.

"Wait," Nelson said. "What if we just cut the power to that module?"

"Good idea," Bryant said, and opened an emergency control panel. She found the switch for the port thruster module and flipped it.

The ship continued spinning, but at least they had control again. Bryant activated the starboard thruster to slow down their spin.

"Captain," Nelson said, pointing out the window.

Bryant looked up just in time to see the alien space station, much closer than it had been before.

"Everybody brace for imp—" Bryant shouted, just before the collision.

"I believe she was going to say 'impact,'" Keejuun said.

"We could ask her," Seevaal replied, scratching her long yellow beard.

"Unfortunately the collision shattered her skeletal structure," Keejuun said. "Their bodies really are quite fragile, you see."

"The bots can't reassemble her?" Seevaal asked.

"They could," Keejuun said. "But she still wouldn't function. Her inner light has been extinguished."

"Are any of them capable of recovery?" Seevaal asked.

"The ones designated Nelson and Wright are in need of repair, but they should persist," Keejuun replied.

"I would very much like to see them when their minds are functional again," Seevaal said.

"I will arrange it," Keejuun replied.

"Ow," Nelson said as the room faded into view. She couldn't tell where she was. Everything was black, but there were stars in the sky. It didn't feel like she was outside, but it certainly looked like it. Her skin felt strangely cool, and she realized she was naked.

She turned her head. Wright lay on a table a few feet away, also nude and covered in new scars. Nelson then realized it wasn't a table Wright lay on, but rather just a tabletop. The rectangular slab of metal floated in space, with no legs or other support. Nelson couldn't see any ground beneath the two tables, and the starry sky wrapped around them in all directions.

Nelson suddenly felt an attack of vertigo. These metal slabs were the only thing that kept them from falling into infinity. She gripped the edges of her table until her knuckles were white. "Wright," she said, then coughed. "Wright!" she repeated, shouting this time.

"Uhh," Wright moaned, beginning to stir.

"Where are we?" Nelson asked.

Wright opened her eyes, then shrieked. "How?" she asked, and started breathing faster. She rolled over onto her stomach, then rose onto her hands and knees.

"Can anybody hear us?" Nelson shouted.

A round door irised open, maybe ten feet away. The opening just appeared in thin air. On the other side, they saw white light. Two metal orbs floated into the room – if it was a room – and the door irised shut again.

The orbs were shiny and bronze-colored. Each had a round, blue sensor on the front, making them look like metal eyeballs. "Please do not be alarmed," one of them said.

But both women were very alarmed. Wright began screaming, and Nelson backed up to the edge of her table, trying to get as far from the orbs as possible. Then she slipped over the edge and landed on the floor.

Huh, Nelson thought, now too distracted to be scared. She felt the floor with her fingers; it felt solid and cool to the touch. The space and stars beneath her were just an illusion. She stood up and started backing away from the orbs.

Wright stopped screaming long enough to ask, "What did you do to the rest of the crew?"

"We did everything we could for the other two," one of

the orbs replied.

Two? Nelson wondered for a moment, but she was too distracted to hold onto the thought.

"You have our sympathies," the orb continued. "Their injuries were beyond our ability to repair."

"But their loss is your gain," the other orb said. "We used some of their parts to restore your bodies. Two of Bryant's fingers are now Wright's. Thompson's spleen lives on in Nelson."

Wright examined her hands, her eyes going wide. She looked like she might scream again in a moment.

"What *are* you?" Nelson asked, getting to her feet.

One of the orbs turned toward Nelson. "My designation is Keejuun, and this is my *translation error*, Seevaal."

"Translation error?" Nelson asked.

"My apologies," Keejuun said. "Our translation program doesn't have a word for my association with Seevaal."

"You might say spouse," Seevaal added. "But different. We have swapped many body parts, so each of us lives in the other. It is the only way for a bonded pair to really understand each other."

"Body parts?" Nelson asked. "But you don't *have* bodies."

"This is not us," Keejuun said. "We can't be here."

"We are too large," Seevaal added. "We can only interact through the drones."

"How..." Nelson began, but paused to put her thoughts in order.

"What is this place?" Wright asked. She still seemed panicked, but she was keeping it together.

"Observation node," Keejuun replied. "One of thousands. We use these to watch you. Some are like this one, others are hidden on your planet. We also monitor your broadcasts."

Behind the drones, hundreds of screens appeared in the

air. Some showed aerial views of Earth, others showed more close-up shots from ground level, and still others displayed movies and television shows.

"So this is what you do?" Nelson asked. "You send these nodes to watch inhabited planets from a safe distance?"

Keejuun shrank back a little. "There is more to it than that."

"What do you mean?" Wright asked.

The orbs turned to look at each other. "There is no harm in telling them," Seevaal said. "They can't go back either way."

Keejuun turned back to Wright. "This may not be easy for you to understand," he said. "Your universe... ends where you crashed."

"Ends?" Nelson asked. "What do you mean, ends?"

"You are in a... ball," Keejuun said. "Like a globe. This node is attached to the outer wall. Your sun is in the center. Your solar system stops just before Jupiter's orbit. Beyond that is a spherical wall made of... video screens. The stars you see are an illusion."

"That makes no sense," Wright said. "We can see the other planets through telescopes! We've sent out probes!"

"You see what we wish you to see," Seevaal said. "We intercept your probes, and return data of our making."

"But what about meteors?" Nelson asked. "Haley's comet?"

"All sent by us," Keejuun explained. "Some meteors are drones sent to plant more cameras. If we neglect to disguise them as rocks, people call them UFOs. They get suspicious about the true nature of your universe."

"Okay, I have a question," Wright said. She took a deep breath. In her head, she rejected three different ways of phrasing her question. Finally she just asked, "Why?"

Keejuun paused before answering. "You were a... science project for my *translation error* classes. Close to nine thousand years ago, by your count."

"All your history before then has been fabricated," Seevaal added. "We live a very long time by human standards."

"Your solar system now sits on a shelf in my office," Keejuun continued.

"But he never forgets you," Seevaal said. "Sometimes he uses you as a *translation error.*"

"She means paperweight," Keejuun clarified. "I couldn't bear to end the project, so it will continue at least as long as I do."

"He wants to see how long your species survives," Seevaal added. "You are always on the brink of global war and you do very little to take care of your planet."

"We have a wager going," Keejuun said. "But it isn't just curiosity. I do care for your people. I hope the experiment outlives my own existence."

Nelson and Wright were speechless.

"I told you they wouldn't understand," Keejuun said.

"It is still valuable data to see their reaction to the truth," Seevaal replied.

"So..." Nelson began, collecting her thoughts. "What happens now?"

"It would be unwise for us to send you back to Earth with this knowledge," Seevaal said.

"It would cause chaos," Keejuun added. "Your world would destroy itself even faster."

"You must live out your days in this node," Seevaal said.

"But please do not worry," Keejuun said. "We will take care of your needs. This room can be anything you need it to be." As he spoke, the floor became a grassy plain, and the walls became a blue sky. A ring of trees circled the meadow, and they could hear birds chirping in the distance.

"We will leave you now so you can discuss our offer," Seevaal said.

"I hope you accept," Keejuun added. "There is much we can learn from each other." Then the outer door irised open again, and the orbs floated out of the room.

Nelson stepped over to Wright's table and sat down next to her. She put her arm around Wright's shoulders and they sat in silence for a few minutes.

"What do you think?" Nelson finally asked.

"They didn't present an alternative," Wright said.

"I think we already know the alternative," Nelson said.

Wright nodded, then took a deep breath. "There's worse ways to live," she said, gesturing at the simulated meadow. She could even smell the grass.

"Agreed," Nelson said, and pulled Wright in for a hug.

A scorched gray cube hurtled through space. The Zambia 12's port thruster module had detached just in time, and now it was on a course for Earth.

I'm not the crazy one, Bradford reassured herself. *I did the right thing. Maybe I got them killed, but they were going to die anyway. At least I didn't die with them.*

She opened a panel on the wall and looked over the supplies. The thruster modules were designed to be used as escape ships in case of emergencies, so each one came equipped with food and water reserves, as well as a waste tube and other necessities.

Is it enough to last for two years? Bradford wondered as she looked through the packets of freeze-dried nutrient bars. It had to be. She'd ration them out, maybe eat a third of a bar each day. She might be malnourished when she arrived, but she was determined to survive.

She had to get back to Earth. She had a whopper of a story to tell them.

Moving On

"Miranda, um… the boss wants to see you." Cheryl took a sip of her coffee as she hovered by Miranda's desk, waiting for a reply.

Miranda barely looked at her. "Tell Jen I'll be right there," she said. On her screen, she corrected the routing number on a corporate share draft.

"No, not Jen, Bruce," Cheryl clarified. Her expression was full of sympathy. Whatever she knew, it couldn't be good.

"Bruce?" Miranda asked, immediately closing the check processing program. *What could he possibly want from me?* she wondered. She locked her screen and headed for the CEO's office.

She passed Paul in the hallway. He looked like he'd just witnessed the murder of a loved one. Miranda shot him a curious look, but he just shook his head and kept walking.

Bruce's door was partly open, and Miranda gave it a polite knock as she entered.

"Good to see you," Bruce said. "Please, have a seat." He was in his early forties with neatly trimmed hair and a business suit. He was the only one in the company who wore a tie every day. Today his eyes were oddly red.

Miranda sat down. "You wanted to see me, sir?" she asked. Bruce was usually very approachable, but there was something about his expression that bothered her. He looked almost as upset as Paul had.

"Thank you for coming on such short notice," he said pleasantly. But then his expression turned grim. "I have some... news."

"Bad news?" Miranda asked.

"There's no good way to say this," Bruce said. He took a deep breath before he continued. "We've had to make some tough choices. We've decided not to renew the contract with ChePix."

ChePix was the software they used to correct and process check images. Miranda spent a good ninety percent of her day using the program.

"So we'll be using different software?" Miranda asked, trying to ignore the feeling in the pit of her stomach.

Bruce took another slow breath. "We've decided to outsource the process," he finally said. "We're eliminating your position, I'm sorry."

Miranda tried not to look how she felt. For the rest of the meeting, Bruce's voice seemed to take on a surreal echoey quality, like Miranda was at the bottom of a well, and he was calling to her from far above. He went over the terms of her dismissal and her generous severance package, all the while assuring her that she was a wonderful employee and it was out of his hands. Fortunately he also gave her the details in writing, or she wouldn't have remembered half of them.

And then it was over. She returned to her department, feeling numb all over. She passed Cass in the hallway. Cass did a double-take when she saw Miranda's face.

Miranda just gave her a tired look and kept walking.

Cass, Paul, and Kim were the only other employees who shared Miranda's position. All four of them were being let go.

As Miranda approached her desk, she noticed some of her coworkers glancing at her, before turning away. *Do they all know?* she wondered. Then she loaded up ChePix and threw herself into her work, blocking out the world until five.

The house was unusually dark as Miranda pulled into her driveway. She went in through the back door and put her purse down on the kitchen table. "Moon?" she called. The house was too quiet. Moon's car hadn't been in the driveway, which usually meant she'd gone out for drinks. But something felt different this time. The house just felt emptier somehow.

The one time I really need someone to talk to, Miranda thought. She went upstairs and put on a T-shirt and pajama pants. Both were dinosaur-themed. As she put her work clothes in the hamper, she noticed that Moon's favorite stuffed cat wasn't on the bed.

Miranda frowned. Then she turned and started opening dresser drawers. All of Moon's clothing was gone.

No, she thought. Her relationship with Moon had always been sort of tentative, hovering somewhere between "friends with benefits" and "open but steady." Maybe they weren't exactly soulmates, but she couldn't stand the thought of losing a girlfriend and a job on the same day.

She grabbed her phone and started to tap out a panicked text. Then she deleted it in favor of a more breezy approach. "U at the bar?" Miranda texted.

"Check the fridge," came the reply.

Just tell me, Miranda thought, but she didn't want to get

into a fight over text. She stomped back down the stairs and ripped the note off the fridge. She didn't have to read it to know it was over. Instead she just sank to the floor, clutching the note in her hand.

She didn't cry. Moon had always been very open about her aversion to commitment, and Miranda had always known she was a flight risk. Moon's feet never touched the ground, and it was nothing short of a miracle that she'd stayed this long.

Still. She'd been both a bestie and a lover. It was like losing two people. And worse, now Miranda had no one to vent to about her job.

Miranda stared off into space for a good half hour, then moved to the couch. She considered calling one of her other friends, but none of them were really close enough. Bawling to a "fun time friend" seemed inappropriate somehow.

And her family was right out. She hadn't spoken to her parents in years, not since they'd found out Miranda's college roommate wasn't just a roommate.

That left her with… no one.

She watched the TV for a while. Then she actually turned the TV on and watched some more. Some insipid sitcom was playing. She'd always hated the show, but she didn't have the energy to change the channel. It was all just moving colors to her anyway.

She fell asleep on the couch without having dinner.

There was a reason Bruce had informed his employees on a Friday afternoon. Miranda was useless on Saturday, wandering around like a ghost haunting her own home. But by Saturday evening she began to get some perspective on things.

For one thing, her job wasn't really all that precious to her. She hated that she'd have to look for employment again, but it wasn't like it was an emergency. She had three months before her final day, which was plenty of time to get some feelers out there. And even if she didn't find a new job right away, she had six months of severance pay to live on while she looked.

And losing Moon wasn't such a big deal either. They'd gotten along well enough, but there'd never been any sort of future there. Moon's departure had always been inevitable. She'd never lied about that.

And finally, this could be a good opportunity to start over. Miranda wasn't a fan of her hometown. Nashville was too conservative, too crowded, and it was getting to be too expensive. She hated the boiling summers and lukewarm winters. She wanted to live somewhere north, maybe a blue state, where she would never have to hear country music again.

Excited by this line of thought, she opened up her laptop and started browsing house listings.

Miranda spent the next few weeks packing boxes and searching for the perfect home. She looked around the west coast, mostly Oregon and Washington. The larger cities were just as expensive as Nashville, but she found that in some of the smaller towns, housing prices were very good. The neighborhoods weren't always pretty, but she lived most of her life online anyway.

She was browsing houses in Oregon when she came across a town called "Sappho's Heart."

"Oh my god," she said out loud. It was just too precious.

Okay, but you can't pick a town based on the name, she thought.

Still, how cool would it be to see that on my address labels?

She decided to research the town. What could it hurt? The more she learned, the more she fell in love. Sappho's Heart was too small to have a thriving LGBT+ community, but it wasn't too far from Salem, which did. *I could be a recluse who only goes into town on weekends,* she thought. She liked the idea of being a recluse.

The houses were just gorgeous, like a town full of storybook cottages. Several of the homes were more than a hundred years old, but the listings assured her that they had modern amenities and proper wiring. And the prices... wow. Most of the homes were half the price of Miranda's, with more square footage.

I'm going for it, Miranda thought, and began to pick out a few favorites.

Reality quickly reared its ugly head. The logistics of moving halfway across the country were a nightmare. Lenders wouldn't even consider her since she wouldn't have a job when she got there. She tried to explain that her severance meant she could spend six months looking for a job, but the underwriters didn't consider that solid income.

She needed to have a job in Oregon before they'd loan her money, but she couldn't exactly jet back and forth for job interviews. She wasn't some IT specialist or stock market hero, she was just an office grunt with a very specific job title. Nevertheless, she applied online and even got a few callbacks. But the employers wanted to meet her face-to-face before hiring her.

This isn't going to work, she thought more than once. She realized she'd have to move into an apartment first. Apartment, then job, then house. But she hated the thought of moving twice. It was already going to cost thousands of dollars to move all her things that far. It would probably be cheaper to sell everything she owned and buy it again when she got the house.

"Ugh," she grunted one morning while browsing apartments in Oregon. Everybody wanted a year-long lease. Miranda didn't want to stay for more than three months. Just long enough to get a job, get a loan approved, and find the perfect house.

"How do people do this?" she said out loud. She couldn't be the first person to move after losing their job. She knew she could afford to live in Sappho's Heart, but getting there was proving impossible.

Her last day at work came and went, and she still didn't have a solid plan for moving. She kept filling out applications, both for loans and for jobs, and she continued browsing apartments.

And then one day, she came across an ad:

ROOMMATE WANTED: SWF seeks quiet roommate. Large house but mostly unfurnished so must bring own bed.

Miranda's eyebrows perked up. She called the number right away.

"This is Katie," the voice yawned. It was late afternoon but she sounded like Miranda had woken her up.

"Hi, my name is Miranda Jackson, I was calling about the room?"

"Yes, hi, do you want to come see it tonight?"

"Actually, I'm in Tennessee," Miranda said.

"Is that far?" Katie asked.

She doesn't know where Tennessee is? Miranda wondered. But the woman had an odd accent, one Miranda couldn't quite place. Her voice was lilting and melodic, like the way elves spoke in fantasy movies. *Maybe she's from another country,* she thought.

"Yes, it's over two thousand miles away," Miranda said. "But I'm sure it's fine. Every house in that city is beautiful. I'd be bringing a lot of furniture, though."

"Good, good, this house is too empty," Katie replied. "I bought it unfurnished and I've only put furniture in my bedroom."

"But I might only stay for a few months," Miranda added. "I'm looking for a house of my own. It's just easier to move to another state if you stay in an apartment first."

"I understand," Katie said. "But maybe you won't feel that way after you move in. I have a lot of room I don't use, and I'll charge you less in rent than a mortgage would be."

"This sounds like a really good deal," Miranda said. *Maybe too good*, she thought. *What's the catch*?

"Would you like to see some pictures?" Katie asked.

Miranda gave her an e-mail address and looked at the pictures of the house. Katie was right, it had a lot of room and very little furniture. Plus it was seriously cute. Miranda pictured herself living there in the roomy fairytale cottage, away from the crowded cities and rude zealots. Maybe for once she'd feel like she actually belonged.

Still, things were moving very fast. The last three months had flown by. It seemed like just yesterday that Bruce had given her the bad news. She didn't want to make a snap decision she might regret later.

Yes I do, she thought. "When can I move in?"

Miranda still owed eighty thousand on her mortgage, but property values had risen in the few years since she'd bought her home, and she managed to sell it for one hundred and twenty thousand. Between that and her severance, she could take all the time she needed to get a job.

Moving her furniture from Tennessee to Oregon cost her roughly five thousand dollars, which was slightly cheaper than buying all new furniture.

The night before the move, Miranda had trouble sleeping. Hundreds of scenarios whizzed through her mind. What if she didn't like Oregon? What if she couldn't get a good job there? What if her roommate was a serial killer? What if the house was a scam, and the address turned out to be an empty lot? What if what if what if…

New rule, she thought. *No thinking about real life in bed. You never solve anything, you just make it harder to sleep.*

Instead, she forced herself to imagine the perfect scenario. She pictured herself living in the new house, getting a job in town, meeting a woman, going on dates, getting married, raising a hippo together… it was hard to say exactly when the musings melted into dreams, but it was most likely somewhere before "hippo."

Miranda had happy dreams for most of the night, but she woke up screaming. "Blood," she gasped, running her hand across her neck. She couldn't remember any details of the nightmare, but she could still see those fangs coming for her. It took another hour to fall back asleep, and the alarm seemed to come too soon.

It took Miranda three days to drive to Sappho's Heart. The sun was setting when she pulled into the driveway, but even in the dim light, the house made an impression. It was even more beautiful in person. It was a one-story coastal-style cottage with white siding, and it was just large enough to still feel quaint. When Miranda went inside, she could have sworn it was still up for sale. While the kitchen was decked out with modern appliances, there wasn't a bit of furniture in sight. There wasn't even any food in the refrigerator. There were, however, heavy curtains on every window.

Katie lived in the basement, leaving the rest of the house for Miranda to furnish as she liked. As for Katie herself, she was a diminutive young woman with pale skin and black hair. She wore black clothing and gave Miranda a "goth chick" vibe. But she was very sweet and easy to talk to.

"So what's the story here?" Miranda asked. "Did you just move in, or are you one of those 'material possessions just trap us in consumerism' people?"

"Come with me," Katie said, and led her downstairs.

The basement was nearly the size of the upstairs, but other than a bathroom, it was all one big open room. One corner was set up like a second kitchen, another had a bed, and another had a couch and a television. There was a table against one wall covered in jewelry, some of which looked unfinished. There weren't any pictures on the walls or other decorations, but the room definitely looked lived in. And almost everything was black.

Katie led Miranda over to a small table in the kitchen area. "This is all I need in the world," Katie explained as they sat down. "I inherited this house, but it's more than I can really use. I'd look for somewhere smaller but I like this basement. I don't have an actual job – I just sell hand-made jewelry online – so I need a roommate to help pay the bills."

The movers weren't scheduled to arrive until the following morning, so Katie offered her bed to Miranda. "It's okay," Katie said. "I can take the couch, I really don't sleep much anyway."

"No, no," Miranda said. "I'll take the couch. I'm too excited to sleep."

In the end it barely mattered. They both stayed up late watching television, and Miranda finally passed out on the couch sometime after three AM.

Katie shook her awake around nine. "Your phone just buzzed," she said. "The screen said something about a moving company."

"Oh, shit!" Miranda exclaimed, grabbing the phone. She called them back, then told Katie, "They'll be here in a few minutes. I have to pee. Will you get the door if I'm not out yet?"

Katie looked oddly bothered at the request, but she nodded.

When Miranda emerged from the bathroom, movers were already carrying boxes and furniture around the house. Katie stood as far from the front door as possible, pointing the movers to various rooms. "I can take over," Miranda said. Katie thanked her and disappeared downstairs. *That was odd,* Miranda thought, but she forgot all about it as she turned her attention to the movers.

The movers worked surprisingly fast, and the van pulled away less than two hours later. Miranda knocked on the basement door and asked Katie if she'd help unpack.

Katie was halfway up the stairs when she balked. "Would you mind closing the curtains?" she asked.

"You don't like sunlight?" Miranda asked.

"Sensitive eyes," Katie said. "Electric lights are fine, but sunlight gives me a headache."

Miranda shrugged and shut all the curtains. The two spent the rest of the afternoon unpacking boxes and figuring out where everything went. They chatted all the while, learning more about each other as they worked. They found they had similar tastes in music as well as movies.

They stopped around sundown. There were still plenty of

boxes left, but there was no rush. They watched a couple of movies together before turning in around eleven. Miranda slept in her own bed, in her own room, in a house she could finally call home. She was out like a light within minutes and didn't wake up again until around four AM.

Ow, Miranda thought. Her muscles screamed at her. Unpacking with Katie had been so much fun that she hadn't realized how much work they'd actually done. She rolled over, trying to find a position that didn't aggravate her sore arms. She was almost asleep again when she heard a thump from somewhere outside her bedroom.

She was on her feet in an instant. She opened her bedroom door just a crack and peeked through. Katie was carefully closing the back door, trying not to make a sound.

"Katie?" Miranda asked.

Katie jumped and made an "eep" sound. "Sorry," she said. "Did I wake you?"

"It's okay," Miranda said. "Were you outside?"

"Yes, sorry," Katie replied. "I was just coming back from my morning run."

"At four in the morning?" Miranda asked. "The sun's not even... Oh. Your eyes. Still... Can't you just wear sunglasses?"

Katie shook her head. "I don't like them," she said.

Miranda looked confused. "So you just... don't go out in the daytime? Like, ever?"

"Please don't make a big deal out of it," Katie said. She bit her lower lip, watching Miranda's face carefully.

Miranda thought a moment, then smiled. "I guess everybody has quirks," she said. "I've had worse roommates. At least you're not playing loud music all night."

Katie gave her a tired smile and then walked down the stairs to the basement. As she passed, Miranda thought she spotted blood on her cheek. Miranda frowned, then shook her head. It was dark and she was still half-asleep. She went to the bathroom, took a couple of painkillers, and went back to bed.

"It's good to have you on the team. I hope you enjoy working here."

The words echoed through Miranda's mind the entire walk home. She couldn't believe her luck. She'd thought it would take weeks to find a job, and that she'd end up having to drive all the way to Salem every day. But here she was, only a week after moving in, job in hand. She would start Monday, working from eight AM until three.

The bookstore was so close she didn't even have to drive. It was in a cozy little shopping center, next to a café and an old-timey drugstore. It wasn't much money, but her expenses were way lower than they'd been before the move. And she still had those severance payments for a few more months.

Is this even real life? she wondered. It was almost too perfect. The storybook town had become her storybook life. The bookstore even had a shop's cat that wandered the stacks and slept on the shelves. It was the kind of thing Miranda had only seen in romance novels.

She was halfway home when she saw the flashing lights. Two police cars were parked in front of another quaint cottage, similar to Katie's but smaller and yellow. Miranda slowly walked past the police cars, trying not to look like she was eavesdropping. One of the officers gave her an annoyed side-eye and gestured for her to move along.

She kept moving, but she listened hard to the conversation between the officers. She couldn't hear much, but she did pick up on the words "victim" and "blood."

Even here? Miranda wondered as she walked on. She shook her head sadly. There was simply no escaping human depravity.

When Miranda got home, she searched the internet for local news. According to the headlines, it was the third such murder to occur in the past two months. The police refused to discuss the specifics of the cases, but there were rumors that the victims had been drained of blood.

Oh come on, Miranda thought. *Why are people in small towns always so superstitious?*

The sun was starting to set. Katie would be up soon. She slept a lot during the day, most likely due to her aversion to sunlight. Miranda looked back to the article on the computer screen, then thought about Katie's strange sleep schedule. A silly thought crossed her mind.

Grow up, she told herself, pushing the thought away.

That night they had a vampire movie marathon. Miranda had suggested it the previous night, before she'd learned about the local deaths. Now it seemed a little disrespectful to watch horror movies, given recent events. But then, murders happened every day, all over the world. Scary movies were either always in poor taste or never in poor taste.

Not that tonight's collection was particularly scary. One of the movies was so old that it was more funny than frightening. The next one was a modern vampire romance with more kissing than violence. Their final movie for the night was an action-fest full of gore and gratuitous nudity.

"This is so dumb," Katie said. "Look at the bumps on his forehead. Real vampires don't look like that."

Miranda laughed. "Did you just say 'real' vampires? Is there something you want to tell me?"

"You know what I mean," Katie replied, sounding more sober than the conversation warranted. "The actual legends. The stories written by classic authors like Stoker."

"The legends contradict each other anyway," Miranda said. "One version says you have to stake them in the heart. Another says you have to bury their head at a crossroads. Some turn into bats, some don't. These are just modern variations of the legends. In a few hundred years these movies will be folklore too."

Katie looked like she wanted to argue, then changed her mind. "I guess you're right," she finally said. Katie leaned against Miranda's shoulder as they watched the rest of the movie.

Miranda's dreams were overloaded with themes of vampires and homicide. Sometimes the vampires were the murderers, sometimes they were the victims, and sometimes they were the cops. She woke up at one AM, just an hour after she'd gone to bed. She heard the back door close, just as she had a few nights earlier. Worried that it might be a burglar, she peeked out her bedroom door. All was silent. She checked both the front and back door, and found both to be locked. Then she looked out the kitchen window and saw someone walking into the woods behind the house.

It was hard to see much more than a silhouette, even with the ample moonlight, but it was a feminine shape and about

Katie's height. *What is she doing?* Miranda thought. The woman wasn't even carrying a flashlight.

Miranda thought about running after her and asking her what was going on. She also considered sneaking after her so she wouldn't lie. But Miranda didn't think she could keep up without a flashlight, which would give her away. Also, she didn't like the idea of wandering around after dark, especially with a murderer on the loose.

A murderer, Miranda thought, the full implications hitting home. *Katie's wandering around out there without so much as a flashlight, while a serial killer is preying on local citizens. Just how crazy is she?*

Miranda paced around the house. *I should call her cell,* she thought, then thought better of it. It seemed possessive, somehow, to interrupt Katie's routine. *I should call the police,* she thought. *But for what? Because a woman voluntarily left her own home?*

At two AM, Miranda gave up and called Katie's cell. There was no answer. She walked downstairs and tried to open the basement door, but it was locked. She put her ear to the door and called the cell again. She could faintly hear a ringtone from beyond the door.

So she's out alone at night and she doesn't even have her phone? Miranda thought. *What if she breaks her leg or something? Or gets attacked by an animal? How will she call for help?*

Miranda started to dial the police, then stopped. *This was her routine long before I moved in,* she reasoned. *The only difference is that I'm here now. It's not an emergency, at least not a new one, it's just a woman who's a little too brave for her own good. Or maybe I'm the coward. Either way it's her life and it's not for me to judge her weird decisions.*

She sat down at the kitchen table, then stood up and paced some more. *I really don't want to see her get hurt,* though.

Miranda hadn't known Katie very long, but she had already grown to care for her. She didn't know if it was love or lust or something more familial – it was way too early to put a label on it. All she knew was that if Katie were to get herself killed, the news would cut Miranda like a knife.

Shortly after three, the doorknob jiggled and the back door opened. Miranda raised her head from the kitchen table where she'd fallen asleep. Katie was a bit startled to see Miranda sitting there. "Can't sleep?" Katie asked.

"Me?" Miranda asked. "What about you?"

"You know I sleep during the day," Katie said.

"And you go walking around in the woods at night?" Miranda asked.

"I like hiking," Katie said. "I like the woods. I can't go during the day, so when else should I go?"

"Unarmed? No phone? Not even a flashlight?"

Katie sighed. "Look," she said, turning out her jacket pockets. She placed three items on the kitchen table: a small flashlight, a taser, and a can of pepper spray.

"Oh," Miranda said. "You weren't using the flashlight when you left."

"There's plenty of moonlight tonight," Katie said. "And I don't like turning on the flashlight until I'm deeper into the woods. The neighbors might see it and call the police."

"That's so dangerous," Miranda said.

"It's nice that you're worried about me," Katie replied. "But I've been doing this for years, and I've never had a problem."

"It only takes once," Miranda said.

"It's my life," Katie said. "I'm not giving up my walks just to make you feel better."

Miranda nodded. She didn't like it, but what could she do? Katie was right, it was her risk to take. "All right,"

Miranda said.

"Sorry I woke you," Katie said. "You go get some sleep. I'll see you tomorrow evening."

Miranda stood up and they hugged, then went to their separate rooms.

The following morning, Miranda watched the local news while she ate a bowl of cereal. There had been another murder overnight, a middle-aged woman who had been killed in her own backyard. The police believed her time of death had been sometime around two AM.

Oh my god, Miranda thought. *That's when Katie was out. What if the murderer had taken a shortcut through the woods? Then Katie would have been his next victim. I've got to talk her out of those late-night walks.*

Just then the reporter turned their mic on the victim's next-door neighbor, who'd had the misfortune of discovering the body. "It was a vampire," the man said. "Had to be. All her blood was gone, and there were two puncture wounds in her neck. I knew somethin' was up when I saw a bat fly by my window last night. He was probably fleeing the scene of the crime."

Freaked out as she was, Miranda almost laughed. She wondered what Katie would think of this guy's take on vampires.

Once again, putting Katie and vampires in the same thought made her pause. Katie – a pale, black-clad woman who lived in a basement because she hated sunlight – left the house at one AM. A woman was murdered at two, and Katie returned home at three.

There's no such thing as vampires, Miranda told herself. But there were people with delusions. There were people who thought they were vampires. Miranda had seen news reports about killers who drank the blood of their victims. *Could Katie be one of them?* Miranda wondered.

"Give me a break," she mumbled. There was no way Katie could be a serial killer. For one thing, she was too tiny. Half of the victims had been men, and big ones at that. The thought of Katie overpowering one of them made Miranda laugh.

Unless she's got vampire strength, she thought. "Oh my god just stop it," she told herself and switched the channel.

Later that day Miranda posted the following to a small online message board:

How Can I Tell If My Roommate Is A Vampire?

I (28F) recently moved into a house in Oregon. My roommate (26F) owns the home, and she has some quirks. She lives in the basement, and can't go into the sunlight because she says it hurts her eyes. She sleeps most of the day and only comes out at night. She has pale skin and always wears black. She goes hiking every night after midnight. There have been some murders in my town recently, where the victim was found without any blood. At least one of the murders happened while my roommate was "hiking."

Also... I think there might be a spark between us. I'm worried that I might be looking for excuses to reject her.

She waited half an hour, then scrolled through the responses:

GlorfBot: Shoot her. If she lives, she's a vampire.

VampHunter: Does she eat garlic? Are there mirrors in the house?

NeverWrong: That's movie stuff. And mirrors don't use silver anymore.

AlwaysInappropriate: Boobs.

AnimeShipper: Aw, this is just like that Mike Meyers movie.

GlorfBot: Halloween? There's no vampires in that.

AnimeShipper: The actor, not the character. The one where he marries an ax murderer.

RejectReality: Call the police. Even if she's not a vampire, she could be a suspect.

MovingMan: What's Oregon like? I want to move there. But not if there's vampires.

SheezanAnteater: There's no such thing as vampires.

NeverWrong: Could be porphyria. Maybe the killer is a hemophiliac.

AlwaysInappropriate: Send nudes.

RejectReality: Seriously, though. Police. Now.

AnimeShipper: She can't send her future girlfriend to jail!

RejectReality: If she's innocent they'll figure it out pretty quickly. She has to have an alibi for at least one of the murders.

AlwaysInappropriate: I can detect vampires. I'll need a naked picture of your roommate.

SheezanAnteater: Can someone please report this guy?

AnimeShipper: What if it's true love?

RejectReality: What if it's true crime?

MovingMan: What if I move to one of the hub cities? Do you think there's vampires in Portland?

Miranda shut her laptop. She wasn't going to find any real help online. She decided against going to the police. There just wasn't enough to go on. She couldn't call the cops and say, "My ninety-pound roommate might be the violent brute on the news." The only evidence she had was that Katie had been out of the house at the time of one of the murders.

Nor could she tell the cops, "I think my roommate's a vampire." For starters, there was no such thing. But even if there was, she still didn't have any hard evidence to support that theory.

But maybe I can get some, Miranda thought. She considered sneaking some holy water into Katie's drink, or maybe some garlic. But she wasn't even sure that would work in real life. She already knew most of the movies were bullshit, but Katie seemed to have some very specific opinions on the subject.

So… What if I just ask her?

"So tell me what this one gets wrong," Miranda said.

She and Katie sat in the living room, watching more vampire movies on the couch. Katie leaned on Miranda's shoulder, as she often did when they watched movies together. Katie smelled nice, and Miranda felt a little guilty for suspecting her of anything.

"Well, for one thing, vampires don't sparkle," Katie said. "But you knew that. But also, vamps can't be good guys. It's just not in their nature. They're basically demons wearing human skin."

"And demons can't be good guys?" Miranda asked.

"Good and bad isn't a thing for them," Katie replied. "It's like asking if a shark is evil. Vampires live to feed, and they don't consider humans to be people. They can act the part of a human, but it's all a ruse to get their next meal."

"What if they turn a really good person, though?" Miranda asked. "Wouldn't some of their original personality remain?"

Katie shook her head. "When a vampire sires another vampire, it's like their way of reproducing. A portion of their own demon splits off and inhabits the new body. The original host is dead, and the demon spawn takes over their mind."

"So how do you kill them?" Miranda asked.

"It's not easy," Katie said. "They have incredible regenerative powers. That's because the only living part is the demon, so damaging the body is like trying to kill a puppeteer by harming the puppet. Still, some of the movie methods do work. Sunlight harms them, and can even kill them if they stay in it long enough. A wooden stake through the heart also works, because the demons are allergic to wood. Anywhere else in the body and they can shrug it off, but the heart pumps wood splinters throughout the body."

"What about garlic?" Miranda asked.

"Vampires have a strong sense of smell," Katie said. "Garlic annoys them, but it won't stop them, especially if they're hungry."

"Holy water?"

"Pure Hollywood," Katie said.

"So where did these demons come from in the first place?" Miranda asked.

"Outer space," Katie said.

Miranda blinked. "Seriously?" she asked.

"Yeah, the original vampires were from a planet called Gythos," Katie said. "But when they ran out of food on Gythos, they built rocket ships and... why are you looking at me like that?"

"Where are you getting this?" Miranda asked. "I thought you were going by the old legends and stories. I never actually read Dracula, but I'm pretty sure Brahm Stoker didn't mention spaceships."

"Oh, ah…" Katie thought for a minute. "It's… a modern theory. The idea is that ancient people often mistook extraterrestrial phenomena for gods and angels. They weren't advanced enough to understand the concept of spaceships or aliens, so when they saw UFOs, they dreamed up mythology to explain it. One spaceship became Apollo's chariot. A weird-looking alien was called a demon or monster. The very concept of religion itself might have been started as a way to explain visiting aliens."

Miranda winced. This was even stranger than she'd expected. "But you still called them demons," she said.

"To me, that's what 'demon' means," Katie said. "A vampire-creature from the planet Gythos, who preys on the blood of humans and reproduces by infecting people with its bite."

"I've never heard anything like this before," Miranda said.

"So it's not a very widespread theory," Katie said. "I frequent some pretty obscure websites."

"Do you… actually believe this stuff?" Miranda asked.

"Oh god no, it's all just for fun," Katie assured her. But she looked away as she said it, as if afraid to make eye contact.

"Good," Miranda laughed. "I was about to have you committed."

"I know, right?" Katie said, but her voice didn't match her eyes. "Let's just… watch the movie. I think I missed some important dialogue."

"I'm not sure this movie has any important dialogue," Miranda said, and Katie laughed. They cuddled up closer and enjoyed the film.

Miranda felt a lot better. She still wasn't sure if Katie believed all the space vampire stuff, but the important part was, she was clearly on Team Human. When Katie talked about "real" vampires, at least real in the sense that they were based on actual legend, she spoke about them with a mouth full of venom. It was as if she considered these imaginary creatures to be her worst enemy. Maybe she was overcompensating to cover for being a murderer, but Miranda didn't think so.

They watched movies until midnight, and Miranda went to bed. The following morning she learned that there'd been another murder. This time, the police estimated the time of death was around eleven PM. Miranda and Katie had been together at the time, so there went the last of Miranda's lingering doubts. She was still quite unnerved by the fact that there was a killer on the loose, and that her roommate kept putting herself in danger, but she let go of the idea that her roommate was a murderer... or a vampire.

Over the next couple of weeks, they got closer and closer. They watched movies together every night and even went out on a couple of dates – after sundown, of course. On Halloween, exactly one month after Miranda had moved in, they shared a brief kiss.

On November first, Miranda was on cloud nine as she worked her shift at the bookstore. She couldn't stop humming, and her boss, Natalie, kept giving her knowing smiles. "You're in love, girl," she said as Miranda skipped by carrying a stack of books.

"Anything's possible," Miranda said, putting the books back on their shelves. She gave the cat a quick stroke as she walked by its favorite shelf. Peaches mewled in protest, either not wanting to be touched or not wanting Miranda to stop, it was hard to say for sure.

"Well I'm glad you're in a good mood," Natalie said. "Because I need a favor. I have to leave early. Would you mind closing up tonight?"

"Not a problem," Miranda said. The bookstore closed at six, and it would take another hour or so to clean up and count the register. With as late as Katie slept, Miranda would still be home in time to have a nice night together. Maybe she'd even pick up a romantic dinner on the way home. Katie loved the sushi restaurant a few doors down from the bookstore.

The sun had set by the time Miranda left the restaurant. She belatedly realized that she'd walked to work. She didn't exactly love the idea of walking home in the dark. There hadn't been any murders since the night she'd had that strange talk with Katie, so it was possible the killer had moved on to another town. But Miranda wasn't about to bet her life on it.

She thought about calling Katie to pick her up, but she didn't have a car of her own. Katie could have taken Miranda's car, but Miranda only had the one set of car keys, which currently resided in her jacket pocket.

Miranda browsed the app store on her phone. She'd never used one of those rideshare apps, but there was a first time for everything. She installed an app and searched for drivers in her area. There were none.

"Small towns," Miranda grumbled.

She sent a quick text to Katie. "On my way home, bringing food." Sushi take-out in hand, she began the walk home.

The street lamps gave off meager yellow light, and the houses Miranda passed – which looked so picturesque in the daytime – now had a sinister quality. The shadows seemed to turn their windows into eyes and their covered porches into gaping maws.

Stop it, she told herself. Sappho's Heart was one of the safest towns in America, if you didn't count the violent murders. She would be home in twenty minutes, watching movies in the arms of her roommate.

The streets were so quiet it was unnerving. The silence felt forced, like the world was holding its breath out of fear. Miranda nearly jumped out of her skin when her phone buzzed. It was just a "thumbs up" to the text she'd sent Katie.

She passed the house where she'd seen the police cars a few weeks earlier. All of its lights were off, and a realtor sign now sat in the yard.

She stood still for a moment, staring at the house. She thought she saw something move in one of the windows. Suddenly she felt even more exposed, as if the house was looking back at her. She continued her walk.

A few houses later, her heart leaped into her throat when a dark figure approached her. It turned out to be a man in pajama pants carrying a bag of trash to the bin out front. He gave her a slight nod before he turned around and headed back inside.

A few minutes later, Miranda's house was in sight. The porchlight was on, like a beacon guiding her to safety. But then she heard the crunch of grass. A shadow fluttered to her left. A dark shape rushed towards her at an alarming speed.

She dropped the take-out and ran, but the thing was much faster. It grabbed her by the arm and pulled her roughly off the sidewalk, into a dark place between two bushes. It was insanely strong, with hands that felt like steel. Miranda opened her mouth to scream, but a hand covered her mouth.

She was shoved and pulled and wasn't even sure which way was up for a moment. Then she wound up on her back, in the grass, staring into the face of a man. She couldn't make out a lot of his features in the dark, but what she saw was more than enough to change her perspective on the existence of vampires.

His eyes glowed orange and were slitted like a cat's. His skin was mottled gray, the skin of a corpse. He held her down with one hand, the other still over her mouth. Miranda banged on him with her hands, but he didn't even seem to notice.

He leaned in, and his mouth opened wide, at least twice as wide as should have been possible. His fangs extended as he turned Miranda's head to the side.

And then he was gone. Another dark shape, moving so fast it was a blur, pulled the vampire off of her and wrestled him to the ground.

Miranda rolled over and climbed to her feet, backing away from the brawling pair of shadowy figures. She tried to tell her feet to run, but she was too fascinated by the fight. And the newcomer looked so...

Katie? Miranda gaped as she watched her roommate tear into the vampire, clawing his flesh with razor-sharp fingernails. Or were they claws? Miranda caught glimpses of Katie's face, and her features had changed somehow. Her face was almost wolflike.

The vampire gurgled as Katie ripped off his head. Then she removed a wooden stake from a sheath on her belt, and drove it into the vampire's chest. The creature shuddered for a moment then lay still. After a few seconds the body dissolved, leaving an empty set of clothing.

Katie stood up and her face reverted to normal. Her

fingernails retracted as she brushed herself off. Still breathing heavily, she looked at Miranda and asked, "Are you okay?"

Miranda couldn't speak for a moment. Finally she asked, "What are you?"

"Long story," Katie said.

"Can you give me a 'back of the book' summary?" Miranda asked.

"My people travel the galaxy killing vampires," Katie replied.

Miranda cocked her head, then shrugged. "Good enough for me," she said.

Katie looked relieved. "I'll tell you everything tonight, I swear," she said.

"I got sushi," Miranda said, looking over her shoulder. The bag still lay on the sidewalk, on its side.

"You read my mind!" Katie said.

The two hugged, picked up the take-out bag, and returned home arm-in-arm.

Dream Sequence

"Never start a story with a dream sequence," the giant hermit crab said, his rhinestone-encrusted top hat glittering in the light of the floating bonfire. "Publishers won't even look at your book if you start it that way. Dreams lack tension, since there's no real danger."

"What if you self-publish?" a platypus in the audience asked.

"Then it doesn't really matter," the hermit crab said. "Since no one is going to read it anyway."

Standing at the edge of the gathering, Scott nodded slowly. He wasn't a writer, but he still took the crab's advice to heart. He had to; it was Thursday, and crabs were always right on Thursdays. At least that's what Scott's soccer ball had always told him. But now it was time to float. He said goodbye to the crab, the platypus, and the rest of the menagerie. His feet turned into little clouds as he rose into the air. Soon the bonfire was just a tiny bright spot on the ground far below.

The neighborhood looked different from above. Instead of the crisscrossed suburban streets he knew by heart, it was now full of stone castles and Egyptian-style pyramids, with the occasional miniature golf course thrown in. And yet somehow he knew his way around. He soon spotted his destination. At the base of a volcano, a small baseball stadium glowed under a futuristic glass dome. Scott couldn't remember exactly why he was supposed to go there, but he knew it was the place to be.

As he lowered himself to the tree line, the stadium changed. It didn't transform like a toy robot, it was more like an optical illusion – the building just looked different from the side than it did from above. It was now a two-story home with pink stucco walls and a ceramic tile roof.

Nadine's house, Scott thought. *I wonder if she's home?*

Propelled more by the question than actual free will, Scott floated closer to the home until he could see through the second-floor windows. Peeking in one window, he saw the inside of an elephant pen at the zoo. The elephants were all on roller skates and one appeared to be doing a crossword puzzle. He moved on to the next window, in which he saw the floor of the New York Stock Exchange. Brokers in hula skirts shouted "Buy" and "Sell" at each other from opposite sides of a raging river, while ticker tapes drifted down from the ceiling.

He reached the third window and peered in. It was Nadine's bedroom. He'd never been in her room before, but somehow he just knew this was it. The wallpaper was salmon-colored with a floral print. There were posters of boy bands on the walls. As Scott watched, the door opened and Nadine stepped through, wearing a pink bathrobe.

Scott was about to rap on the window when she took off the robe. She was naked underneath, and her body was more beautiful than he had ever imagined. *Oh my god,* Scott thought. His hand still hovered at the window, but now he lowered it. He couldn't get her attention now; she'd know he'd seen her.

His eyes traveled up and down her body, taking in every curve, every freckle, every minute detail. *I should turn away*, Scott thought. But he couldn't. He was transfixed by her beauty. As he watched, she puttered around her room, getting ready for bed. She slung her robe over the back of a chair, then opened her dresser and rooted around, looking for clothing.

Scott reached into his pocket and withdrew his phone. It was not a conscious decision, and certainly not something he would have done in real life. But his morality seemed to be napping and his primal instincts took over.

He took more than a dozen pictures as she set a couple of pieces of clothing on the bed. He continued snapping shots as she got down on the floor and did ten sit-ups, followed by ten push-ups, and finally ten jumping jacks.

Finally she stood up and grabbed her clothes off of the bed. First she put on a pair of white panties, then pulled an oversized T-shirt over her head. As her head poked through the T-shirt, she spotted Scott outside the window. She froze, her eyes wide, her face full of shock.

She marched over to the window and reached for Scott. Her hand phased right through the glass. It seemed like her arm stretched to double its length as her fingers clasped around Scott's throat.

Nadine pulled him through the glass so that they were face-to-furious-face. "How *dare* you," she said, and her teeth turned into fangs. Then her mouth opened impossibly wide, and she pulled Scott into her maw.

Scott woke with a jolt, and didn't fall back asleep for another hour.

"I had the strangest dream last night," Nadine said. She and

Scott sat around a lunch table, along with Rani, Denise, and Nic.

"Me too," Scott said, taking a bite out of his hot dog.

"You first," Nadine said.

Scott was about to speak, thought for a moment, then changed his mind. "I… can't remember," he lied. "What was yours?"

"I was in my bedroom, and I could swear I was being watched," Nadine said. "And then I looked out the window and…" She paused, trying to remember. Then she looked at Scott and cocked her head. "Why do you look so strange?" she asked.

He'd stopped chewing, and his skin had gone pale. When Scott realized everyone was staring at him, he swallowed his bite and then started coughing.

"You okay, man?" Nic asked, starting to stand up.

Scott gave a thumbs up and wiped his mouth. "Swallowed wrong," he gasped, then coughed a bit more.

"So anyway," Nadine said, "I looked out the window and —"

"Can I borrow someone's phone?" Rani interrupted. "I need to check my Flitter."

"What happened to yours?" Nadine asked.

Rani rolled her eyes. "My mom took mine when I stayed out too late."

"Who were you out with?" Denise asked.

"Nobody you know," Rani said, winking.

"Here, take mine," Scott said, unlocking his phone and handing it over. He was just glad someone had changed the subject.

"Come on, girl, what's his name?" Denise asked.

"Promise not to tell anyone?" Rani asked, logging into the Flitter app.

"Me? Gossip?" Denise asked.

"I won't tell either," Nic said.

"We all know you don't have any friends, Nic," Rani said. "Okay, so you remember that rich guy I met at that party last month?"

"Really?" Nadine and Denise asked together.

"No," Rani said. "But this is the guy that grooms his dog."

"A career man," Scott said sarcastically. "Nice."

"Can he get me a discount?" Nic asked. "I have this shiba —"

But Rani suddenly shrieked.

"What's wrong?" Denise asked. All the students in the lunchroom had turned their heads toward their table.

"Where did you get these pictures?" Rani asked, glaring at Scott.

"Let me see," Nic asked, getting up.

"No!" Rani said, putting her hand over the phone. "Nadine, did you let him take these?" She handed the phone over.

Nadine's eyes widened as she scrolled through the photos. Other students started to crowd around them but Rani and Denise stood and blocked their view. Then Nadine turned the phone over and just stared at Scott, her mouth wide open.

Their homeroom teacher, Mrs. Knisley, stepped forward. "Break it up, everybody," she said, and several students returned to their tables. Then she leaned over to look at Nadine, whose face had gone pale. "What's wrong with her?" she asked.

"Scott took nude pictures of her!" Rani blurted.

Mrs. Knisley squinted at Scott. "Both of you come with me," she said, and led them to the principal's office.

"I swear I didn't do it," Scott said. *Unless I was sleepwalking*, he thought. But that didn't make any sense. There was no way he could have traveled all the way to her house, climbed up a ladder and taken those photos, then returned home, all in his sleep. He'd never sleepwalked in his life, not so much as a step, and suddenly he was driving across town?

"Then how did the photos get on your phone?" Principal Kean asked. Mr. Kean sat behind a black wooden desk, while Mrs. Knisley sat between Scott and Nadine on a wide black couch.

"I don't know," Scott said. "You believe me, don't you Nadine?"

Nadine just stared, unsure what to believe. *I've never done jumping jacks*, she thought. "We have a tall fence..." she said, thinking out loud.

"See?" Scott said. "I didn't even know that. How could I have gotten onto her property to take the pictures?"

"You expect us to believe someone else took the pictures and put them on your phone without your knowledge?" the principal asked.

Just then there was a knock at the door. Mrs. Knisley stood and opened it. Nic stood outside the door, accompanied by a police officer. "Sorry to bother you, sir," Nic said to the principal. "This policeman wanted to see you."

The officer stepped forward. "I'm Officer Porcine from the twelfth precinct," he said. "We're warning all the schools about possible phone hacks. Someone has been creating A.I. images of students in compromising positions, then putting them on other students' phones."

"The pics are A.I.?" Scott asked, looking both relieved and confused. *Then how did I dream I was there?*

Nic stood against the wall, his hand on his chin. He probably should have left after letting the officer in, but he had to see how this turned out, and no one seemed to notice he was there anyway.

"Thank you, officer," the principal said. He looked a bit astonished himself, but was glad he wouldn't have to expel anyone today.

The officer turned and left.

"Of course you *will* delete the photos," Principal Kean said.

"I want to delete them myself," Nadine said. "I need to see that they're gone."

Mrs. Knisley currently held the phone. She handed it to Scott so he could unlock it, then gave it to Nadine. She went through and deleted the entire set. Then she scrolled through his gallery to make sure there weren't more.

"If that's all, you two are dismissed," the principal said.

Scott and Nadine stood and left the office. Lunch was almost over, so they headed for their lockers instead of returning to the cafeteria. "I can't believe that happened," Scott said.

"You *swear* you didn't take those pictures?" Nadine asked.

"I'd never do anything like that," he replied. "And I couldn't have if I'd wanted to. I swear."

Rani and Denise came walking up to them. "Is he expelled?" Denise asked.

"It was all just a misunderstanding," Nadine said. "His phone was hacked."

Denise looked skeptical. "Someone hacked his phone," she repeated. "...and they put pictures *on* it?"

"The police confirmed it and everything," Nic said, coming up behind them.

"Then who took them?" Rani asked.

"The officer says they were A.I.," Nadine replied. "I… guess that makes sense. Some of the pictures were of me doing exercises I don't do. But they looked so real."

"Technology's getting crazy good," Nic said. "So, are we still on for the game this Saturday?"

"I'll be there," Scott said, thankful for the chance to talk about something else.

The others also nodded in agreement, and they broke up to go to class.

They played tabletop RPGs every Saturday. This week it was "Knight Times," a fast-paced dungeon crawler with lots of combat. It was their third session of the campaign, and the party was already up to level eight. Nic was the DM, and they always played in his kitchen.

Scott was the first to show up. He'd made sure to get there early because he wanted to talk to Nic.

"And you promise you didn't take the pictures?" Nic asked.

"For the last time, I swear," Scott said. "But…"

"But what?" Nic asked.

"It's crazy," Scott said.

"It's already crazy," Nic said. "Who puts dirty pics on other people's phones?"

Scott sat down on one of the folding chairs. "The night before Rani found the pics, I… well, I dreamed that I took them."

Nic frowned. "Seriously?"

"Yeah, I mean, I don't believe in psychic powers, but how could I dream about it before it happened?"

Nic stroked his chin for a moment. "Well, I see two possibilities. One, you were sleepwalking. Two, you were awake when you took the pictures, but something's wrong with your head and you mistakenly remember it being a dream. I've heard of a psychological condition where memories don't feel real."

"I told you, I couldn't have taken them," Scott said. "What if I'm still dreaming now?"

Nic shook his head. "Nope. I'm here, and I perceive you, therefore you're not dreaming. *I* might be dreaming, but this doesn't feel like a dream to me."

"But I don't know that," Scott said. "Maybe you're just saying all this in my dream. Prove to me you're not part of my dream."

"How am I supposed to do that?" Nic asked.

Scott thought a moment. "Take off your clothes and yodel."

Nic laughed. "How would that prove you're not dreaming?"

"It wouldn't," Scott said. "But it would prove I *am*. But since you won't, maybe that means I'm awake."

Nic thought a moment. "You dream about me naked a lot?"

"God no," Scott said. "No offense, but ew. It's just something that would only happen in a dream."

"Try counting," Nic suggested. "Read a book. Do some math. Anything that uses the analytical part of your brain. It's really hard to do that in a dream."

"Our game today should take care of that," Scott said.

"Now I have a question for you," Nic said. "Sometimes we do things in dreams that we wish we could do in real life. If you had the chance to take those pics, and you knew there would be no repercussions, would you?"

"No!" Scott said. "That's horrible. I'd never violate someone's privacy that way."

"That's the right answer," Nic said. "But is it an honest answer? You did make the choice the other night. You made it in a dream, but it was still all you."

"I've done all kinds of crazy stuff in dreams," Scott said. "One time I drove around in a giant shoe. Does that mean I want a shoe-shaped car?"

"Dreams are random," Nic said. "But choices are still choices. I've always wondered if dreaming was like being drunk. Your inhibitions are asleep, so we finally see the real you."

"Not in a million years," Scott said.

"But you wish you could see her naked, right?" Nic asked. "I mean, she does have a nice body."

"Who talks like that?" Scott asked.

"Isn't this how guys talk?" Nic asked.

"Maybe on TV…" Scott said.

"But am I wrong?" Nic asked.

"Okay, fine, yes," Scott admitted. "I am a straight male, and I like looking at attractive girls. If we were in a one hundred percent consensual situation, yes, I would love to see her naked. Same goes for Denise and Rani."

"But it's not like Denise and Rani, is it?" Nic asked. "You like Nadine."

"Huh?" Scott pretended to study his character sheet.

Nic shook his head. "I've seen how you look at her. You want to ask her out."

"No," Scott said. "Wait, is it obvious? I mean, no. Why?"

"Because I want to make sure that's not the only reason you're here," Nic said. "If you like hanging out and playing games with us, great. But if you're just here because you think Nadine might eventually fall in love with you…"

"I like the games," Scott said. "It's why I'm here. I mean it." He stared at his character sheet a bit before he continued. "Though if she did fall in love with me, that'd be cool too."

"You know she likes girls, right?" Nic said.

Scott looked up. "Wait, seriously?"

"You haven't noticed?" Nic said. "The way she and Rani hang on each other?"

"Rani too?" Scott asked, astonished.

"Rani's bi, or she wouldn't be going out with the dog groomer," Nic said. "She and Nadine aren't exclusive or anything, but I thought you should know before you go hitting on anyone. As far as I know, Nadine's only interested in girls."

"Oh," Scott said.

There was a knock at the door, and Nic stood up. "Take my advice," he said, walking into the living room. "Keep your dreams as dreams." Then he opened the front door. Nadine and Rani came in and put their bags down.

"You two doing okay?" Scott asked. As they sat down, he watched them closely, looking for any signs that they were a couple.

Nadine seemed a little uncomfortable around him at first, but after a few minutes they got back into their normal rhythm. The four talked about their characters and discussed the events of the previous week's game.

There was another knock at the door, and Nic stood up to answer it. Denise walked in and set her backpack on the floor beside her chair. "What?" she asked, finally noticing the way the others were staring at her.

"Your… outfit?" Nadine said, pointing.

Denise looked down and saw that she was in her underwear. She wore a pink bra with a little blue bow in the middle, and yellow panties with a floral pattern. "What the *hell*?" she exclaimed, then ran into the bathroom and slammed the door.

"Whoa," Scott said.

"You have any extra clothes I can give her?" Nadine asked Nic. He nodded and walked out of the room.

Rani stood up and talked to Denise through the door. "You left the house like that?"

"I swear I had clothes on before I got here," Denise said through the door. "Jeans and a T-shirt. It's a brand new T-shirt with a d20 on it. I was going to show it off today."

Nic returned with a robe. "Have her put this on," he said, handing the robe to Rani. "Then if you want, you can take her to my mom's room and find something of hers. I think they're about the same size."

Rani handed Denise the robe, and they retreated to the bedroom on the other side of the house.

"It's starting to fall apart," Nic muttered.

"What is?" Scott asked.

Nic shook his head. "Nothing, just... it's been a weird week."

Denise and Rani returned a few minutes later. Denise was now wearing a yellow sun dress.

"You were right," Denise said, "Your mom's clothes fit great. I'll bring this back next week if that's okay."

"I'm sure she won't mind," Nic said.

"Where *are* your parents anyway?" Scott asked. "I haven't seen them in forever."

"They go out on weekends," Nic said.

The five friends finally sat down and played their game for the rest of the day.

I really need to pee, Scott thought, rushing through the school hallway. Class was in session, but he just couldn't wait any longer. Mr. McNair would be mad at him when he finally showed up. He might even make him stay after school. But it was better than wetting himself in class.

The halls were empty as he rushed to the bathroom. He reached it only to find that the boys' had a big "out of order" sign across the door. He pressed on the door anyway, but it wouldn't budge. Which was odd, because he didn't see a lock on the door.

He turned to the girls' room. *Everyone's in class*, he thought. *It should be empty. I'll be in and out before anyone comes in.* Looking around nervously, he pushed open the door.

The girls' room was much larger than the boys'. It was nicer, too. It had more than twice as many stalls, there was a comfortable-looking sofa against the far wall, and there were three video arcade machines near the sinks. Everything smelled like lilacs and the floors weren't nearly as sticky.

I knew theirs was better, Scott thought as he headed into one of the stalls. He latched the door behind him, then noticed that there was no toilet, just a little bench in the back of the stall. *Weird,* he thought. He was about to pick another stall when he heard giggling. Someone had come into the restroom. He peeked through the door crack and saw Nadine and Rani walk past. They stopped in front of the sinks. Then they started to make out.

Scott's eyes bulged as Nadine lifted up Rani's shirt. *How far is this going to go?* Scott wondered. He found it mildly interesting – and ultimately distracting – that Rani's bra was identical to the one Denise had been wearing at the game the previous weekend. And that was when the illusion started to break down.

This has got to be a dream, he thought. He'd had lucid dreams before, and it was always interesting to see just what triggered the part of his brain that noticed inconsistencies.

He could ride a Komodo dragon all over town without thinking anything of it, but the minute he saw a green stop sign, his brain might say, "Nope, that's too far." *The logic center of the brain sleeps with one eye open*, Scott thought.

Denise's bra had been on his mind, so obviously his dreaming mind used that image for Rani's. And why not? He'd never seen Rani's bra in real life, so of course his brain would just use the last bra he'd seen. *It's like a video game using shared assets to save hard drive space*, he thought.

Now that he knew it was a dream, he no longer feared getting in trouble. "Hello ladies, need a third?" he asked as he opened the stall door. The two girls gasped and Rani quickly pulled her shirt down.

"What are you doing here?" Nadine asked.

"The boys' room was out of order," he said. "Now come on, let's make this dream more memorable." He stepped forward and put an arm around Nadine's waist.

"Hey, boundaries!" Nadine shouted. She tried to pull away but Scott tightened his arm.

Rani slapped him, hard. "What the hell do you think you're doing?" she asked.

Scott put a hand to his face, stunned. He couldn't remember feeling that much pain in a dream before. *It's my dream*, he thought. *Shouldn't they be nicer to me?*

Suddenly his bladder was screaming at him. *I have to wake up now or I'm going to wet the bed*, he thought. He tried pinching his arm, but all he felt was pain. "Slap me again," he said. "Harder."

The girls just stared at him like he'd sprouted goat horns.

"Seriously," he said. "I need to wake up now." When they didn't comply, he reached out and grabbed Rani's breast, making a "honk honk" noise as he did so.

She kicked him in the crotch so hard he doubled over in

pain. "Why can't I wake up," he moaned as he lay on the bathroom floor, curled up with his knees to his chest. Then he finally lost control of his bladder.

The girls ran off to get the principal. Scott rocked back and forth, his pants wet, his eyes watering. For just a moment he thought he saw Nic standing by the door, shaking his head in disapproval. When he blinked again, Nic was gone.

Principal Kean spoke calmly but looked furious. "It's most disappointing to see you in here again, Scott. And for sexual assault?"

"It's okay," Scott replied. "I'll wake up in a minute, and this'll all go away." He sat on one of three metal chairs in front of the principal's desk. *Wasn't this a couch before?* Scott wondered idly as he touched the armrest.

Now Mr. Kean looked concerned. "I assure you this is the real world, Scott. Have you been having trouble distinguishing reality from fantasy?" He started typing on the computer.

"Have you ever had one of those dreams where you keep looking for a bathroom and can't find one, because you have to go in real life?" Scott asked.

"Not that I recall," the principal said.

"Seriously?" Scott asked. "Never?"

"I rarely remember my dreams," the principal said. "Actually it would be closer to say that I have no memory of ever having had a dream."

"That can't be normal," Scott said.

"We're talking about you, not me," Principal Kean said. "So you think you're dreaming right now?"

"This has to be a dream," Scott said. "Nothing makes sense. The bathroom was closed..."

"Yes, the boys' room is going under repairs at the moment," Mr. Kean confirmed. "A pipe burst. You should have used the one on the other side of the school. Not the girls' room."

"But it was locked," Scott said. "And it doesn't even have a lock."

"There's a latch in the upper right of the door," the principal said.

"But the girls' room was larger…"

"This building wasn't always a school," the principal said. "It was converted from an old factory. Some of the rooms aren't as symmetrical as they should be."

"But," Scott said, struggling to understand. It had all seemed so dreamlike. "They had so many stalls…"

"It's not uncommon for girls' rooms to have more stalls than boys' rooms," Mr. Kean said. "If you stop and think for a moment, I'm sure you can reason out why."

"…and then the stall had no toilet," Scott continued.

"There are three stalls like that," Mr. Kean said. "The cheerleaders sometimes use them to change when they don't want to walk all the way to the gym."

"…and the girls were in there during class…"

"Yes, and they'll spend this Saturday in detention for that," the principal said.

"And Rani's bra looked just like the one Denise wears," Scott said.

"First off, it disturbs me that you know that," Mr. Kean said. "Secondly, girls often go shopping together. Is it possible they bought them from the same store?"

"But it all seemed so… surreal," Scott said. "Even you look sort of blurry."

The principal took a deep breath. "Please be honest with me, Scott. Are you on drugs? I assure you, I will do my best to get you whatever help you need."

"I've never..." Scott began, but once again there was a knock at the door.

It was Mr. Kean's secretary, Mrs. Fenople. "I'm sorry to bother you sir, but we just got a call from the CDC."

As the door closed behind her, Scott thought he saw Nic out in the hall.

"Is there a pandemic?" Mr. Kean asked.

"Nothing like that," Mrs. Fenople said. "But they wanted to warn us about a medicine recall. The local stores received a shipment of Cleer-Breethe allergy pills that—"

"Those are the ones I use," Scott interrupted.

"Well, this batch was laced with LSD," Mrs. Fenople said. "The CDC says that some of our students could have taken it accidentally, and we should watch for any strange behavior."

The principal shut off his computer. "Looks like you're off the hook again. Please report to the school nurse," he ordered.

"Yes, sir. Thank you, sir," Scott said as he stood up and left. Once he was in the hallway, he thought he saw the principal standing with his arms outstretched in a T-pose right before the door shut.

As he walked back to his locker, he realized that his pants were soaked. He was surprised that he'd forgotten, as they were starting to reek. Class was in session – it had let out while he was in the principal's office, but now seventh period had started. Scott shook his head. He couldn't go back like this, and he didn't have a spare change of pants at school. Instead he headed for the gym, took a shower, and put on his gym shorts.

On his way out of the gym, he looked at the clock. School would let out in fifteen minutes. *No point in going back now*, he thought, so he went back to his locker, packed his backpack, and headed for his car. *At least I'll beat the traffic*, he thought.

Nic was waiting for him by his car.

"Hey bud," Scott said. "Why aren't you in class?"

"LSD scare," Nic said. "They're letting anybody who takes 'Cleer-Breethe' allergy pills go home early. You know, as a precaution."

"Sure, that sounds safe," Scott said. "Let's fill the streets with potentially-tripping teenage drivers. What could possibly go wrong?"

"Pretty sure they just don't want any accidents to happen on school property," Nic said. "If we wreck somewhere else, we can't sue the school."

Scott opened his car door and then stood there for a moment. "I didn't know you had allergies," he said.

"As far as they know, I do," Nic said with a chuckle. Then he looked serious. "Are you... feeling anything strange?"

"I've seen a couple of weird things today," Scott admitted. "Did some stuff I wouldn't normally do. I thought I might be dreaming."

"Like I said, try reading a book," Nic suggested.

Scott shrugged and pulled a textbook out of his backpack, then flipped to a random page. "In 1862, Abraham Lincoln ratified the fourteenth amendment, which prohibited slavery from being practiced in the United States," he read. "Eight months later he was assassinated by John Wilkes Ford while watching a play at the Booth theater."

Nic winced a little, but Scott didn't notice. "So the text looks normal?" Nic asked. "It's not blurry, or dancing off the page?"

"Looks fine," Scott said, tossing the book onto the

passenger seat of his car.

"Then I'm pretty sure you're wide awake," Nic said. "Just promise me if you start to feel weird, you'll pull over."

Scott agreed and said goodbye. He tossed his backpack into the car, then sat down in the driver's seat. He briefly glanced at the textbook lying in the next seat. The photo on the cover depicted a man writing numbers on a blackboard. Above the picture, the title "Algebra II" was printed in bold letters.

He frowned a little. A voice in the back of his mind told him that something didn't add up. But then he shook his head. *It's just the LSD making you paranoid*, he thought. Then he started the car and drove home.

Where is everybody? Scott thought. He'd seen this place before, in a... video game, maybe? Yes. This was the military complex from... Call of Zombies? Ghost Prototype? Something like that. But in the game, the hallways were full of soldiers and the undead. This place was just empty.

Maybe all the monsters are asleep, he thought. *What time is it?*

He peered at his watch, but the numbers looked fuzzy. The first number could have been a three or a nine, it was hard to tell. It seemed to oscillate back and forth between the two.

Cheap watch, he thought. He walked through the wide halls, looking for his friends – they'd said they'd meet him at the arcade. *Why is there an arcade in an army base?* he wondered.

Because they have locations all over the place, he reasoned. Bob and Dexter's was more than just an arcade, it was also a restaurant, a sports bar, and a bowling alley. Why wouldn't the soldiers want a place to hang out?

He turned a corner and saw the arcade, but it was closed.

Not just closed, but out of business, by the look of things. He peered through the gate and saw that all the machines were gone. The carpet was covered in lighter square patches where the arcade games had once been. *Where are we going to spend our Friday nights now?* Scott wondered.

Then he turned and left. As he walked away, a tentacle wrapped around his arm. Scott found himself eye-to-giant-eye with a colossal squid. "Don't believe the stereotypes," the squid whispered. "Look at me. Just because I have tentacles, people think I do porn. But all I want is to be a ballet dancer."

"Understood," Scott replied with a smile. Now he realized he was dreaming, which was a great relief because it meant his favorite arcade was still in business. Though probably not in a military base.

The squid looked left and right, searching for anyone who might be watching. Then it leaned in closer and whispered, "He's up to something, you know."

"Who?" Scott asked.

"You know," the squid said. Then it swam away, jetting through the rippling floor tiles as if it were swimming.

There was a commissary across the hall. The lights were off and the doors were closed, but Scott could swear he saw a pair of eyes staring back at him through the window. He knew that stare.

"Nic," Scott said as he sat up in bed. There was something about Nic, something he needed to know. But the dream had faded; it was nothing more than ephemeral shapes and colors now.

It was Saturday. Game day. Scott ate breakfast, alone in his quiet house, not questioning who had put out the plate of bacon and eggs. It seemed like he never saw his mom these days. She always set out Scott's breakfast before she left for work, seven days a week. Most days she didn't get home until Scott was in bed. If Scott happened to stay out late, his mom was already asleep by the time he got home.

It probably should have bothered him more than it did, but as far as Scott was concerned, it was just how life was at the moment. Every family had a different dynamic, and Scott's was the type that just didn't run into each other that often.

He finished breakfast, got his gaming bag together, and headed for Nic's place.

As usual, Scott was the first to arrive.

"Hey," Nic said, as Scott sat down at the kitchen table. "There's something I wanted to talk to you about. Before the others get here."

"What's on your mind?" Scott asked, unpacking his bag.

"You've been noticing strange things, haven't you?"

Scott frowned. Somewhere in the back of his mind, a tiny voice was screaming at him not to trust Nic. *But he's my best friend*, Scott thought. He took a deep breath. "Like what?" he asked, trying to feign nonchalance.

"You've been having intense dreams, right?" Nic asked. "And maybe a little trouble distinguishing them from reality?"

"Chalk it up to the LSD that got in my system," Scott said.

"Do you really believe that?" Nic asked. "I mean, first you almost went to jail for taking photos. Then you almost got in trouble for grabbing Rani. Both times you were saved by Deus Ex Machina so blatant, even the worst writers wouldn't use it in a story."

Scott nodded. "And you were there both times," he said.

"You don't think I had something to do with..." Nic said, trailing off.

Scott had a crazed look in his eye. "You've been watching me wherever I go," he said. "In both my dreams and in reality. Or are they both dreams?"

"I was wondering that myself!" Nic said. He took a few steps backward as Scott stood up.

"Like you don't already know," Scott said, stepping closer to Nic. "The squid was right about you."

There was a knock at the door. "Come in!" Nic shouted. "Quick!"

Nadine and Rani let themselves in and looked at the guys strangely. "What's going on?" Nadine asked.

Nic was backed against the wall, and Scott looked like he was about to boil over.

"Nic's been lying to us," Scott said. He put a hand on Nic's shoulder. His other hand was balled into a fist.

"We're both being lied to," Nic said.

"What's this about?" Rani asked. "Who's been lying about what?"

"He's crazy," Nic said. "Keeps babbling about squid!"

"Shouldn't you two be in detention?" Scott asked, turning to look at Nadine and Rani.

"They let me out because of the allergy thing," Nadine said.

"I don't have allergies," Rani said. "But my pharmacist called the principal and talked him out of punishing me. He said he'd filled my anxiety meds wrong."

"And you don't find that oddly convenient?" Scott asked.

"I do," Rani said. "I've been wondering about it ever since. I was just telling Nadine on the way here—"

"It's true, she was," Nadine added. "Lots of weird

coincidences this week."

"That's because none of this is real," Scott said. "My dreams keep leaking into reality. I get in trouble, but I don't get punished. And have any of you seen your parents lately?"

Nadine and Rani looked at each other, frowning. "And you think Nic knows something?" Rani asked.

"I'm just as confused as you are," Nic exclaimed. "That's why I kept following you, Scott. You looked like you knew something, and I thought you'd believe me."

"You're lying!" Scott shouted, pulling his fist back. Nadine stepped forward to stop him, but Rani grabbed her by the arm.

"All of you just calm down," Denise said.

Everyone turned to look at her. She stood by the kitchen table, just a few feet away from Scott and Nic. She wore a white one-piece jumpsuit, which made her look like something out of sci-fi.

"When did you get here?" Nic asked.

"I was here all along," Denise said. "You just couldn't see me. I can explain everything."

Scott released Nic. They both stared at her, waiting for her to speak.

Denise looked like she was trying to figure out where to begin. She pulled out a chair and sat down, then gestured for the others to do the same. Scott was about to say something when she finally spoke. "You're all in my basement," she said.

"Your basement looks a lot like Nic's kitchen," Nadine said.

"This isn't real," Denise explained. "Look, it started as an experiment. A voluntary experiment – you all consented to help me test my invention, you just can't remember. You're all asleep in stasis tubes, and we're sharing a dream together. You're the only real people in the dream world; the rest are all NPCs."

No one spoke for a moment. Scott looked like he had too many questions to pick one, while Nadine looked like she didn't believe a word of it. Nic and Rani just looked thoughtful.

"How long have we been here?" Rani finally asked.

"A few months," Denise said. "Sorry. The experiment was only supposed to last a couple of hours. The police are looking for you, but I'm not a suspect, so they haven't thought to check my basement."

"So all the weird things that happened..." Scott began, looking confused.

"You had to be able to dream," Denise said. "Or you wouldn't believe the 'reality' parts were reality. But the software wasn't very good at generating dreams. Its solution was to make your dreams as weird as possible. But sometimes the software gets confused and generates dream elements in the reality scenes. Hence the photos you took appearing in both places."

"And that time you showed up in your underwear?" Nic asked.

"Textures failed to load," Denise said. "I'm still working on that glitch."

"Are you controlling everything that happens?" Rani asked.

"The computer is trying to simulate your normal life as accurately as possible," Denise said. "But whenever you got in trouble, I'd step in and bail you out."

"Wait wait wait," Nadine said. "I still don't get it. So the original experiment was only supposed to take a few hours. Why are we still asleep? Did something go wrong?"

Denise shook her head and sighed. "Do you have any idea how hard it is to find a gaming group that consistently meets every weekend?"

Road Hog

ED02500.04.01

From above, the planet of Magnar barely even looked inhabited. It seemed to have very little vegetation or water, and most of its surface was covered in arid wastelands. The shuttle passed over the occasional domed city, sparse dots of civilization that punctuated an otherwise bleak-looking environment.

There was only one place the shuttle could legally land. If it veered even slightly off course, it would be vaporized by the planetary defense satellites. The Magnarans did not like visitors and went to great lengths to avoid interplanetary contamination.

Tabi looked out her window, shaking her head. On a planet like this, finding their target would either be very difficult or very easy. "We're almost there," she told her partner.

Sycathe didn't respond. She was fast asleep, taking up both of the seats on Tabi's right. They almost always had to book three seats when they traveled together, as very few commercial shuttles were built with Grunthians in mind. At just over two meters tall, Sycathe was actually small for her species, but her wide frame was more than most vehicles could comfortably accommodate. Not that Grunthians cared about comfort.

"Wake up, Syca," Tabi said, nudging her partner. When Sycathe still didn't react, Tabi extended a claw from her index finger and gave her a good poke.

"Corn dog!" Sycathe said, all four of her eyes fluttering open. Then she blinked a few times, trying to figure out where she was. "What'd I miss?"

"Not much," Tabi replied. "The planet's mostly dirt. Hope we find Hogan quickly."

As the shuttle set down, Port Accountant Ghee Sinrak marked the arrival time on his log. He stood at attention as the passengers disembarked. Most were Magnarans on official business. Some were suppliers who immediately proceeded to the back of the shuttle to help unload their cargo. The last to exit were the pair Ghee needed to see. As the mismatched pair of bounty hunters stepped down the ramp, Ghee motioned for them to come forward.

He scrutinized them as they approached. The Galean resembled a humanoid cat with black fur and a white mane. The Grunthian looked more like a shaved ape with extra eyes and arms. *How did these two even meet?* Ghee wondered. But it didn't matter. He just wanted them off his planet as quickly as possible.

"Tabi Thene-Zeer and Sycathe Exbac," the accountant said. It wasn't a question, but they still nodded in reply. "Come with me," he said, and led them into his office.

"Thank you for allowing us this opportunity," Tabi said as she sat down. Sycathe remained standing, as the remaining chair did not look like it would hold her weight.

"It was against my better judgment, but we do need this woman caught," Ghee replied. He shuffled through some papers before handing a few documents to the bounty hunters. "Please sign this non-disclosure agreement," he said. "Once you leave Magnar, you will discuss nothing you've seen here. You will take nothing from our planet. You will leave nothing on our planet. You will not cause any damage, major or minor, in our cities or out in the wastelands. If you break these rules, you will be subject to severe fines and possibly imprisonment. Do you agree?"

Tabi nodded her head and signed the paper. Sycathe picked up the pen with one of her smaller, frontal arms, then looked lost in thought. "We can't take anything? Are we allowed to eat?"

"Of course there are exceptions for biological functions," Ghee snapped.

"We understand," Tabi said, nudging Sycathe. The Grunthian looked like she had more questions but signed anyway.

"Thank you," Ghee said. "Now, I have arranged passage to the town of Freedirt. Hogan's band has been active in that area, so someone there may have information for you. Do you have any questions?"

Sycathe looked to Tabi, who shook her head no. "I think we've got all we need," Tabi said.

Ghee looked relieved. "Then be on your way. Your possessions should be unloaded by now. Pick them up and proceed to terminal three. Your transport leaves in three hours."

The bounty hunters stood up and left.

Given their three-hour window, they took a winding route

to the terminal. Hubport was a delight to explore. It was built on top of a huge lake – they would later learn that every body of water on Magnar had a city over it – and it was full of crisscrossing walkways that took them under beautiful hanging gardens, over small islands surrounded by crystal clear water, and through parks full of trees and fountains.

They stopped for a bite to eat at a food cart, and enjoyed a meal of spicy, cheese-filled sausages. The food was delicious but a little on the pricey side. They bought a few more snacks for the road and proceeded to the terminal.

After all the exquisite sights they'd seen so far, the hoverbus looked like it was from another planet. It had to be at least fifty years old, with rusted bumpers and dirty, cracked windows. The other passengers were also quite a bit different from those who had been on the shuttle. They were still Magnarans, with the same rough, charcoal-colored skin broken up with orange lines in lightning-bolt patterns, making them look a little like humanoid volcanoes. But these were the working class, exhausted from a long day of cleaning apartments, repairing toilets, mopping floors, and serving spicy, cheese-filled sausages.

The bounty hunters filed onto the bus with the off-duty workers, where they were the target of many suspicious stares. As the bus sped over the wasteland, Tabi tried to strike up a conversation with one of the Magnarans, but he just shook his head and looked out the window. Outside, the cracked, dry dirt seemed to stretch on forever.

They didn't see any other traffic on their journey. They passed the occasional boulder, and at one point they drove by the burned-out remains of an old hovercar. Roughly half an hour into the ride, a red light flashed overhead, and the passengers braced themselves.

"Attention passengers," the driver said over a

loudspeaker. "There are signs of raider activity in the area. Please remain calm." Metal plates slid over the windows, and the bus came to a stop. There was a shudder and a bump as the bus descended to the ground.

Most of the passengers remained perfectly stoic, as if this were a daily event. Others looked around nervously. Up front, the driver spoke into his headset. Tabi could only hear his half of the conversation, but he seemed to be confirming safety protocols and discussing coordinates.

"We'll be okay," one passenger whispered to her daughter. "The raiders know we're not worth the effort."

"Why, momma?" the little girl asked.

"The bus has thick armor," the mother explained. "And they know we don't carry valuables."

"But you said they like to hurt people for fun," the girl replied.

"You know how hard it is to crack open a rocknut?" the mother asked, and her daughter nodded. "You really have to like rocknuts to make the effort, right? So if you knew a rocknut was empty inside, you wouldn't waste your time."

The girl seemed to understand, but she still looked nervous.

After ten minutes the windows slid open again. "False alarm," the driver announced. "Sorry to worry anyone."

They arrived at Freedirt fifteen minutes later. The city was surrounded by a wall made of scrap metal. As the bus approached, a pair of guards pushed a large panel aside, allowing the vehicle to enter. The bus came to a stop in the middle of an open-air market, and all the passengers stepped off.

Tabi and Sycathe took a look around. Architecturally, Freedirt was about as different from Hubport as it could possibly be. The merchant stalls looked like they were welded together from materials found in a scrapyard. Other buildings were made of mud bricks, and most were in a state of disrepair.

The market was full of activity. Stone-skinned citizens shopped and talked. They were dressed in homemade clothing that favored utility over style. The smell of cooking food wafted over from open-air restaurants. Musicians played for spare credits, and several people danced in the street.

"People seem happier here than in Hubport," Sycathe remarked.

"They have less," Tabi said. "But what they do have, they appreciate more."

They walked around a bit, getting a feel for the place. Occasionally they'd strike up a conversation with a local resident, and ask them if they knew anything about Rhoda Hogan and her gang.

Most of them remained tight-lipped, but one suggested they check out the town arena. There was a man named Jacek there who might be able to help them.

The arena wasn't difficult to find. It was the largest building in town, and the sound of revving engines echoed from its walls. When they asked for Jacek, an attendant took them up the stairs to a large balcony that overlooked the arena floor. Down below, three beat-up hovercars raced around an oval track. Though their engines were electric, they revved loudly and produced every bit as much smoke as an ancient diesel engine.

While there were plenty of seats around the track, only a handful of spectators were in attendance. Only one person occupied the balcony. He sat in the front row, watching the race with a wistful expression on his face. He had pale gray skin punctuated with jagged orange lines. While most of the

Magnarans had yellow eyes, Jacek's were so pale as to be almost white.

"Sir, you have some visitors," the attendant said. Even though Jacek stood and turned towards them, the attendant continued to describe the newcomers. "One's a cat person – Galean, I think, with black fur. And the other is a Grunthian, though she's not as big as I thought they'd be."

"Thank you, Kej," Jacek said. "I can take it from here."

Tabi approached him, staring into his vacant eyes. "You're bl…" she began, then stopped herself.

"It's okay," Jacek said. "It is what it is, no reason to pussyfoot around it. Get it? Pussyfoot?"

Tabi gave him a polite chuckle. "But you still watch the races?" she asked.

"Every day," Jacek replied. "And I can even tell you who's winning. The red car's in the lead, right?"

She glanced at the track and nodded, then chastised herself for nodding. "Yes, it is," she said.

"Yep," Jacek said. "No two engines sound the same."

"I was told you might know where I can find Rhoda Hogan," Tabi said.

"Have a seat," Jacek said, and the two sat down. Sycathe continued to stand. She was used to it.

"We're bounty hunters," Tabi said. "We've come to bring Hogan to justice."

"You know, I was the best racer this town ever saw," Jacek said. "Only lost three races my entire career."

"That's impressive," Tabi said. "But Hogan—"

"They don't let me race anymore," Jacek said.

"I'm sorry," Tabi told him. She was about to ask about Hogan again, but stopped herself. She put her hand on Jacek's shoulder. "It must be tough," she added.

Jacek smiled at her. "Driving's the only thing I ever really loved. Before I was a racer, I drove an enforcer car for the Tusks."

"The Tusks?" Tabi asked.

"Rhoda's gang," Jacek said. "Wasteland raiders. They're the reason Freedirt has walls. And why travel between towns is so dangerous."

"Tell me about her," Tabi said.

"She's human, nothing special. Your friend there would tear her apart in a fair fight," Jacek said. "But she'd never allow a fair fight. She lives in her car. Spends all day in it. Sleeps in it. And what a car. 2376 Vorpal Comet. Neon piping, turbo microfusion engine, decked out in weapons. She calls it the Razorback. You know, I got to ride in it once..." He trailed off, remembering.

"Where can we find her?" Tabi asked.

"Her gang lives in Geardox," Jacek said. "It's eighty-three kilometers south of here."

"Is there another bus to Geardox?" Tabi asked.

"I'm afraid not," Jacek said. "But I suppose you can take my car. It's not like I have any use for it."

"Wow," Sycathe said as the bay door opened.

"I call her the Molten Lightning," Jacek said. "Isn't she a beaut?"

The hovercar was a 2466 Venus Coldstar, modded with turbo jets and two energy cannons. It was painted black with red lines that resembled lava. Despite its age, it was in perfect condition. Someone had been keeping it clean, waxed, and well-maintained.

"We can't take this," Tabi said. "It's too nice."

"Borrow," Jacek corrected. "And I expect you to return her with a full charge."

"We're looking for a fight," Tabi said. "It's going to get a few scratches."

"It's not like I'll be able to see them," Jacek said.

"And if it gets destroyed?" Tabi asked.

"Then I'll know she died doing what she loved," Jacek said. "I was a criminal for years," he continued. "I have a lot to atone for. The people of Freedirt love me, but they don't know how bad I was before I came here. Please, take the car. Use it to bring down Hogan's gang. Make the world safer. Working for Hogan is my biggest regret, but I can't stand up to her now. Maybe I'll sleep easier at night if you tie up that loose end."

Tabi tried to come up with another argument, but her heart wasn't in it. She knew Jacek was right, and what's more, deep down she couldn't wait to get behind the wheel of this classic hot rod. "Okay," she finally said.

Jacek handed her the keys and she slipped into the driver's seat. She couldn't believe how comfortable the seats were. She strapped herself in and started the engine. Sycathe got into the backseat, where she sat sideways so her legs weren't as cramped.

Tabi lowered the driver's side window. "Thanks," she told Jacek. "I promise we'll be careful with your car."

Jacek shook his head. "You're not going to bring down Rhoda by being careful. Just do what you have to do. And good luck."

Tabi revved the engine and sped out the door. There were a few stares as they drove down the street towards the gate. But Jacek had called ahead, and the guards knew that he'd given Tabi the keys. They pulled the gate aside and waved her on through.

Then Tabi put the pedal to the metal and they zoomed off into the sunset.

"Look at that," Tabi said, pointing out the window.

"Dust storm?" Sycathe asked.

"I don't think so," Tabi replied, tightening her grip on the steering wheel.

They'd driven roughly thirty kilometers with no change in scenery. Now Tabi squinted out the driver's side window, where three lines of dust seemed to be on a path to intercept her hovercar.

"Drive faster," Sycathe suggested.

"This is as fast as it goes," Tabi said. There was a button on the dashboard marked "Turbo," but she wanted to save it for an emergency.

As the other vehicles gained on them, Tabi was finally able to make out more details. It looked like one hovercar flanked by a pair of hoverbikes. The vehicles had a matching color scheme – black with hot pink details. The car had a stylized boar's head painted on its armor-plated hood. All three vehicles were well-armed.

"Get your gun ready," Tabi said.

Sycathe drew her energy rifle and made sure it was warmed up. Then she lowered the back windows and positioned herself so she could fire if needed.

The pursuers fell in line behind them. They were only about twenty meters away now. There was a thump against the back windshield, and suddenly it was covered in pink paint. "They've tagged us," Tabi said.

"A warning?" Sycathe asked.

"Probably," Tabi replied. "Let's show them we have teeth."

Sycathe faced backwards and held her rifle out the window. She managed to squeeze her head out just enough to target a hoverbike. She fired a blast of energy and the bike swerved. A glint of red light pinged off the bike's Levatech emitters, and it shuddered for a moment before flipping forward, throwing the driver to the ground. The bike bounced off the ground a few times before skidding to a halt.

"Good shot, now let's get out of here," Tabi said. She tapped a button on the dashboard. A blast of smoke billowed out of the back of her hovercar, turning the air black behind them. Then she hit the turbo button. Jets of flame erupted from a pair of small turbines near the rear of the car. For the next ten seconds, their speed nearly doubled.

But it wasn't enough. The other car burst through the smoke, and the remaining hoverbike sped past it, using its own turbo jets to close the gap.

"Get 'em, Syca," Tabi said, and her partner drew a bead on the other bike. But right as she was about to fire, three blasts hit their car, throwing off her aim. The car swerved as Tabi tried to regain control.

The bike caught up with them and pulled up to the passenger side of the car, keeping pace. The rider – a man in black leather with a helmet shaped like a boar's head – waggled his finger at them in a gesture that seemed to say, "Naughty, naughty."

Sycathe aimed her weapon but the biker hit his brakes and fell back behind them.

Thunk! Thunk! There were two impacts from somewhere behind them, and suddenly Tabi's car began losing speed. "Something's draining the battery," she said as she scanned the control panel.

There was only a small corner of the back window that wasn't covered in paint, and Sycathe pressed her face against the glass to see what was going on. "EMP magnets," she reported. The biker shot her an obscene gesture before falling back to ride beside his partner.

"If that's how they want it," Tabi said. She spun the car around so that she was face-to-face with her opponents, then fired the front-mounted energy cannons.

The bike swerved to the side, but the enemy car just charged ahead. Its armor absorbed the energy blasts, and it sped forward with the intention of ramming Tabi's car head-on.

Tabi shifted into reverse but the car would no longer move. "Out," she ordered as she opened her door.

Sycathe kicked her door open, then ripped the door off its hinges and hurled it like a discus. The door smashed through the oncoming car's windshield. It swerved and spun, barely avoiding Tabi's car as it whooshed by. No longer hovering, it skidded for another half a kilometer before it came to rest.

The hoverbike turned and fled. Tabi drew her energy pistol and fired off a few shots, but it was long gone.

"Come on," Tabi said, surveying the damage. Once they removed the EMP magnets, they had to reboot the hovercar's engine before it would hover again. Even then, it shuddered and threatened to give out at any moment. "I think the battery's about had it," Tabi reported.

"How about that car?" Sycathe asked, pointing at the smoking ruin of the hovercar that had tried to ram them.

They went to investigate the wrecked car. The driver was dead, having been impaled by the door. They were able to pull the battery, which worked just fine in their own car.

They cleaned the paint off their back windshield using some rags and cleaning solution they found in the trunk of the wrecked car. Unfortunately they weren't able to do anything about the missing door, but otherwise they had a functioning car again. Satisfied that they'd salvaged everything useful from the wreckage, they drove on to Geardox.

It wasn't a long drive, but the sun had set by the time they reached the outer gates of Geardox. Like Freedirt, it was surrounded by walls of scrap metal. But that was where the similarities ended. While Freedirt was populated by destitute blue-collar workers, Geardox looked more like a giant biker bar. The streets were filled with leather-clad ruffians, most armed and carrying alcoholic beverages.

Curiously, the city had a more diverse population than that of Freedirt. Roughly a third of Geardox's citizens were off-worlders, including some humans, Vhelrans, and some species Tabi had never seen.

Tabi and Sycathe turned a few heads as they drove through the crowded streets, but it wasn't because they were aliens. Several people stopped what they were doing to admire their car. Some even reached out and touched it as it drove by.

"I'm not sure I like this attention," Tabi said.

"We should rent a garage," Sycathe suggested.

Once they dropped off the hovercar in a secure parking bay, they went out to explore the town. One of the first things they noticed was the pervasiveness of the Tusks logo. Roughly one out of every ten people wore the gang's colors, and many wore jackets emblazoned with that hot pink boar's head.

"We're going to have to be very careful when we're asking questions," Tabi said. They pushed their way through the crowded streets and entered a bar.

The place was packed and the music was loud. Tabi's sensitive ears could barely take the heavy metal beat. There were no empty seats at the bar, where boisterous drunkards sang along to the speakers. A tired-looking bartender raced to keep up with all the orders. Some customers crowded around long green tables playing holographic billiards.

Tabi spotted a table where four Tusk-jacketed Magnarans talked and laughed. *As good a place to start as any*, she thought.

She approached the table and leaned over so she could be heard. "Hey, I'm new in town," she said.

"No shit," one of the Magnarans said, and they all laughed.

"I hear the Tusks are the biggest badasses around these parts," she said.

"You heard right," another Tusk said, and bumped his fists with his friends.

"So how do I become a Tusk?" Tabi asked.

They burst out laughing again. "Beat it, narc," one said.

"No, I mean it!" Tabi said. "I'm a great driver. I know they could use me."

They looked at each other with expressions that said, *Is she for real*? Finally one of them, the only woman in the group, rolled her eyes and pointed to a flyer on the wall. It showed a picture of a car and read:

RUNNER TRYOUTS – ARENA – EVERY THORK-NIGHT AT SUNDOWN

"What's a thork-night?" Sycathe asked.

Rather than answer, the Tusks just started laughing again.

"Come on," Tabi said. "I can't even think in this place."

There was an influx of new customers blocking the entrance, so they left through the back door. As they stepped out into the alley, they saw a human couple having sex by the waste bins. Tabi started to avert her eyes when she noticed the woman was unconscious. "Hey!" she shouted, marching towards the man.

He didn't even slow down. "You want her next?" he slurred. "That's cool, give me a minute."

"She's not even awake!" Tabi yelled. She put her hands on his shoulders and pulled him off of his victim.

"Yeah, so?" the man asked, taking a half-step back. "She'll never know, so who cares?"

"Get lost," Tabi growled, extending her claws.

The man glared and tried to look tough, which was a bit difficult since he was naked from the waist down. "If you wanna fight, I'm game," he said. He reached into his jacket pocket and retrieved a switchblade. Once extended, the blade began to glow bright red. Then his jaw dropped as he looked over Tabi's shoulder.

Sycathe charged forward, her teeth bared, and the man lost all control of his bladder. He turned to run, but the mad Grunthian grabbed him by the head and threw him as easily as one might throw an apple. His flying body vanished in the darkness farther down the alley, and they never even heard him land.

"I could have taken him," Tabi said as she kneeled to check on the woman.

"I know," Sycathe said. "How is she?"

"Still breathing," Tabi said. "Let's take her somewhere safe."

They found a nearby motel and paid for a room. Then they set the woman on one of the beds and watched over her while she slept.

"Should we call the police?" Sycathe asked.

"You think this town has police?" Tabi asked. "And even if

it did, they'd be more likely to arrest us than to help this poor woman. The rapist was wearing a Tusks jacket. They obviously own this town."

The woman started coughing. Tabi helped her sit up and handed her a glass of water.

"Thank you," the woman said between hacks. "Where am I?"

"Safe," Tabi said. "You're in a motel. There was a man—"

"Bastard drugged me," the woman said, clenching her fists. "If I ever get my hands on him again…"

"If it helps, I think I might have killed him," Sycathe said.

"Serves him right if you did," the woman said. "Thanks for your help. I'll be going." She started to stand up.

"Can I ask you some questions first?" Tabi asked.

"Cops?" the woman asked with a laugh. "Here in Geardox?"

"Bounty hunters," Tabi admitted. "We're here to apprehend Hogan."

The woman laughed even harder. "Not gonna happen."

"She can't be that tough," Tabi said. "I know she has a nice car, but my friend here demolishes cars with her bare hands."

Sycathe raised one of her massive hands and gave a little wave.

"You can't get to her," the woman said. "She lives in the arena parking garage. It's walled off and guarded. You'd have to fight your way through hundreds of Tusks just to get to her floor."

"What if we challenged her to a fight?" Sycathe asked.

"Sometimes she agrees to duels, but she makes sure the odds are greatly in her favor," the woman replied.

"I still think our best bet is to join the Tusks," Tabi said.

"There's tryouts every Thork-night," the woman said.

"That's four days away."

"I don't want to wait that long," Sycathe said.

Tabi nodded. "We'll call that plan B," she said. Turning back to the woman, she asked, "What's your name?"

The woman thought for a moment, like she was trying to come up with a fake name. "Laika," she finally replied. "Why?"

"Because we could really use your help, Laika," Tabi said. "What can you tell me about where Hogan sleeps?"

According to Laika, Hogan only left her car for exercise and bathroom breaks. The rest of the time she drove around the four-story parking garage, the fourth floor of which had been converted into Hogan's extravagant mansion. It included such luxuries as a personal drive-in movie theater and her own personal car wash. Sometimes she drove up to the roof to watch the stars.

The bottom three floors of the parking garage served as Tusk headquarters, and it was impossible for non-members to gain access. The second floor had a bridge that led to Hogan's personal box at the arena. She spent part of every day parked on the balcony, watching the violent races.

"What if we got up to the roof somehow?" Tabi pondered. Two hours had passed, and Laika was asleep again. They'd managed to keep her from leaving by offering her ten percent of the reward.

"I'm a good climber," Sycathe said.

"You're not so good at stealth, though," Tabi replied. "They'd see you right away and shoot you down."

"Maybe we could just buy a ticket," Sycathe said. "We watch a few matches, then grab Hogan from the balcony."

"Too many witnesses," Tabi said.

"We'd sneak up during an exciting match," Sycathe said. "The fans would be watching the race."

"Someone would still see us," Tabi said. "And I'm sure she has guards. Besides, what's your plan for getting back out?"

"Can only Tusks enter the races?" Sycathe asked.

"Good question," Tabi said. "Maybe just being backstage would give us a chance to find a way to Hogan. Hey, Laika…" She stood up and nudged the woman's shoulder.

Just then there was a knock at the door. Laika sat up. Her comm unit was in her hand. "Sorry," she said, yawning.

"Sorry for what?" Tabi asked. The knocking escalated to a banging.

"Their offer was higher than yours," Laika replied.

Sycathe stood up and drew her rifle.

"Wait," Tabi said, grabbing her things. "Maybe we can still—"

The door burst open. Several Magnarans in Tusk colors stood in the doorway, their weapons aimed at the duo.

"Come with us," one of the Tusks said.

Sycathe growled and rushed forward, firing her rifle at the intruders. Two went down, but there were more in the hallway to take their place.

"Wait!" Tabi shouted, reaching for her pistol.

And then the Tusks opened fire.

"Where am I?" Tabi asked as the world faded into view. She felt unusually groggy, like she'd slept for days.

"The Dead End," a man said next to her. "It's what we call this place. Once you wind up in here, your next stop is a Roadkill Match."

Tabi sat up. She was on the floor of a prison cell with thick iron bars. Three other people shared her cell, all

Magnarans.

She looked at the man who'd spoken. He had bumpy, light gray skin with random yellow fissures. "You were out for a while," he said. "I heard they had to turn their stun guns to maximum, because of your partner."

"Sycathe!" Tabi shouted, looking around. "Where is she?"

"I don't know," the man said. "The guards mentioned something about having to find a stronger cell."

"I have to find her," Tabi said.

"You'd have to get out of here, first," the man said.

Tabi stood and put her hands on the bars, giving them a bit of a shake. They didn't budge. She pulled on the door, but it was firmly locked. She patted her pockets, looking for her tools. She realized she was wearing a plain gray jumpsuit, just like the other prisoners.

Her shoulders slumped, and she sat back down next to the Magnaran.

"Sorry," he said, patting her on the shoulder. "What did they get you for?"

"We're bounty hunters," Tabi said. "Me and… Sycathe. She's Grunthian. We were hired to capture Hogan."

The Magnaran smiled. "My name's Goranth," he said. "But they call me 'Wildboar.' Until a few days ago, I was Hogan's right-hand man. But she and I had a disagreement, and here I am."

"What was the disagreement?" Tabi asked.

"The usual," Goranth said. "She likes things the way they are, and I'd like to make the world a better place. The government of Magnar treats its working-class citizens like dirt. I want the Tusks to lead a revolution. But Rhoda's too comfortable – she lives like a queen here. If I were in charge —"

"There he goes again," another prisoner interrupted.

"Thinkin' he has a future. We're in the Dead End. This is it for us. Might as well—"

"I'm not giving up, Trag," Goranth replied. "As long as I breathe, there's hope."

"Hope is for fools," Trag said. "No one survives the Roadkill matches. You should accept reality."

"What's a Roadkill match?" Tabi asked.

Trag chuckled. "Ever fought a car bare-handed?"

"No, but my partner has," Tabi said absently. She was really worried about Sycathe. If the Tusks didn't have a prison strong enough to contain her, then their only alternative would have been to... She shook the thought away. There was no point in dwelling on the unknown, especially when the known was keeping her pretty busy.

Goranth picked up on her worries. "You're more than just partners, aren't you?"

"It's complicated," Tabi said.

"I'm sure it is," Goranth said. "If it makes you feel any better, I know Rhoda. She won't just execute your friend without spectacle. Everyone gets a fighting chance, even if it's a ridiculously small fighting chance."

In a weird way, that actually did make Tabi feel a little better. If anyone could fight their way out of an impossible death trap, it was Sycathe.

"Ladies! Gentlemen! And those who eschew the gender binary! Are you ready for some action? Some thrills, chills, and blood spills? We've got it all! So welcome to tonight's... Roadkill Match!" The emcee sounded so playfully exuberant that he might have been announcing ice cream and clowns instead of an execution.

The arena was approximately three kilometers in

circumference. On the south end, four prisoners stood chained to the high, smooth wall. On the north end, Hogan's hovercar revved its engine. The Razorback was even more intimidating in person. It was gleaming black with neon pink piping, and covered in barbed wire. Flames spewed from its tailpipes, and pink smoke billowed out behind it.

Near the center of the arena, several weapons were scattered across the floor, including energy pistols, AON blades, and some spiked metal rods.

Tabi turned her head to look at Goranth, who was chained up about three meters away. "Does anyone ever reach the weapons before she hits them?" she shouted.

"Sometimes," Goranth shouted back. "But only half the pistols are charged, so it's still a gamble!"

The audience cheered with rabid enthusiasm, ready to see some blood. It was a packed house, and those close to ringside threw popcorn at the prisoners.

"The rules are simple," the announcer continued. "Anyone who survives for ten minutes gets to go free. But as easy as that sounds, no one has ever gotten out alive. Will tonight be the night?"

"I have an announcement," another voice said over the loudspeaker. The audience gasped as the Razorback's top folded down. Rhoda Hogan stood up in her car, holding a microphone. She was human, with pink hair and flame tattoos across her face. "That man is a traitor," she said, pointing across the arena. "Goranth was my trusted ally for years, but all this time he wanted more. Well, tonight he's going to get more than he bargained for. Tonight he rests in pieces!"

She sat back down and revved her engine. The audience went wild.

"Then without further ado, let the match begin!" the

announcer shouted, and the Razorback burst forward. On the far side of the arena, everyone's shackles came undone. The prisoners scattered, unsure which way to run. One tried to climb the wall, but a node on the lip of the arena wall shocked him with an electric jolt. He stumbled back to his feet and ran in a random direction.

Goranth ran straight for the Razorback. Trag ran beside him, then veered off to the right. Hogan had already passed the center of the arena, and she sped straight for Goranth with fire in her eyes. She'd almost reached him when she suddenly swerved left instead. Her front bumper - which was wrapped in barbed wire – cut Trag in half at the waist. Hogan cackled as her wipers cleaned the blood off her windshield. Then she winked at Goranth and turned towards him again.

While Hogan played with Goranth, teasing him and herding him around the arena, Tabi made a beeline for the weapons. That fourth prisoner – Tabi never did learn his name – managed to pick up an energy pistol. But when he tried to fire it, it only emitted some harmless sparks. He tossed it aside and looked for another weapon. He was halfway to the next pistol when the Razorback rammed into him so hard his torso landed in the stands. It crashed into a bench next to a spectator who cheered as if he'd caught a home run ball.

"We're only two minutes in and it's already two down, two to go!" The announcer shouted. "That's twos all around. Will the survivors make it to four?"

Hogan zoomed by Goranth again, missing him on purpose. He lunged at the car as it went by, trying to grab onto the doors, but he missed and stumbled. Then Hogan turned and set her sights on Tabi.

Tabi quickly dove for the nearest weapon, a spiked metal club. It wasn't much but it was better than being empty-handed. She stood at the ready, telegraphing that she would throw the club at Hogan as her car approached. Hogan fell for it, tilting slightly away and giving Tabi time to dive to the side. A bit of barbed wire ripped across her shoulder as the Razorback passed. Tabi winced in pain and rolled to her feet. The Razorback had already turned around again, and it was headed straight for her.

This time Tabi leaped forward, landing on the hood of the hovercar. Her Galean dexterity served her well as she balanced on the hood. She brought the club back, ready to smash it through the windshield.

Then Hogan braked hard and shifted into reverse. Tabi was thrown to the ground, landing on her side. She lost her grip on the club, which went flying several meters away. Worst of all, she felt a sharp pain in her left shin as she landed, and she thought she heard a snap. Getting back to her feet was agony, but the Razorback was already headed towards her again. Tabi stood and limped away, knowing she had seconds to live.

Her reprieve came from two directions. First, a blast of blue light shattered Hogan's windshield. Goranth had found a working pistol. The Razorback swerved to take on the bigger threat.

With Hogan distracted, Tabi started limping towards the weapons again, but a commotion in the stands demanded her attention. Spectators were running and screaming from… something. There were too many people in the way to figure out what was causing the uproar. Tabi stepped aside as one of the security officers flew through the air and landed in the arena with a crunch.

Sycathe pushed through the crowd like she was cutting her way through the jungle. Everywhere she went people fled or were tossed aside. More guards shot at her, but she grabbed the nearest spectators and used them as shields.

Then she threw the spectators at the guards.

She reached the edge of the arena and hopped down to the floor.

"How —" Tabi started to ask, but Sycathe ran up and hugged her. "Ow," Tabi moaned.

"They locked me in a metal room," Sycathe said, releasing her from the crushing hug. "Like a bank vault. But not a very good one. Only took a few punches to pop the lock."

Tabi could see the cuts and bruises on Sycathe's knuckles, and knew her friend was exaggerating. But it didn't matter now. For good or ill, they were together again.

On the other side of the arena, Goranth barely dodged the Razorback as it tore across his back. He dropped the pistol and desperately tried to reach it again before the hovercar turned around.

"He needs help," Tabi said.

"On it," Sycathe said. She picked up the club Tabi had dropped and charged the hovercar.

Hogan never knew what hit her. One moment she had Goranth dead in her sights, ready to pulverize him beneath her front grill. The next moment there was an angry four-armed gorilla monster grabbing her rear bumper, smashing her trunk to pieces with a club.

I almost feel sorry for Hogan, Tabi thought as she watched her friend tear into the vehicle. She limped over to one of the scattered pistols, tested it, and took aim. She couldn't get a clear shot with the car lurching and Sycathe in the way, so she held the gun steady and waited for an opportunity.

Rhoda gripped her steering wheel for dear life. Goranth was shooting at her and the Grunthian was turning the rear of her car into scrap metal. She didn't usually use the Razorback's energy cannons in Roadkill matches, but now she brought them online and took aim at Goranth. She fired off several blasts, but the car continued to bounce around from the chaos going on behind her. All her shots went high above Goranth's head, and a few even went into the audience.

The spectators dove for cover, and many started to flee. A stampede formed in the stands. The shrieks and shouts from panicked viewers drowned out the sounds of battle. "Everyone stay calm," the emcee announced, but no one was paying attention.

Steady, steady... Tabi thought as she held her energy pistol in both hands. Her leg was screaming at her, but she refused to tremble.

Hogan turned the wheel sharply, deftly swinging Sycathe so that she collided with Goranth. But Sycathe continued to hold on with one hand. Hogan drove low to the ground so that she dragged the Grunthian behind her, putting Goranth at her back. Now if Goranth continued to shoot at her, he'd hit Sycathe instead.

But this move put Hogan directly in Tabi's sights. She squeezed the trigger, firing a single blast that crossed the arena and hit Hogan in the neck. The Razorback veered wildly out of control, dipping in the front until it tumbled end over end, finally landing on its roof. Flickers of flame rose from the engine.

"Syca!" Tabi shouted, then spotted her friend lying safely on the ground, several meters from the burning wreckage. She slowly crossed the arena, dragging her useless leg behind her.

Sycathe got to her feet and ran to the car. With one hand she lifted the car, and with another she pulled Hogan from the driver's seat. The woman was badly burned and unconscious, but she was breathing. Carrying Hogan under one arm, Sycathe leaped away from the Razorback just as it exploded.

"The winners are... Goranth and Tabi?" the dumbfounded announcer reported. The audience – at least, those that were still watching the match – roared in approval.

Doors opened around the arena walls, and Tusk guards entered to greet the winners. For a moment Goranth was afraid they'd put him back in restraints, but instead they congratulated him on his victory. A few even bowed. Medical staff came along and put Tabi and Hogan on stretchers. Sycathe demanded to stay at Tabi's side and followed her all the way to the recovery room.

"You sure you won't stay here with us?" Goranth asked. "We could sure use your help."

Tabi smiled and shook his hand. "You'll do just fine without us," she said.

"Well, you're welcome back anytime," Goranth said. "Want me to arrange a transport to Hubport?"

"No thanks, we have to meet someone in Freedirt," Tabi said.

They strapped Hogan into the passenger seat of the Molten Lightning. The car had been fully repaired thanks to Goranth's team of top mechanics.

Goranth smiled as he watched the car leave town. As the newly-appointed leader of the Tusks, he had his work cut out for him. He planned to turn his followers into an army, one that would force the Magnaran government to grant more power to its citizens. It would be a long road, but he was ready for the journey.

Tabi and Sycathe returned the car to Jacek, took the bus back to Hubport, and surrendered Hogan to the local authorities. The next flight off-planet wouldn't depart for another two days. As an extra bonus for capturing Hogan, the government put them up in a luxury hotel for the remainder of their stay.

That evening they sat on a pair of comfortable deck chairs, on a balcony that overlooked an indoor forest. Tabi reached for one of Sycathe's hands.

"You know, this hotel might not even be here next time we visit," Tabi said, gently stroking her friend's hand.

"What do you mean?" Sycathe asked.

"If Goranth has his way, there won't be such a big divide between the upper and lower classes. Luxury rooms like this one will give way to smaller, more affordable housing units, so that Hubport can house more people."

"So no more room service?" Sycathe asked.

"That's right," Tabi replied.

"No more gold faucets? In-room massages? Cute little scented soaps?" Sycathe asked.

"Right again," Tabi confirmed.

"But more people would get to live here, where it's clean and safe, instead of taking the bus to their metal shacks each night," Sycathe said.

"And they'd have better access to clean water, child care, nutritious food..." Tabi added.

"Then I don't think it's such a big loss," Sycathe said.

"I knew I liked you for a reason," Tabi said, scooting her chair over until it was touching Sycathe's. She nuzzled her cheek against her partner's gigantic arm as they watched the sunset through the city's glass dome.

New World

The darkness was endless and all-enveloping. Crys tried reaching out into the inky blackness but her arms wouldn't move. She couldn't remember where she was or how she'd come to be here. She couldn't feel anything on her skin. She wasn't sure if she even had skin. Nothing existed but her mind and the black void. And even her mind was suspect.

I'm still asleep, she thought. That had to be it. This was just sleep paralysis. Soon she'd either fall back into deeper slumber, or wake the rest of the way up. It bothered her, though, that she couldn't feel anything. It was like her mind was so disconnected from her body that she couldn't even access her nerve endings.

This is just a dream, she told herself. She tried to calm herself down by taking slow, deep breaths. Then she realized she couldn't breathe. She wasn't suffocating, but she couldn't draw a breath or even feel her chest rise and fall. It was like her body was frozen in time, but her mind was still going.

Don't panic, she thought. *It's all part of the dream.* But she knew she wasn't dreaming. Her mind was too alert for this to be a dream. She tried opening her eyes, but she couldn't even tell if they were already open.

What's the last thing you remember? she asked herself. A jumble of memories bubbled to the surface, but they weren't in any particular order. She couldn't tell what was recent or what was in the distant past. No, it was worse than that – all her memories felt like they were from eons ago. *How long have I been asleep?*

Maybe I'm in a coma, she thought. That would have explained a lot. The paralysis, the memory loss, the inability to completely regain consciousness. She listened for medical equipment, perhaps the rhythmic beeping of a heart monitor, but there was nothing but silence. There wasn't even any ambient noise. No gentle thrumming of an air conditioner, no dripping water or buzzing flies, no distant wind or voices. It was as if her ears had been switched off like a microphone.

Her heart beat faster, a sensation that surprised her. It was the first tangible feeling she'd experienced since waking. That was something – if nothing else, it proved she wasn't dead. A light came on. It was very dim, an amber glow so dark it was almost brown. Crys thought she saw movement in the distance, a roughly humanoid shadow just to the side of her field of vision. Then it moved again, crossing in front of her and disappearing to her left. The movement was warped and blurry, like it was on the other side of a fish tank.

This brought on two realizations. First off, her eyes were open. She couldn't blink, nor did she feel like she needed to. Secondly, she wasn't lying on a bed, but suspended in a vertical position.

This triggered a memory. Actually it was more like déjà vu. She could almost half-remember being placed here, wherever here was. But that felt like a hundred years ago. She'd had a lifetime of dreams since then, and she could no longer sort the dreams from the memories. The word "gel" floated around her mind, and it seemed very important, but she just couldn't make it mean anything.

Gel, she thought. *Gel, gel, gel. Gel!* She almost had it, but it was like sifting through a bucket of quarters to figure out which one tasted like cabbage. *Like what?* she asked herself. Even her analogies were still asleep.

Another collage of images spun through her memory carousel until the wheel came to a stop on a single image. A woman. It wasn't Crys; this woman was Caucasian and completely bald. She was nude, and suspended in a glass tube filled with some sort of… some sort of…

Gel, she thought again. Glad to finally be on the trail to something meaningful, she studied the image more closely. A wire hung from the ceiling and led to a single sensor stuck to the woman's chest. Beyond that connection, the woman floated freely. No, floated was the wrong word. There was no bobbing or swaying, no movement at all. The gel held her perfectly still.

Does she dream? Crys wondered. The woman's eyes were open, but she looked at peace. There was no light in those eyes, no spark that would indicate consciousness. But Crys knew the woman wasn't dead. The woman was in a deep sleep, where she would remain for ages.

I miss her already, Crys thought. In another couple of weeks, Crys would be placed into a tube herself. Then, someday, the two would wake up and see the new world together.

But I'm already in a tube, Crys thought. The memory battled with her present consciousness as she tried to work out the sequence of events. *That was before, when April went in*, she thought.

A voice sounded in her head, and at first Crys thought it was real. But it was only another part of the memory. "They don't need to breathe or eat," the voice said. "Whatever their body needs, the gel provides." It was a woman's voice. She sounded mature and good-natured, like a kindly grandmother. But there was an edge to that voice that made Crys doubt the sincerity of that kindness. "This gel can keep them alive for more than a thousand years," she continued.

But the woman wasn't talking to Crys. A man with a deep voice replied, "It'll have to work longer than that. It'll take a thousand years just for the waters to recede. Then the plant life needs time to regrow before the oxygen levels return to normal."

"We'll just have to pray the tubes hold out," the woman said.

"Which ones will you wake first?" the man asked.

"Those we need," the woman said. "And after that, those who'll stay in line."

"And the ones who won't follow your orders?" the man asked.

"They don't need to wake up at all," the woman said.

I shouldn't be hearing this, Crys thought. They didn't know she was in the room. She'd been checking April's vitals when they walked in. Now she stayed hidden in the forest of wide-eyed, sleeping survivors. She had every right to be in the room - it was her duty to check the tubes - but if they discovered her now, they'd know she'd overheard them.

Fortunately they left soon after. Crys leaned against a tube, releasing a long, slow breath. *Maybe they were just joking*, she thought, but they'd sounded dead serious. *Maybe I should tell someone*, she thought, but there was no one to tell. Most of the citizens were already asleep, and techs like Crys would be among the last to go in.

But that was a long time ago, Crys thought. The memory dissipated as a blurry shape once again moved into her view. The humanoid form stopped and stood in front of her.

It was hard to make out any details, but the figure seemed to look Crys up and down as if appraising her. Then one of its arms raised and started touching something on her tank.

The next couple of hours were a living nightmare. Having gel pumped from her lungs, getting used to the feel of air on her skin, learning how to breathe normally again, puking up liquid... it was like being reborn. Though they washed her off thoroughly, hours later she still found herself picking gel out of unmentionable places.

Now she lay in a recovery bed, in a room filled with hundreds of coughing, groaning survivors. "Crystal Pérez?" She turned her head at her name and started to sit up. "Whoa, don't get up, stay comfy," the man said.

The man loomed above her, holding a tablet computer. He had pale skin and short, brown hair. Crys frowned. Something about the hair bothered her. "I'm Andrew Stanley, but you can call me Andy. Good to meet you."

Crystal shook his hand but didn't say anything.

"Says here you're part of Tech Unit Three," Andy said.

Crys nodded. She tried to speak, but her voice wouldn't work.

"Don't worry about it, most of these are yes or no questions," Andy said.

He read more of her dossier. "Looks like you were a military technician before joining our unit."

Crys nodded.

"Good, good," Andy said. "Denver likes people who can follow orders." He continued looking over her dossier, then frowned. "I see you left your religion blank."

Crys cocked her head, then opened her mouth to answer. "Why..." she said, but started coughing.

"It's okay," Andy said, then handed her a pen and some paper. "Just write it out."

Crys took the pen and thought for a moment. Then she wrote, "Why does my religion matter?"

"It doesn't," Andy said. "Don't worry, you're not going to be ostracized for being the wrong religion or anything. But Denver wants complete psychological profiles on everyone, and that includes religious beliefs."

Crys wasn't sure she believed his answer, but she wanted to move on. "I was between churches when we went into stasis," she wrote. It wasn't a lie, but it wasn't exactly the truth. She'd had to leave her previous church due to their position on homosexuality. She'd considered looking for a new one, but she hadn't felt the need to rush. She considered herself agnostic these days, if she thought about religion at all.

"Good enough," Andy said. "One other thing. You list your birthplace as Mexico City, but your last address was in Florida."

Crys nodded.

"Were you in America legally?" he asked.

Ugh, Crys thought. *Why does this bullshit matter anymore?* It wasn't like those borders still existed. She pointed to the word "Why" on the piece of paper.

"Psychological profiles include criminal records," Andy said.

Her dossier still sat in front of Andy. Though it was upside down to her, she pointed to the section that showed her military service.

"Gotcha," the man said. "They granted you citizenship for serving."

Crys nodded, though the full story was a bit more complicated than that.

But it was enough to satisfy him. "Well, it says your programming skills are top-notch," Andy said. "That's good. We'll need more people like you. We're only a couple of months away from breaking the surface, and everyone's going to have to pitch in to make it work. Your skills will be invaluable."

Crys nodded and forced a smile.

"Well, that's all I need for now," Andy said. He stood and reached for her hand. "It was nice meeting you."

You too, Crys mouthed, and shook his hand. Then he left and headed for another recently awakened patient. Crys frowned and rubbed her chin. Something about the interview had set her on edge. She watched Andy talking to the other patient, several beds away. Like Crys, the other patient was completely bald. But Andy had at least a month's worth of hair growth.

I thought they were supposed to wake the techs up first, Crys thought. She supposed they'd needed a couple of administrative types to keep track of who got woken up and where to put them, but a full month? And just what had they been up to during that time?

It had been three days since her awakening, and Crys was already hard at work. Though her specialty was programming, they had her working in data analytics. Her job was to scan the database of sleepers and determine which ones should be revived the soonest. There were over fifteen thousand tubes in the compound, and only a handful of med techs to help with their revival, so only ten to fifteen sleepers could be awakened each day.

Sleepers were assigned a "priority rating" between one and ten. Med techs were given a rating of ten, because having more available meant they could step up the timetable for waking everyone else. Other tech positions also ranked high on the list, which was why Crys had been awakened as early as she had been. Those who had served in the military generally ranked higher than those who hadn't, because they had discipline and skills that would help once the colony breached the surface.

The sleepers with no listed skills or applicable experience generally ranked in the middle, usually between four and six. Those lower than four often had criminal records or a history of violence. They would be revived last, once the colony had established a functioning society, with the resources they needed to deal with those who had trouble following the rules. Low priority was also given to those with certain medical conditions, so they could be sure they would be properly cared for once revived.

At least, that was the plan. As Crys sorted through the data, she found several discrepancies. Someone had changed the algorithm, and many sleepers had been assigned low-priority ratings for reasons Crys couldn't discern. When she tried to correct these entries, she found that they were protected and could not be altered. She tried to peek into the code and see the new algorithm, but the computer informed her that she didn't have the clearance required to view the code.

How am I supposed to do my job if I can't see the new rules? she wondered.

But at least her position came with some privileges. Crys poked her head up from her screen and looked around the lab. Seven other techs sat glued to their screens, and there were no supervisors in sight. What Crys was about to do wasn't exactly against the rules, but it might have been seen as wasting time when she should have been working. Still, she had to know, and the tablet in her room couldn't access this database.

Now sure that she wasn't being watched, Crys typed a name into the search box. April's dossier came up right away. She had a priority rating of eight, and she was scheduled to be revived in less than a week. *I can't wait to see you,* Crys thought, staring at her girlfriend's file photo.

"Andy?" Crys asked, entering the tiny office.

The man looked up from his computer and put on an overly wide smile, but he couldn't hide the impatience in his eyes. "What can I do for you?" he asked.

"I'm looking for an old friend of mine," Crys said. "She was scheduled to wake up today, but she's not in any of the recovery rooms."

"Well, there's a lot going on," Andy said. "Perhaps her awakening was delayed."

"No, I saw it myself," Crys said. "In the database, her status says revived."

"Don't use the database for personal reasons," Andy grumbled, then started typing. "Name?" he asked.

"April Rosenthal," Crys said.

"Ro... sen...thal," Andy said, hunting and pecking at the keyboard. "Ah. There were complications waking her. She's in the infirmary."

"Oh god," Crys said, and turned toward the door.

"Wait!" Andy shouted, and Crys hesitated. "She's in surgery right now. They won't let you see her."

"What happened?" Crys asked.

"It says... Preservation failure on her right arm," Andy said, making a poor attempt to mimic concern. "Possibly gangrene, they're not sure. It says they may have to amputate."

Crys looked sick. "How soon will I be able to see her?"

"I don't know," Andy said. "I suggest you wait until tomorrow, then ask at the infirmary."

Crys nodded, and neither spoke for several seconds.

"Was there something else?" Andy asked. He tried to sound sympathetic, but Crys could tell he was anxious to be rid of her.

Crys hesitated. She'd been wanting to tell someone about the discrepancies in the database, but she had the feeling that Andy wasn't safe. She'd have to keep her worries to herself until she found someone she could trust. All the more reason she wished April was awake.

"No, thank you," Crys said, and stepped back into the hallway. Her footsteps echoed loudly in the empty corridor. There wasn't a lot of activity on the administration level yet. Just a long hall full of mostly empty offices. At the end of the hall she saw the door to Director Denver's office. For some reason, just seeing the door gave her chills. She'd only met the director once. She doubted he'd remember her now, but he'd definitely left an impression on her.

The director was one of those people who had a presence. Even if you had no idea who he was, you knew he was important when he walked by. His self-confidence was like a beacon, and he had a face that demanded authority. Even now, Crys thought she could tell he was in his office. She could just feel it.

As if to confirm her suspicions, she heard yelling from the other side of the door. A man's voice – it had to be Denver's – boomed through the hallway. Crys couldn't make out any words, nor could she hear the other side of the conversation, but she knew the director was upset about something. She'd have hated to be the one on the receiving end of his tirade.

I really should head back, Crys thought. But part of her

wanted to tiptoe closer to the door and see if she could hear anything more clearly. Finally she shook her head. *Not my business*, she thought. She was about to head for the stairwell when she passed the restrooms. She realized that she'd been ignoring the call of nature for over an hour now, as more important things had been on her mind.

All the restrooms in the compound were unisex. What's more, everyone was expected to use the urinals when possible. The waste recycling system converted urine back into drinking water, so it was best to keep it separate from solid waste.

Crys entered the restroom and stepped up to one of the two urinal stations. There were two cups hanging on the wall, each attached to the wall by a hose. She grabbed the female cup and pulled it out of its sanitizing holder. Then she unzipped her pants and slid the elongated cup between her thighs. She was about to release her bladder when the door opened behind her. Angry footsteps stomped across the room until a man stood at the urinal station next to her.

She nearly choked when she realized it was Director Denver. Staring straight ahead, he picked the male cup off the wall in front of his station, then pulled it down to his pants. He continued to stare at the wall, silently fuming.

Crys couldn't pee. Her bladder had seized up. She hadn't taken a breath since he'd walked in, and she wasn't even sure if her heart was still beating. She could hear the director urinate, though the sound was nearly drowned out by the deep, angry breaths he was taking.

Finally he turned toward Crys, his face livid. "Let me ask you a question," the director said. "Two people are drowning. One is your husband of fifteen years. The other knows the cure for a deadly disease that's been killing millions. You can only save one. What would you do?"

Her brain locked up for a second, but her fear of looking

like an idiot overrode her fear of answering. "I suppose I'd have to save the one with the cure," Crys said.

"Exactly," the director said. "You know it. I know it. Why can't everyone else see it?" Then he put his cup back into the sanitizer and zipped up his pants. "A brain-damaged baby could see it," he mumbled while washing his hands. "Everybody wants to play favorites..." Then he walked out the door and was gone.

What was that about? Crys wondered, finally able to pee. She left as quickly as she could after that, not wanting to spend any more time on the administration level.

The waiting was the hardest part. Crys sat on her bed, in a room she shared with five other women. She was trying to read a book on her tablet, but her mind kept wandering. She thought about spending some time in the gym, but she knew if she walked out that door, she'd head straight for the infirmary. And she'd already stopped there once on the way back from the administration level. She didn't want to annoy anyone.

"Come back tomorrow," they'd said. As if it were that simple to postpone your worry for a loved one.

I should sleep, Crys thought. She had a work shift in the morning, after which she'd check on April. If she went to sleep now, she'd get a full eight hours in, and wake up refreshed and ready for the new day. *Yeah, right*, she thought. As if she was going to sleep a wink tonight.

She could hear two of her roommates snoring from the bunks above her. On the opposite side of the tiny room, the other triple bunk bed was two-thirds full. *Stacy must be working the overnight shift*, Crys thought, seeing the empty bottom bunk. Then she remembered Stacy had a boyfriend.

They couldn't possibly… Crys thought, wondering how people made relationships work in this environment. There was so little privacy.

What's it going to be like when April wakes up? Crys wondered, already trying to think of places they could be alone. She supposed she'd have to ask Stacy for tips. Then she wondered if April would even be healthy enough for that sort of shenanigans. That thought took her into a downward spiral of worry and doubt. What if April didn't like her anymore? What if there were complications from the surgery? What if, what if, what if…

What if you stop making up things to worry about and go to sleep? Crys thought. She was about to put down her tablet when a notification popped up:

This Sunday – Worship Service – 8 AM – Mandatory – Auditorium

Mandatory? Crys thought. *We'll see about that.*

"She's still under the effects of the anesthesia," the nurse said. "She won't be awake for a few hours."

"I don't care," Crys told him. "I just need to see her."

"Suit yourself," the nurse said, and led her into the back. They passed more than a dozen beds before they reached April. Her sleeping form was as beautiful as ever, though her skin was paler than usual and her right arm was completely covered in bandages.

"You didn't have to remove her arm?" Crys asked.

The nurse pulled a folding chair off the wall and handed it to her. "We found a donor," he said. "You can stay as long as you want, just don't get in the way."

Crys sat and stared at April, memories flooding her mind. Med techs moved all about the room, prepping the nearby beds for patients, performing a minor surgery just two beds away, and even restraining a psychotic patient who had apparently lost his mind during the long sleep. But Crys ignored it all. As far as she was concerned, April was the universe.

Hours later, the nurse tapped Crys on the shoulder and reminded her to eat. She reluctantly headed for the cafeteria where she gobbled down a square of bean curd that tasted like chicken, then rushed back to the infirmary. When she got back, a doctor was standing over April, who was now starting to stir.

"Just in time," the doctor said as Crys approached. "April, you have a visitor."

April's eyes couldn't quite focus yet, but she smiled weakly when she recognized Crys. "You're here..." she slurred. "Turtle soup..." Then her eyes shut again.

The doctor chuckled. "She'll be in and out for a while," he said. "Stick around if you like. Don't be alarmed if she says something strange. Just let us know if she complains of any pain."

Crys nodded, and the doctor left to tend to other patients.

"Love you," Crys said.

"They weren't dead," April murmured.

"Who?" Crys asked.

"The arm girl," April said weakly. "I heard them. While they worked on me. They said... something about her profile..."

"What are you talking about?" Crys asked, but April started to snore.

An hour later the doctor checked up on them. "Everything all right?" he asked.

"She hasn't complained of any pain yet," Crys said.

The doctor nodded. "Good, I'll be back in…"

"Doctor?" Crys asked. "What can you tell me about the arm donor?"

"Not much," he replied. "Not everyone can be revived. What happened to your friend's arm, happened to the other woman's brain. It's sad, but at least parts of her get to live on in other people."

"Rose," April said suddenly. "Her name was Rose." Then she resumed snoring.

The doctor looked concerned. "You should probably come back tomorrow," he told Crys.

"But I want to be here when she wakes up again," Crys said.

"I need to run some more tests," the doctor said. "It'll be easier if you're not in the way. Please just come back tomorrow."

"Let me know if anything happens," Crys said, standing up.

She slept more soundly that night, though something in the back of her mind bothered her.

The following morning she stopped at the infirmary on the way to work. The nurse recognized her right off. "She's been asking about you," he said, and pointed Crys toward April's bed.

April was awake, lucid, and munching on a protein bar. Her eyes brightened when she saw Crys.

"Hi!" she said, putting down her food. Crys leaned in for a hug.

When they finally released each other, Crys pulled the chair off the wall and sat down. She was going to be late for her shift but she didn't care. They chatted and reminisced, and Crys told her everything that had happened since waking up.

"What was that you said yesterday?" Crys asked. "About Rose?"

"Who's Rose?" April said.

"The arm donor?" Crys asked.

"I don't remember," April said. "They told me I'd have a lot of false memories. It's bad enough dreaming for a thousand years. Going from that to medical sedation will make anyone say funny things."

"At least you came out of it okay," Crys said.

"Yeah," April said. "I'm okay. But you want to see something... weird?" She held up her bandaged arm. With her left hand, she separated a couple of the bandages until Crys could see the dark brown skin underneath.

"What the heck?" Crys asked.

"I mean, beggars can't be choosers," April said. "I'm lucky it was a match at all. I could have wound up with some muscley man's arm that went down to my knees."

"Does your new arm work okay?" Crys asked. "I mean, can you feel with it?"

"Hard to say," April replied. "I'm still on painkillers, so I haven't felt much yet. It itches though. I can't wiggle my fingers, but the doctors aren't expecting it to be completely functional for a while. They may have to go back in and connect some nerves."

"I'm sorry this happened to you," Crys said.

April chuffed. "I'm the lucky one," she said. "I could have just as easily died in my tube, like the woman who gave me this arm. Any of us could have."

Crys nodded, but she was starting to wonder if that was actually true.

Three days later, Crys once again sat at April's bedside. The bandages were off, and April would be free to go by the end of the day. She couldn't grasp anything yet, but she could wiggle her fingers and bend her elbow.

"The doctors say it'll be at least a week before it's really usable," April said, holding up her hand and trying to make a fist. The fingers trembled but wouldn't quite close. "The nerve connections are there, but it's like my body has to relearn the neural route."

"Have they given you a job yet?" Crys asked.

"They want me to take it easy for another week," April replied. "Then it's going to be light duties only – nothing that involves heavy lifting. Possibly data entry, but I don't know how fast I'm going to be able to type."

"They're not going to care about speed," Crys said. "We've still got months to go before we start terraforming the Earth. Right now they're just trying to make sure everyone's able-bodied and ready to work when they need us. They didn't even punish me for missing work this week. Though they did warn me not to let it happen again."

April nodded. "What will they do if you—"

Just then the doctor tapped Crys on the shoulder. "Sorry to interrupt, but it's almost eight AM."

"What happens at eight?" Crys asked.

"Worship service," the doctor said.

"Oh," Crys said. She hadn't even realized it was Sunday. "I'll just stay here with April if that's okay."

"She can go too," the doctor said. "They've been putting pressure on us to get as many patients to attend as possible." He gestured towards the other beds, where doctors and nurses were helping patients into wheelchairs.

Crys thought that a couple of them didn't look healthy enough to move, but then, she wasn't a doctor.

Crys and April looked at each other and shrugged. Then Crys helped April get dressed and they joined the crowd forming in the hallway.

Crys and April were among the last to arrive at the auditorium. April was a little shaky on her feet, and Crys had to help her walk. They picked a mostly empty row towards the back so that they wouldn't have to move April past a lot of people.

The auditorium looked a bit like a college lecture hall, only cleaner and much larger. It could seat more than a thousand people, but only a couple of hundred were awake so far. Crys wondered if these meetings would still be mandatory once more were awake than could be seated. But that was a long way off. The majority of the sleepers would remain in stasis until the world was habitable.

It didn't seem like they were tracking attendance, and Crys wondered what would happen if she missed the next meeting.

Once everyone was seated, the lights dimmed and a meek-looking man stepped out on the stage, pushing a wheeled metal podium. Once he had the podium centered, he locked the wheels in place. Then he stared out at the audience like a deer stuck in headlights. "Ladies and gentlemen," he muttered, "Please welcome Mrs. Cora Denver." Then he shuffled off while a woman stepped onto the stage.

Mrs. Denver looked like she was in her sixties. Her short, brown hair was graying at the tips, and she wore a conservative yellow dress, which she no doubt referred to as her "Sunday best." When she smiled, it was the smile of a woman who was about to invite you in for a cup of tea and some ribbon candy, and if Christmas was coming, she'd also ask for your sweater size.

A few audience members clapped as she stepped up to the podium, but she waved for them to stop. "I'd like to start with a prayer," she said. "Heads down. Our Dearest Lord, we thank you for…"

As the woman prayed, Crys looked around the room. Most of the audience had their heads bowed and their eyes closed. Even April prayed, her mismatched fingers interlocked in her lap. A few prayed with their eyes open, mouthing the words along with Mrs. Denver. Only a couple appeared to abstain like Crys.

Something about the makeup of the audience bothered her. It wasn't as racially diverse as she'd expected. Crys had been a tech on-site a thousand years ago, when people were first being placed in the preservation tubes. The groups going in hadn't seemed so overwhelmingly Caucasian.

She might have let it go if not for her job ranking the sleepers. When she thought back to all the nines and tens she'd assigned, she was sure a fair percentage of them had been people of color. More than this room represented, anyway. She resolved to do some more digging when she went back to work.

"…Amen," Mrs. Denver concluded, and everyone raised their heads. "Before we get started, I'd like to make a few announcements. So far we have revived two hundred and seventeen sleepers. I want to thank everyone who made this possible, particularly the med techs. You're doing a fantastic job, and we couldn't do this without you." A few people clapped.

"It's going to be a slow process," she continued. "Within the next few weeks, we'll be sending remote drilling devices to the surface to get some readings. Some will send back video, so we can have some idea of what's going on up above us. If the conditions look right, the next batch of remotes will break the surface and release some drones, which will map the area and spread some seeds in the hopes of getting vegetation started again. After that, we'll start sending manned crews. We already have some volunteers, but there's a link to the signup page on your tablets."

Crys had already added her name to the volunteers list. She was very excited about the possibility of getting picked. She'd be one of the first to see the surface again. Maybe she'd even be the first to set foot on the soil. She'd be like Neil Armstrong for the new era.

"We will keep you updated at these weekly meetings," Mrs. Denver said. "So please make sure you attend. We've arranged it so that hardly anyone has other duties on Sunday mornings. That does not mean the time is your own. This time has been allotted so that we can keep you informed, and so that everyone has time to commune with the Lord. Are there any questions?"

A couple of hands shot up. Mrs. Denver pointed to one man and he stood up. "With all due respect, ma'am, for those of us who don't worship, would it be possible to get these updates on our tablets?"

Mrs. Denver gave him a warm smile. Though Crys was pretty far away, she thought she saw daggers in the woman's eyes. "I realize not all of you are believers," Mrs. Denver said. "And that's fine. You don't have to pray, and it's not my place to judge you if you don't. But I'd still appreciate your attendance. You don't have to be a Christian to find valuable lessons in the scripture. As the last survivors on Earth, I'd like us to feel a sense of community. If we don't have unity, we'll fall into chaos."

The man sat down. Mrs. Denver asked if anyone else had

any questions, but the others had already lowered their hands. "Very good, then," she said. "I'd like to begin with a devotional…"

She continued to speak for two hours, during which time Crys nearly nodded off twice. She'd been to her share of sermons when she was younger, and this one wasn't particularly memorable. Mrs. Denver focused on verses that stressed the importance of working together, and of being of one mind. She had a decent voice for reading scripture, but she was all over the place when she tried to ad-lib.

"So in conclusion," Mrs. Denver said, "Do not let yourselves be unequally yoked. We will all have to work hard, struggling as one, if we're to make it through this. If someone isn't pulling their weight, encourage them. If someone is working counter to our goals, report them. The Promised Land is waiting for us, if only we have the strength to make the journey." Then she led them in one more prayer before she dismissed the audience.

April wasn't required to return to the infirmary, so Crys helped her get settled into her new room. It was three doors down from the room Crys lived in, and it was every bit as cramped. Crys still had another hour before she had to report to duty, so they sat on April's bed and talked about the sermon. As they talked, two of April's new roommates came in, changed clothes, and left. After a few more minutes Crys and April realized they were alone.

Alone together. It was the first time they'd had this much privacy. They stared into each other's eyes, suddenly aware of the possibilities. Then they leaned in and kissed. It was the best feeling either had experienced since waking up.

The door opened. "Get a room, you two," another roommate said.

"If only one were available," Crys muttered, and April laughed.

Crys browsed through the database, ranking dossiers and searching for potential errors. She worked as fast as possible, staying ahead of quota so she'd have time to do some research of her own. Several persistent questions pestered her subconscious, and she'd sleep better once she found some plausible explanations.

First she wanted to know more about that arm donor. April couldn't remember it now, but she'd said the donor's name was Rose. Utilizing her database skills, Crys looked for sleepers named Rose, cross-referencing them by race and medical status. Soon she had the woman's profile on her screen.

Rose Johnson. Age twenty-six at the time of preservation. African-American. Divorced. No siblings or children. Previously worked as a secretary. No religious affiliation. No military service. Cause of death...

Crys frowned. The blank that would have listed her cause of death simply said "Project 431." She'd come across references to the project in a few other dossiers in the past couple of weeks, but she hadn't found anything to give her more context. She'd even asked her supervisor what it meant, but he'd told her it was classified. At the time she'd been annoyed that they didn't trust her. But now that annoyance was replaced by an eerie foreboding, like she was searching for knowledge that might get her killed.

They wouldn't tell her what Project 431 was all about, but with a little more data she might be able to deduce it. She performed a global database search for the term to look for commonalities. She found that thirty-six people had died of Project 431.

Crys pulled up their photos and felt a shiver go up her

spine. Of the thirty-six people on her screen, twenty-nine of them were people of color. Then she did a double take as she recognized one of the few white faces. It was the man who'd raised his hand at the Worship Service, the one who'd asked if non-believers could leave. He had just been assigned Project 431 status an hour earlier.

Nope, Crys thought, and cleared her search history. If her suspicions were correct, she needed to stop investigating right now. There was no one she could report this to, no one in whom she could confide. Her only choice was to forget she'd found this. Going forward, she needed to do her job and not make waves.

Hopefully it wasn't too late.

"Let's skip Worship Service tomorrow," April whispered. They sat together in the cafeteria, eating squares of beef-flavored bean curd.

"I thought you liked Worship Service," Crys said.

"I like you more," April said. "And I can pray on my own time. My room's going to be empty of roommates for two straight hours tomorrow, and I don't want to waste it listening to the old lady ramble."

"I don't think it's a good idea," Crys replied. She hadn't told April what she'd found in the database, for fear of putting her in danger.

April looked hurt. "You do know I'm talking about sex, right? You, me, alone for two hours? Bucking like funnies? My tongue, your p—"

"I just don't want to get in any trouble," Crys interrupted.

"You weren't so paranoid before," April said. "Back before the world fell apart, you were a real daredevil.

Remember that time under the bleachers... during graduation?"

"Back then I thought we were all going to die anyway," Crys said. "But we survived, and now our lives are dependent on keeping certain people happy."

"Don't be so dramatic," April said. "Nobody's going to execute you for skipping church."

"You might be surprised," Crys whispered.

"Crystal," April said. "I haven't had an orgasm in a thousand years. You work hard. We deserve this. It's not like they take attendance."

Crys thought it over. It really wasn't much to ask. And she longed to be alone with April. Right now, she wanted it more than anything else in the world. The size of the congregation would be larger this week, as more sleepers had been revived. Surely they wouldn't miss a couple of faces. The more she rationalized it, the sillier her worries seemed.

She took a deep breath and looked into April's eyes. With a soft, seductive smile, she said, "Sure. I can't wait."

Their date went off without a hitch. Nothing interrupted them, and no one came looking for them. For two hours, they were the world to each other. It was just what they'd needed, and afterward they felt closer than ever.

Crys kept looking over her shoulder for the rest of the day. She pulled up her own dossier several times throughout her work shift, as well as April's a few times, worried she might see the dreaded "Project 431" added to their profiles. But no such updates occurred. There were no warnings or reprimands, no indication that their absence had been noticed at all.

It still took several days for Crys to finally relax, but eventually she fell back into her normal routine. A few weeks passed. Crys and April continued their Sunday morning dates. Occasionally they found other places to be alone, and they gradually became more daring.

April was assigned a data entry job, but she had to leave it because her new hand was useless at typing. They transferred her to the laundry facilities, but that was just temporary. She was on the shortlist for a data analysis project that would start soon. Remote tunnellers would be returning with soil samples, and April hoped to be on the team that studied the soil for plant viability.

One day, Crys dyed her hair blue. She'd always kept her hair purple or blue in the distant past, and it was finally long enough to be worth the effort again. Such acts of self-expression were perfectly acceptable in the compound, though wasting resources was frowned upon. Crys assured anyone who asked that she'd used excess dye that was destined to be recycled. April's laundry duties included dying bleach stains out of uniforms, so she had plenty of access to castoff dye.

When the data sorting project was complete, Crys was transferred to a team that made preparations to break the surface. There were twenty on her team, and only four of them would be on the first trip. But Crys liked her odds. They would need a programmer with her skills in case something went wrong with the software during the expedition.

When the departure date was finally scheduled, Crys was elated to see her name on the crew list.

The tube-shaped tunneling vehicle, which they had

informally dubbed "The Elevator," slowly crawled through the rock on its way to the surface. Crys, Alex, Jake, and Mira all wore pressurized suits, even though they wouldn't be leaving the tube. This trip was just to get a quick look and release a payload.

They looked at each other nervously as the vehicle shuddered. The Elevator slowed to a crawl, and the lights flickered as it diverted more power to the engines.

"Please don't get stuck," Mira muttered.

"Have a little faith," Alex said, his eyes glued to the control panel on his left. Several indicators flashed red for a moment, then went back to yellow.

"Don't worry," Jake added. "If we break down, the trip back is pretty quick."

"Don't even joke about that," Mira said. They'd already ascended more than five miles, and the surface wasn't too much further. But if the engine gave out and they couldn't fix it, they'd have to use the rear escape hatch and rappel their way back to the compound.

The Elevator shuddered again, then suddenly picked up speed. The lights stopped flickering, and everyone breathed a sigh of relief.

Like the others, Crys sat buckled in a chair, her helmet in her lap. They sat with their backs to the wall in the round control room. Each had access to two small instrument panels, one on each side of their seat. Crys looked around the room, studying the faces of her coworkers. Their expressions ranged from terrified to excited. This would be the first time anyone got to see the surface with their own eyes.

They'd already seen some video. A week earlier, a few of the smaller, automated tunnellers had returned. Their grainy footage hadn't painted a pretty picture. The oceans had receded, but the land was barren.

But we'll fix that, Crys thought, giving a half-smile to the others. These four would be part of history. The first to break the surface in the new world. The majority of the population still slept. After all, there was no reason to wake them up until the world was inhabitable.

Crys took another look at her comrades. She wasn't the type to make everything about race, but she did think it was funny that out of twenty people, these were the ones who'd been chosen. Of the four, only Mira was Caucasian. *They probably consider us the most expendable*, Crys thought. She'd meant it as a joke, a bit of self-deprecating whimsy to keep her mind entertained, but now that she thought about it…

She'd recently learned that Mira was transgender. She'd gone by "Mark" just a few weeks before, but now she wanted everyone to start treating her as a woman. Crys didn't have a problem with it, but she could only imagine how the powers-that-be had taken the news. There was no way they'd allow Mira to transition. The logistics of it were way beyond upper management's ability to care. The more Mira fought for her rights, the more she'd make herself a target.

Is that really how we got the job? Crys wondered. *Because it's so dangerous, we might not come back?* Now that the thought was loose, it bounced around her head like a hyperactive housecat. Jake saw the look on her face and tilted his head in concern. Crys responded with a thumbs-up and a fake smile, but he didn't look convinced.

"We'll be past the bumpy part soon," Jake said. "Just keep it together." Though he'd misunderstood the reason for her anxiety, he did end up being right about the turbulence. Just a few minutes later they reached softer ground, and the ride became much smoother.

"We're here," Alex said as the vehicle came to a stop.

"Where?" Mira asked, looking at her control panel.

"We've broken the surface," Alex clarified. "The Elevator is currently sticking halfway out of the ground."

Crys gasped. All her previous worries vanished. All she could think about was that they were finally above ground. It didn't feel any different, and they couldn't see anything yet, but just knowing where they were took her breath away.

"I'm going to get some video," Jake said, tapping on his instrument panel. All around the control room, monitors flickered to life. The feed was fuzzy at first, but then it came in clear.

Mira shrieked. The screens showed a cracked landscape with lava-filled crevasses and smoking volcanoes in the distance. In the foreground, a tyrannosaurus rex and a triceratops fought tooth and claw in a battle to the death.

"Jake," Alex said, not sounding a bit surprised.

"Just kidding," Jake said, and cut the video.

Crys laughed. "How long have you been planning that one?"

"More than a month," Jake said. "Here's the real feed."

This time the video showed a sandy plain. There were no plants or animals in sight. Judging by the airborne ribbons of sand, it appeared to be a windy day.

It wasn't a particularly interesting shot, but all four of them were at a loss for words.

"We're really here," Mira said finally.

"And we have a job to do," Alex added. "Jake, get the drones ready. Mira, perform a full environmental scan. Crys, monitor the incoming data and look for anything that might indicate life."

Everyone turned to their stations and began working. Ten minutes later, a hatch opened on the side of the Elevator, and dozens of tiny drones were released into the air. Some dispersed seeds over the nearby ground, while others flew miles away to release their cargo. The drones took scans of the surrounding land as they went, transmitting data back to the Elevator.

"What's the air look like, Mira?" Alex asked.

"Surprisingly close to breathable," she replied. "There must be some plant life out there somewhere."

"Should be good enough for our adaptadils, then," Alex remarked. The adaptadil seeds had originally been developed for terraforming Mars, but humankind never got around to using them for that purpose. The seeds would sprout into trees that could survive in a wide range of temperate zones. They also bore highly nutritious fruit and were unusually efficient at converting carbon dioxide into oxygen.

"Looking at these numbers, we might have a proper air mixture within a year," Crys added. "Temperature's a little on the warm side, but it should cool down once more plants take root."

"Excellent news," Alex said. "Well done, team."

Everyone continued to gather data. As more drones transmitted their findings back to the Elevator, the crew began mapping the surrounding landscape. Mira finished scanning the local environment and moved on to studying the readings from the drones. Jake loaded up the returning drones with more seeds before sending them out again. Crys read stats and numbers into her personal voice recorder, as a backup in case something happened to the Elevator's database. Alex relayed their findings to the compound.

Four hours passed. The seed supply went dry, and the drones had scanned as much of the land as they could without exceeding their range. Jake called the drones back and they prepared to reverse back through the tunnel. Alex sent a final report to the compound before closing up shop. They strapped themselves in and were about to start the engines when the communication console lit up.

"A message from the compound?" Alex asked. He tapped a couple of keys. "Huh? It just says Initiate Four Three One. Anybody know —"

"Everybody get out, now!" Crys shouted. She unbuckled her harness, put on her helmet, and dove for the escape hatch.

"What the hell?" Jake asked, unbuckling his restraints.

"Crys!" Alex shouted, but she was already gone.

"She must have had a good reas—" Mira started to say, but then the room filled with fire.

Crys dangled from a metal cable, about a hundred feet below the Elevator. A jet of flame burst from the open hatch, and several bits of debris rained down past her. None of her crewmates had gotten out.

Despite Jake's earlier joke, the trip back wasn't particularly quick. The Elevator hadn't taken a perfectly vertical path to the surface, but had rather zig-zagged its way up to avoid dense deposits of impenetrable rock. This was good for Crys, as it meant she could stop to rest now and then, and she didn't have to worry about falling to her death if she lost her grip.

But it still wasn't easy or safe. The displaced dirt and rock had collapsed in places, and more than once she had to dig a little to move forward. Her backpack contained a small shovel, but it may as well have been a spoon. Though she only had to travel about seven miles, it took her more than a day to reach the compound. By the time she arrived at the hatch, she was exhausted and severely dehydrated.

When she reached the outer hatch of the compound, she typed in her security code only to find it was denied. Thinking she'd mistyped, she tried it again, but to no avail. *Good thing I helped set up the security system,* she thought, and typed in the master code.

It wasn't Sunday, but over three hundred people sat in the auditorium, waiting to hear the announcement. Many conflicting rumors had spread about the tunneling crew, and the news sounded dire. April stared nervously at the empty stage, desperately hoping that her girlfriend was okay.

Mrs. Denver stepped out on stage. "Thank you for coming," she said. "It is with great sorrow that I must inform you that we've lost all communication with the tunneling crew. We suspect that something terrible has happened to them."

April gasped. It couldn't be true. Crys couldn't be gone, not like this.

"Due to this tragedy," Mrs. Denver continued, "We've decided to slow down the timetable on our surface expeditions. We don't want to lose more people. If there's something dangerous up there, we want more time to prepare for it. There's nothing to be gained from haste. We have enough resources down here to last for decades. I know some of you were anxious to see the sunlight again, but you may have to accept that it will be your children or even grandchildren who finally break the surface."

There was a commotion from somewhere behind her, and she cast an annoyed look backstage. Then Crys emerged from behind the curtain, helmetless but still in her dirt-covered pressure suit.

"You," Crys said with an angry glare. The audience gasped.

"Miss Pérez," Mrs. Denver said with surprise. She was clearly perturbed, but she hid it with the biggest smile she could muster. "I'm so happy you're alive. Is the rest of your crew here?"

Crys stepped closer to the podium so she could be heard through the microphone. "You set us up to die," she said. "You wanted the mission to fail. You want to keep everyone here so you can control them. So you can convert them to your religion. You want—"

"I assure you, this wasn't my doing," Mrs. Denver said, signaling to security. "I'm just as surprised as you are that the tunneller exploded."

I thought she didn't know what happened to the tunneller, April thought. Several nearby audience members murmured something similar to each other.

Two security officers grabbed Crys by the arm and dragged her offstage. For just a moment, Crys locked eyes with April. *Laundry,* Crys mouthed, which confused April.

"I'm so sorry for that," Mrs. Denver told the audience. "Something up there must have driven her crazy. She'll need to be debriefed so we can figure out just what horrors wait for us on the surface. Please dismiss. We'll schedule another meeting when we have more information for you."

Then she rushed offstage, leaving the confused audience to their speculations.

Crys sat in the director's office, handcuffed to a chair. She was alone, as the two security officers had remained outside in the hallway. After a few minutes, Mrs. Denver entered and sat down at the desk.

"I thought this was your husband's office," Crys remarked.

"He's my son," Mrs. Denver replied curtly. "He's pretty but he doesn't know shit. We used him for recruitment speeches, but I've always been in charge."

"Maybe he knows more than you think," Crys said.

"Doesn't matter," Mrs. Denver said. "I have a proposal for you."

"Oh, this should be good," Crys muttered.

"Show some respect, dear," Mrs. Denver said. "I might be the last person you ever speak to. You made me look bad down there, but I can still use you for damage control."

"Is that how you view everyone?" Crys asked. "In terms of how you can use them? Or is it just those who aren't white Christians?"

"That is a baseless accusation," Mrs. Denver said. "If you want to remain alive, you will take my offer. While you were on the surface, you witnessed something. Something so horrific and dangerous that it killed your crewmates and drove you mad. Do you understand?"

"I understand you're a con artist," Crys said. "You really expect me to lie for you? You're going to kill me either way. You can't have me walking around knowing the truth."

"If you refuse my offer, you will be executed as a traitor," Mrs. Denver said slowly. "But if you play your part and stick to the story, we'll simply put you back in the tubes. Maybe they'll wake you again in another thousand years. At least you'll get to live."

"Bullshit," Crys said. "If I go back into the tubes, you're going to use me for spare parts, just like you've been doing to anyone else you can't control."

"Ah," Mrs. Denver said. "You stumbled onto that as well? Maybe you were right. I can't afford to keep you alive."

"You call yourself a Christian, but you don't believe in any of it, do you?" Crys asked.

"Of course I don't believe in that tripe," Mrs. Denver said calmly. "It's simply a means of control. You can make people do anything if you threaten them with eternal damnation." She stood and walked to the door. "Now if you'll excuse me," she said, "I have an execution to plan."

April paced around the laundry room, not sure what she was looking for. *Why did she send me here?* she wondered, rifling through dirty clothes for clues. She was on the verge of giving up when the laundry hatch opened and a large article of clothing fell into the heap.

It was a pressure suit. It wasn't unusual for special equipment to be sent to the laundry room. "If they can wear it, we can clean it," April's supervisor had once told her. April rushed to the suit, looking through it for a note or some other piece of evidence. But the suit didn't even have pockets. Then she spotted a blinking red light. Attached to one cuff was a voice recorder. And it was still recording.

Another mandatory meeting took place a few hours later. Citizens all over the compound were given another break from their duties so they could attend the event. The first thing the arriving audience members saw was one of the preservation tubes sitting in the middle of the stage. Crys stood inside, wearing a plain gray uniform. She banged on the glass, screaming at the top of her lungs. But only a faint murmur could be heard through the thick glass.

Mrs. Denver stood beside the tube. When the people stopped trickling in, she began her announcement immediately. "My loyal citizens," she began. "A sad duty has fallen to me today. We've had our first major crime since the awakening. As most of you know, Crystal Pérez was one of the four crew members on the recent mission to the surface. It was meant to be a historic moment – literally groundbreaking – one that would change our lives forever."

She paused for effect, then continued. "But some people don't want us to move forward. Crystal would rather we stagnate down here, never making progress. And so she sabotaged the mission, destroying the tunneller and killing her three crewmates. This sort of traitorous behavior will not be tolerated."

Crys banged even harder on the glass, screaming at her captor and pleading with the audience. "And so," Mrs. Denver continued, "It is with a heavy heart that we must carry out her execution. And we must do it here, now, in front of an audience, so that none of you will entertain similar traitorous thoughts."

Her hand moved to the control panel on the side of the tube. "But we're not monsters. We will make it as humane as possible. When I activate this button, it will fill the tube with preserving gel, the same gel that kept all of you alive for the last thousand years. It will numb her and put her into a deep sleep. Once she is beyond consciousness or pain, I will introduce a new chemical into the mix, one which will dissolve her body, bones and all. I promise she will feel nothing."

Mrs. Denver pressed the first button, and the tube began filling up with gel. Crys panicked as it rose above her ankles. She could already feel its numbing effects on her skin. She reached for the ceiling, looking for any sort of latches or buttons she could press, but there was nothing. As the gel reached her knees, she gave up trying to escape. She knew there was nothing she could do, and she didn't want to go out crying like a coward. Instead she stood still and stared straight ahead, resigned to her fate.

The gel was at her waist when a voice came over the auditorium speakers.

"You made me look bad down there, but I can still use you for damage control." Some of the audience members looked confused. It was Mrs. Denver's voice, but she wasn't speaking on stage.

"Is that how you view everyone?" another voice asked. "In terms of how you can use them? Or is it just those who aren't white Christians?"

"That is a baseless accusation. If you want to remain alive, you will take my offer. While you were on the surface, you witnessed something. Something so horrific and dangerous that it killed your crewmates and drove you mad. Do you understand?" Up on stage, Mrs. Denver's eyes widened. She tried to speak into the microphone on the podium, but it had been silenced.

"Don't listen!" she shouted. "It's a trick!"

But the speakers were louder, and drowned her out. "I understand you're a con artist. You really expect me to lie for you? You're going to kill me either way. You can't have me walking around knowing the truth."

"If you refuse my offer, you will be executed as a traitor. But if you play your part and stick to the story, we'll simply put you back in the tubes. Maybe they'll wake you again in another thousand years. At least you'll get to live." The audience began to glare at Mrs. Denver. Several got to their feet.

"Bullshit. If I go back into the tubes, you're going to use me for spare parts, just like you've been doing to anyone else you can't control."

"Ah. You stumbled onto that as well? Maybe you were

right. I can't afford to keep you alive." A pair of security guards grabbed Mrs. Denver by the arms and began to escort her off the stage. Several more audience members stood and made their way to the platform.

"You call yourself a Christian, but you don't believe in any of it, do you?" In the tube, Crys stood on her tiptoes and held her breath. The gel seeped up over her nose and mouth. The numbing agent was making her lightheaded, and she began to lose consciousness.

"Of course I don't believe in that tripe. It's simply a means of control. You can make people do anything if you threaten them with eternal damnation. Now if you'll excuse me, I have an execution to plan." At this, the audience rushed the stage. Some overpowered the security guards and pulled Mrs. Denver off the platform, into the mass of angry people.

"I think she's waking up," a voice said.

There was a distant, rhythmic beeping that Crys found irritating. Something grasped her arm. A hand? She opened her eyes and saw two blurry people at the foot of her bed. The closer one leaned forward and touched her face.

"April?" Crys asked weakly. "Am I dead?"

"Everything's fine," April said, kissing her on the forehead.

Behind her, the other figure came into focus. Crys stiffened. It was Mrs. Denver's son, Director Hampton Denver.

"No, it's okay," the director said as he saw her panic. "I'm not like my mother."

"You're not?" Crys asked skeptically.

"She and I never saw eye-to-eye on things," he said.

"What happened to her?" Crys asked.

"She's in a stasis tube," the director said. "The mob tried to kill her, but security managed to stop them. You owe a lot to your friend here. She hijacked our speaker system and incited a riot."

Crys turned to April. "You did that for me?"

"I'd do anything for you," April said.

Another year had passed. The new tunneller – this one called "the Lift" – burst through the ground.

"Air reads as breathable," Wesley reported, reading from his instrument panel.

"Pulling up video now," Donovan said.

The four crew members looked at the video screen in awe. What had once been a barren landscape was now full of lush vegetation.

"I think it's time," Crys said. "Who gets to be the first to set foot in the new world?"

"Oh, that honor has to go to you," Donovan said.

"You're sure?" Crys asked.

The other three crew members agreed. Crys had earned her place in the history books.

Think of something profound to say, Crys thought as the outer hatch opened. A fresh breeze swept into the tunneller, and it was the sweetest fragrance they'd smelled in over a thousand years.

Crys stood in the doorway, one foot hovering over the dirt. The other three lined up behind her, equally anxious to experience the surface world. "One small step for a woman..." Crys began.

"...And one giant push from her girlfriend," April finished, before playfully shoving her out the door.

Story Nuggets

Easy Prey

It was nearly midnight and the sidewalks were empty. No cars had passed in over an hour. The street lamps remained unlit since the previous month's earthquake. The City Works Department insisted that repairs were scheduled, but Requiem Cove always seemed to be at the bottom of the list. There would probably be another earthquake before they got around to it.

A lone pair of footsteps broke the silence. A young woman – she couldn't be more than twenty – strolled down the sidewalk. Her designer heels clopped like horseshoes against the concrete.

The Jackelthorn watched her with great interest. *This is almost too easy,* it thought as it tiptoed through a yard and fell in step behind her. It continued to walk on the pointy tips of its feet, staying on the grass and behind cover. It zipped from object to object, hiding behind trees, trash cans, and mailboxes as it followed the woman.

How is she so casual? the dark creature thought. Its head was suddenly abuzz with questions. Why was she out so late? Where had she come from, and where was she going? Why couldn't she take a cab or ride with a friend? These streets were dangerous even when there weren't monsters about.

It usually didn't think so hard about where its food came from. This was its first month on the surface, having broken through during the earthquake. It wasn't alone. Dozens of Underdwellers had taken advantage of the disaster, and now they were scattered throughout the city, each having claimed their hunting grounds.

The creature didn't mind easy prey, but something about this woman gave it pause. *Is this what it feels like to have a conscience?* it wondered. But no, that couldn't be it. Earlier in the week it had camped out in a preschooler's closet, and it could still taste the child's succulent flesh whenever it belched. Decency was not in the Jackelthorn's vocabulary.

It scratched its chin with one of its long serrated talons. Maybe it was the woman's confidence that caused the creature's doubt. She should have been scared out of her mind, but she walked with the poise of someone who owned the night.

It's probably just for show, the Jackelthorn thought. *She walks without fear so attackers will assume she's armed. But I have nothing to fear from a taser or a gun. So why do I hesitate?*

But it just didn't feel right. Despite its hunger, the creature trusted its instincts and loped away, off to another street in pursuit of less confusing prey.

Almost got him, the woman thought, watching the Jackelthorn through the eye in the back of her head. *Too bad, he looked tasty. But the night is young, and there's plenty more streets left to hunt.*

Several of her mouths let out a low chuckle as she walked on into the night.

Unity

The world had expected saucers, but instead they got teacups. The cup-shaped ships swarmed across the globe, coming to a stop above every major city. As a show of power, the cup hovering above the Pentagon tipped, pouring out a burning oily liquid that melted the building into molten rubble. The Air Force attempted to bring the cup down, but their weapons couldn't penetrate the alien shields.

Intergalactic war was inevitable, and the odds didn't look good for Earth. In a last-ditch effort to unite the world, the US president arranged a teleconference with all the major world leaders.

"Greetings," he began. "For years we've stared into the void with high-powered telescopes, wondering if anything was out there. And now we have our answer. I'd always dreamed of a day when we could exchange knowledge with visitors from beyond our solar system. I'd hoped this discovery would lead to an age of enlightenment. But now we've seen the cruel reality. Instead of scientists, they sent conquerors. Instead of illumination, they brought destruction. My long-held dream has become a living nightmare.

"But all is not lost, my friends. With your help, I believe we can defeat them. Right now we have hundreds of scientists searching for a way to breach their shields. Our weapons manufacturers are working overtime on new armaments. If we pool our knowledge and work together, we can bring them down.

"I know we'd had our differences, but now is the time for the world to unite against a common foe. We have to send these invaders a message: That we aren't just going to roll over and let them take our home. We can't go on holding grudges. We have to let go of the past and fight for our future. If humankind is to survive, we have to hold hands and pull each other up this hill.

"Together we can show them what it means to be human. We are survivors. We are fighters. But most of all, we are problem solvers. We're not going to give up our land, we're not going to give up our lives, and we're not going to give up our freedom! Are you with me?"

The other world leaders stared at him for a few seconds.

"Nah," one said.

"Meh," said another.

"I mean, it just seems like a lot of work," another replied.

"Oh, okay," the president said. "Well... thank you for your time."

He ended the call.

"This job isn't so bad," the ex-president said as he drove the tunneller into the rock. "Even if it is a little boring. Get it? Boring?"

"Yes, sir," his former aide said, shaking the precious gems from his drill. All around them, humans pushed high-tech tunnellers into the cavern walls. The devices were easy to operate and went through the rock like it was butter.

Looking like human-sized anteaters, the alien overlords watched their human slaves mine for minerals. It was three hours into the shift, and it was almost time for them to break for lunch.

"Seriously, though," the ex-president continued. "Six-hour days? Four-day weeks? Free medical and dental? If I'd stayed in office for thirty years I still wouldn't have been able to accomplish this much for my people."

"Yes sir," the former aide repeated.

"I'm going to have to talk to Commander Zordex," the ex-president said. "I know they only plan to stay until their vault is full, but maybe they could leave a few overlords behind. I could use a couple of out-of-the-box thinkers on my staff."

"Less talking, more working," an overlord said.

"Yes sir!" the ex-president said proudly. He went back to work with renewed vigor, whistling a happy tune.

The House On Guille Court

The house was nondescript, the kind of house they use for establishing shots on television when the main characters visit the neighbors. Inside, however, was something else. Which is to say, something besides a house. The floors were made of ice cream, and the walls were nothing but sheets of falling sand. Who knew what was holding the ceiling up, certainly not Fadeline "Rhymes-With-Madeline" Roberts, who'd only gone inside to get away from the hornets.

Fad had lived on this street for her entire life, all sixteen years of it, but she'd never seen anyone go in or out of this house. It had actually become a running joke in the neighborhood. "That idea is as unsellable as the house at the end of Guille Court," they'd say. But there'd never been any realtor signs in the yard, either. Whoever owned it, they never used it, but also didn't want to part with it.

The way word gets out, it was odd that it hadn't attracted any squatters. *Maybe not so odd after all*, Fad thought as she climbed onto a giant ice pop to keep from sinking into the floor.

Am I dreaming this? Fad wondered, but her day had been too coherent to be a dream. She'd spent all day at school, where she'd read, wrote, and solved complex math problems. She'd eaten and talked to friends and ridden the bus, and nothing unusual or even exaggerated had occurred.

Until the bus dropped her off, that is. It never actually turned onto Guille Court, but instead let Fad out at the entrance to the street along with six other students. Fad often took a roundabout way home, following the creek that ran behind the houses on her street. Today she came across something new on the ground by a log, and she kicked it, thinking it was a bundle of rags. Unfortunately it was not a bundle of rags, but in fact, a hornet's nest that had fallen from a tree.

She ran blindly at first, more concerned with speed than destination. But after ten or twelve stings she decided to seek shelter. 110 Guille Court was the closest house by then, and she couldn't have been happier to find the back door unlocked.

But now she wasn't so sure. She'd heard of hornet stings causing hallucinations – no, wait, that was in a movie she'd seen. But it didn't matter, as she didn't feel like she was hallucinating any more than she felt like she was in a dream. She didn't feel drowsy, her vision wasn't doubled, and the world didn't have that "blurry edge" filter they used on TV.

The ice pop felt appropriately cold and slippery. It even left orange residue on her palms, a detail she doubted she'd have noticed in a dream. And the room smelled like an ice cream shop. She couldn't remember ever having smelled anything in her dreams.

A giant slice of cheesecake bobbed nearby, and she crawled over to it, grateful to get off the freezing ice pop. She sank a little into the cheesecake, but it held her weight. She wiped her hands over her mouth and got a taste of the most glorious dessert she could imagine.

The sand stopped falling, and beyond the walls she saw an endless desert in every direction. *Where'd my neighborhood go?* Fad thought. She was glad the hornets were gone, but she hoped to be able to go back home at some point.

That was a lie. She hated her home. Her parents always fought, and Fad felt like it was her fault. It had been a difficult year for her. She'd been missing a lot of school due to her migraines, which she believed were brought on by the stress of keeping secrets. Maybe her headaches would disappear if she came clean, but she couldn't. She just couldn't. Her parents were too religious; they'd kick her right out if she told them.

Maybe I should just live here, Fad thought. There was plenty of food, maybe not the nutritious kind but it was certainly tasty. She started to think of more practical questions, such as if there was an actual floor below the ice cream, and whether the freaky house had a bathroom somewhere.

The sand began to fall again, but this time it was white instead of yellow. After another thirty seconds, during which Fad tried to come up with a joke about "dessert deserts," the sand stopped once again. This time the house was surrounded by a grassy field.

So what happens if I go out there? Fad wondered. Would she find herself in a new world? Would she be able to get back? It wasn't worth the risk, not just for a field.

But then the sand fell again, stopped, and this time the house was in the middle of a carnival. Rollercoasters roared in the distance, clowns gave out balloons tied to bags of cotton candy, and a merry-go-round ride blared out happy-but-obnoxious music. The air smelled of pizza and corn dogs. Parkgoers passed by, somehow oblivious to the house full of ice cream smack dab in the middle of the midway.

Fad loved carnivals. Some of her earliest memories were of the state fair, where she'd ridden her first Ferris wheel and danced in front of the fun house mirrors. She had fourteen dollars in her purse just begging to be spent on funnel cakes and ride tickets.

But she stayed on her cheesecake. She wanted to go have a good time, but then what? Carnivals sucked once you ran out of money.

Besides, she was really starting to suspect it would be a one-way trip. If the carnival visitors couldn't see the house, then that meant Fad wouldn't be able to see it either once she left.

...if she even could leave. What if the walls were just like video screens? The door she'd entered through had disappeared, or maybe it was still there, invisible due to the illusion of the carnival.

The sand picked up again. It was closer to brown this time, but it flowed just the same. When it stopped again, the house was in the middle of a zoo, with tigers pacing behind bars and elephants trumpeting in the distance. Peacocks walked alongside visitors as they bought birdseed at vending machines. A zoo employee passed by with a lorikeet on her shoulder.

If there was one thing Fad liked better than carnivals, it was zoos. *It's like the house knows*, she thought. Everything felt like it had been created for her. The cheesecake, the orange ice pop – two of her favorite desserts. Even the floor was mint chocolate chip, which she'd been craving on the bus ride home.

Is the house trying to tell me something? Fad wondered.

As an experiment, she pulled a pen out of her purse and threw it at the wall. The pen went right through and landed on the pavement. *So I can pass through*, she thought.

But then the sand flowed once more, and parted to reveal the living room of her own home. Her parents were arguing, as usual.

"She's faking it and you know it!" her father shouted.

Her mother crossed her arms and yelled, "The doctor says her headaches are real!"

"That guy's a quack!" her father yelled back.

Fad buried her face in her hands. *They're even louder when they don't think I'm around,* she thought.

But she couldn't stay on her cheesecake forever. Her parents would go nuts if she didn't come home. For good or ill, it was time to do the responsible thing and go back to reality.

Fad took a deep breath and climbed across the cheesecake until she reached the wall.

"Bye, Mom and Dad," she said, and waited for the carnival to come around again.

Connection

"This transmission won't last long," the voice said. "You have to listen! It's very important!"

"I hear you," Vogram replied, turning up the volume. "What's the message?"

"Write this down," the voice said. "The Army of Snod will strike at midnight tonight. South entrance of the archives building. Their comm frequency is one-oh-three point seven."

"Got it," Vogram said. "What else can you tell me?"

"I'm about to cut out so listen carefully," the voice continued. "The leader is armed with an EMP hammer. The rest have guns. Six in all. Shockblasters with rapid-fire mods."

"I'm relaying the data now," Vogram said, tapping a few keys. "Good work. Anything else?"

"I've only got seconds before my battery runs dry," the voice said. "So pay attention. The leader's name is Talz Cybo. He's an anarcho-machinist from the technofields. His people never take prisoners. They believe biological life is on its way out."

"Great," Vogram said. "Thank you for the—"

"Wait there's more!" the voice said. "But I might not get it all out before I lose contact. Cybo's first-grade teacher was Mrs. Henderson."

"Is this really important?" Vogram asked.

"It is!" the voice insisted. "It was her resolve that inspired him to gather a following. You can use that against him!"

"I don't see how..." Vogram said.

"And I don't have long, but you have to know Cybo's favorite color! A lot of people think it's blue, but it's actually dark purple!"

"You're messing with me, aren't you?" Vogram asked.

"Don't you see? Purple is the key to defeating him!"

"I'm hanging up now," Vogram said, and switched off the communicator.

Eight kilometers away...

"They don't suspect a thing," Talz Cybo said as he shut off the radio.

"You really think prank calls are the way to go?" Ryca asked.

"They'll never suspect an attack now," Cybo reassured her. "And even if they do, they'll be guarding the wrong building."

"You've got them right where you want them," Ryca said.

The two pored over a map of the campus, circling the locations of surveillance cameras. A door slid open, and Cybo's assistant Jecho entered.

"Sir, I brought you the robe you wanted for the attack tonight!"

Not looking up from the map, Cybo held out his arms so Jecho could slip it on him. "Comfortable," he said. And then his skin began to burn. He shrieked when he looked at his sleeves. "You idiot! I said purple! Not blue! Purple..."

His skin melted away until he collapsed in a pile of cybernetic implants.

"He really doesn't like blue," Ryca remarked.

"My bad," Jecho said. "Wanna grab dinner?"

"Sure," Ryca said, and they left arm-in-arm.

And The Corn Has Ears

"The plants are watching us again, Mona Jean."

The tiny eyestalks turned to see how Mona Jean would respond.

"Oh no," Mona Jean said. "You're not getting out of this fight just because you're afraid of some stupid plants. So what if they're looking?"

"I'm just saying it makes me uncomfortable," Darryl replied. "Can't we talk about this inside?"

"No, we're going to settle this right here," Mona Jean replied. "I've been telling you to fix the tree swing for weeks. You said you'd have it done before the barbecue. And guess what tomorrow is?"

A patch of crabgrass turned its eyestalks until a dozen tiny eyeballs pointed at Darryl.

"But I haven't got the ladder fixed," Darryl whined, leaning against the tree. Just above his shoulder, a clump of moss opened its eyes and looked at Mona Jean.

"You've had three weeks to fix that ladder," Mona Jean said. "You're obviously not going to. Just go down to the hardware store and get a new ladder."

A flower garden sat against the side of the house. Mona

Jean's prize begonias woke up and watched the argument with fascination.

And so it was all over the farm, and for that matter, all over the Earth. It had been two years since plants started growing eyes, and scientists were baffled. Nearly every form of plant life had developed the feature.

The eyes looked like those of a human, complete with irises and sclera. They focused and dilated like their human equivalent. They reacted to movement and even appeared to listen to conversations.

And yet, no one could figure out why. It wasn't a survival feature. The plants weren't more difficult to kill. The grass didn't cringe when being mowed, the trees didn't shy from a woodcutter's ax. As far as anyone could tell, the mutation was completely superficial.

"It's just not in the budget, Mona Jean," Darryl said, and the plants seemed to hang on every word.

"How come it's only in the budget when you want something, but not when I want it?" Mona Jean asked.

"We've been over that, Mona Jean," Darryl said. As he talked, he casually sat down, forgetting the tree swing was hanging by a thread. "I only make so much mo— Augh!"

One end of the swing crashed to the ground, and Darryl flipped head over heels. More and more plants awakened to watch their antics. Soon the entire farm was a field of eyes, all centered on the bickering couple.

One hundred and forty million miles away, three Martians sat on a leafy couch, laughing at a video screen.

"See, that's why I love this show," Spinso remarked. "The characters are so relatable."

"You only say that because you fell off the jobo-stool yesterday," Lyka replied.

"Did he?" Tooka asked. "I wish I'd seen that."

"He flipped over just like the 'Darryl' creature," Lyka said. "It wouldn't have happened if he'd fixed the zabra-hook like I warned him."

"I'll get to it, I'll get to it," Spinso said.

Behind them, a kroza-gem glittered on the wall. They didn't know it, but it wasn't a natural gem at all. Like many of the minerals that adorned their cavern home, it was actually a hidden camera.

Meanwhile on Neptune...

Author's Notes

This is the fourth in a series of short story collections, which started with Geek Cutes and continued with Rainbow Nightmares and Gender Rolls. In my head I've been referring to this series as "Random Xinery." Since most of the stories are unrelated, it's not necessary to read the collections in any particular order. Though if you enjoyed "The NPC," the other three collections also contain stories starring Brant's gaming group.

The NPC

This story came to me in a dream, but it went in a completely different direction once I started typing it. Originally it was going to be more about Harriet's obsession with her lucky coin. It's her favorite possession until she finds herself starving and has to spend it on food. At the end of the story she meets another rabbit-person, who has somehow acquired the coin. The other Hareborn gives Harriet the coin, but she spends it again to buy something for her new friend. After all, what's a lucky coin when compared to finally meeting a kindred spirit?

* * *

Different

My influences for this story are pretty obvious. You've got your typical "aliens take over a small town" body-snatcher type story, combined with the "group of kids fight something supernatural" 80s nostalgia fad we've seen in movies/TV recently. I won't claim I added much to either genre, but as someone about the same age as the kids in the story, it was certainly fun to write.

Playing God

This story is not meant as a diatribe against capital punishment, though I could see it being interpreted that way. My feelings on CP are complicated, but overall it's safe to assume that I'm not a fan. That said, please don't take this story literally. Do I actually think prison executioners and wardens deserve to die? Of course not. This is just a ghost story, not a political statement.

Sometimes I think 90% of sci-fi is coming up with new technology, then explaining why the new technology is evil. I get it. Conflict makes fiction worth reading. A story about science that goes right is, well, a boring story. But over the years, I think the trend has seeded society with a distrust of science. We're taught from birth that every breakthrough comes at a price, and that every discovery is a monster in the making. I worry that this is one of the reasons we have so many anti-science people in the government. Everyone thinks that new equals bad, simply because the movies tell them so.

That said, "science gone wrong" is still hella fun to write.

Eyes

I'll be honest, this isn't my favorite story in this collection, and I'm not sure how it ended up being one of the longest stories in the book. It's sort of a "discount 1984" – I'm not saying it's bad, just that other authors have done so much more with the concept.

Unfinished Business

This story was inspired by a couple of memes and comic strips. Could a person die and become both a ghost and a zombie? The punchline often involves the ghost being embarrassed by the antics of their mindless undead body.

You have to accept a lot of bad science to make a serious zombie story. For example, rotted muscle tissue should make a creature weaker, if not immobile, and yet the movies often depict them as super strong. And that's just the tip of the iceberg. Arguably that's what makes zombies so scary – the fact that we know they're impossible, but here they come anyway. Supernatural stories only need to be internally consistent, not scientifically explainable.

The Answer

I almost called this one "Saphstronauts" before I came to my senses. I really like stories that explain the nature of the universe in unconventional ways.

Moving On

I was in the process of moving to another state when I wrote this. I once heard that moving can be more stressful than losing a loved one, and at the time I certainly believed it.

But... just a few short months after the move, my wife passed away suddenly. And now I can tell you with full authority, nothing, NOTHING matches the stress of losing someone so close to you. She was my right arm, my other half, name your cliché. I'd spent the last thirty years with this woman, learning our secret couple's language, and I don't know how to communicate with anyone else.

Dream Sequence

Yes, I know, it has a punchline for an ending. Not everyone appreciates getting dragged along only to be thrown off a cliff. But as a gamer who rarely gets a chance to game, I thought the joke was too good to pass up.

I'm still not sure how I feel about the main character. Does Scott subconsciously want to sexually assault his friends? Are these impulses indicative of his actual desires, or are dreams just dreams, with no deeper meaning?

Road Hog

A while back I designed a role-playing game set in my Bloodhunters universe. This story is based on an adventure I wrote for the RPG. Like most stories set in the Bloodhunters universe, this one is meant to be a little bit cheesy. Catlike aliens, rock people, electric hovercars that still blow smoke as they rev their engines… it's all part of the fun.

New World

I could have made this story a lot longer and answered some of your potential questions. Is this the only compound? Did they also preserve any animals? What exactly destroyed the Earth? Did anything else take up residence on the Earth's surface during their slumber? But I wanted to leave it open in case I decide to return to this universe later.

Story Nuggets

Sometimes a concept just isn't grand enough for an entire

novel, and sometimes it isn't even worth a short story.

Easy Prey – Everything's afraid of something, and even monsters have their own monsters. I love stories that reveal what monsters fear.

Unity – I love grand speeches in movies, and the really good ones make my skin tingle. But I thought it would be funny to see one fall flat.

The House On Guille Court - So what was Fad's secret? Was she gay/trans/pregnant? Doesn't matter. The takeaway is that her parents weren't safe people to tell. I don't want to encourage runaways, but it is an unfortunate consequence of having an unsafe home. Parents, do better.

Connection – The first draft had the caller talking as fast as possible because they knew the connection wouldn't last long. They finished the message, but the connection didn't cut out after all. The final line was, "So, uh… what do you want to talk about?"

And The Corn Has Ears – The first line in the story was a writing prompt that popped into my head one day. What am I supposed to do, ignore that kind of thing?

Special thanks to Kaius and Jaymes.

About The Author

Xine Fury is the substance of things hoped for, the evidence of things not Xine.

Also By Xine Fury

The following books are also available.
Bloodhunters v1: Bad Blood
Bloodhunters v2: Blue Blood
Bloodhunters v3: New Blood
Blood Samples (A Bloodhunters Prequel)
Geek Cutes
Rainbow Nightmares
Gender Rolls
Nomads of Zyden

www.ingramcontent.com/pod-product-compliance
Lightning Source LLC
Chambersburg PA
CBHW070458010826
48976CB00022B/2035